RIAPOKE

By

Bryan Nowak

Bryan Nowak- Sterling, VA
www.bryannowak.com
bryanthewriter@bryannowak.com
ISBN: 978-1-7347274-2-5

Fourth Edition
April 2022
United States of America

1

THE DANGERS OF CAMPING

The morning shone through the canopy of trees like beautiful cascading mini waterfalls of light. Had they not been so low on provisions, Carl Jensen might have allowed a lengthier stay in the warmth of the sleeping bag. Next to him, the sleeping mat belonging to Mary Conway, a stunning brunette he had befriended on the trail, lay unrolled. He wasn't into one-night stands, however this relationship stretched out the better part of a week. Mary grew on him. She must've gotten up to tend camp.

Carl pushed the tent flap aside, revealing the beautiful mountain vista. The spot was Mary's idea. Consulting the map in their cross-country hike, the trail curved slightly inward deep into the Virginian forest. Their camp site was strategically located near a lake and small town. The lake promised a place to run water through a filter and the town, although small, provided a place for additional provisions and a hot meal for a change. Reconstituted trail food ensured nutritional needs were met, but a burger and fries helped them push farther toward their destination.

The camp site stood seventy-five feet off the trail in a little stand of pines. Trees provided a wind break from the breeze blowing off the mountain. From a small break in the foliage, Carl focused a pair of binoculars on the tops of houses and buildings in the distance as well as a taller structure featuring a large neon coffee cup, suggesting a cafe or restaurant. Pulling the laces of his boots tight, Carl stood and stretched, enjoying the serene picture the rural townscape painted.

Mary didn't appear to be in camp. While nothing more than a summer fling, a little notice that she left for town ahead of him was the polite thing to do.

Carl was just about to walk off into the underbrush with a roll of toilet paper and a metal trowel when something stopped him. Mary's pack, boots, and hiking stick leaned against a fallen log. While he knew little about Mary, no good hiker ever went anywhere without a pair of trusty boots and hiking stick. It didn't make sense.

Wondering if Mary took off running around naked in the woods made Carl smile. Mary proved, on more than one occasion, to be wildness incarnate. This summer stood out as one of the more memorable adventures he'd had.

Walking toward the dark woods for a morning constitutional, the rubber sole of his boot stepped in something wet and squishy. He had more than once stepped into bear or fox poop and desperately hoped this was not the case now. He stooped to examine the dark, slick liquid. It looked like reddish oil; likely a logger's vehicle probably broke down here and the careless asshole just let it leak fluid from a broken line or something.

Some people are so inconsiderate.

Something else caught his attention a few feet ahead of him, in the shade of the tree. A clump of fur lay balled up in the dark. Fairly long for an animal, its brunette color marred only by streaks of blood and dirt that matted the fur. The metallic smell of blood stung Carl's nostrils.

"What the frigg?" he murmured to no one in particular.

Whatever took the unfortunate creature was less than kind. Turning the fur over with a stick laying nearby, he noticed the hair still had skin attached to it, perhaps ripped out or cut off by a hunter in haste to harvest the animal.

Carl decided to search for another spot to relieve himself when the sunlight caught the mass of hair, blood, and dirt just right. In the ball something metallic glinted back at him. Jabbing at the mass with a stick, a small piece of metal fell out. Carl recoiled in horror at recognition of the piece of jewelry. A cross. More precisely ... Mary's cross.

Backing away from the horrifying site, he tripped over the moist patch on the ground. The liquid gave up its true identity. Blood.

"Hold it right there!" a voice yelled at Carl, breaking the silence of the woods.

Carl turned around and couldn't believe his eyes. A police officer happened to come walking up the trail at this exact moment he discovered this horrifying mess.

"Officer, I need your help."

The police officer drew his pistol. "Hold it right there. Don't move a muscle."

"Officer, I can explain. Something awful has happened to my friend. We need help."

Aware someone else was standing behind him, opposite the officer, Carl turned to see who it was. His gaze swept over the landscape just in time to catch the swing of something black toward his head.

Carl Jensen clung to a remaining question as the woods, tent, and the little town faded.

Why isn't this officer helping me?

———

UNFAMILIAR SMELLS WOKE HIM. All around the walls danced like caricatures of themselves, as if an artist painted on the disproportionate shadows being cast in an infinite number of directions. Carl wondered if he was dreaming before realizing this was the inside of a dark cave, lit with flickering torches.

Trying to lift his head and neck, the pain seared through him like a sword thrust through an eye socket and down into his neck. Only one eye opened in response to the desire to see.

To the left, chained to the wall, a woman hung lifeless. It took a moment or two to recognize the broken body of Mary. Half of her beautiful hair had been ripped out and a laceration above the right eye bled over the woman's face.

Carl's hands and arms screamed out in pain, confirming he was also bound to the wall. The ropes seared his hands and arms as the weight of his body pulled down on them. He attempted to stand, but his legs refused to cooperate.

"I see our friend Carl is awake now, Master," a voice called out in front of him. "Shall I knock him out again?"

"It is not my will, high priest. Let the tribute witness the ceremony. The fear will make the heart all the tastier."

Tasty? What the hell is this guy talking about?

Carl tried to say something; however, his lips and tongue refused to work in unison.

"Proceed, high priest," the deep voice bellowed through the cavern.

"Yes, Master," a black-robed figure responded.

Two other figures emerged from the side of the cave. Their robes were white, in contrast to the other man, and looked like monks' robes with Native American ornamentation. Carl couldn't recall ever seeing anything like it.

The figure in black approached Mary. Saying something unintelligible, he reached up and grabbed her collar. Pulling it away, the man's other arm came up with a small blade and plunged down in an arc, cutting the shirt off. With Mary's breasts exposed, the man stepped back as if to admire them. The one identified as The Master spoke up in a language which sounded to Carl like the language the priest had spoken.

Two figures, clad in white, approached the man in black and handed him two daggers in exchange for the short-bladed knife. Carl spied the opulently bejeweled handles of the blades glinting in the firelight. The black-robed figure slid one of these daggers in a sheath on his belt while keeping the other in his right hand. The Master stopped speaking, and the man in black plunged the dagger deep into Mary's stomach. A harsh scream escaped Mary's lips the moment before death or pain rendered her mute.

Carl wanted to avert his eyes or even register some sort of protest. Any attempt to move his neck or even speak was met with excruciating pain.

The man in black rolled up a sleeve and plunged his arm deep into the wound he'd inflicted. Working the blade upwards in a sawing motion, he cut and plied away portions of the chest cavity, with disturbing imprecision. Mary's innards spilled out onto the floor in a sickening pile of human tissue. The sleeves of the black robe became slick as they sopped up more and more blood from the gruesome display. The robed figure held up Mary's excavated heart.

"With this heart, I thank thee for the most holy of sacrifices. I declare this heart Holy and this sacrifice worthy of The Master." Turning from the now still body, the man in black brought the heart to the altar at the front of the cave.

Carl tried to follow the ghastly proceedings. The injuries from the beating he'd received proved so severe that even the simple act of lifting his head hurt too much. The Master let out a sigh, clearly satisfied with whatever he had done with the heart.

In the briefest of moments, the man in black stood before Carl. "You are selected to make the ultimate tribute to our Master. You shall become one with him and the name of Carl Jensen will be written among the stars for all eternity. This is indeed a great day."

A sharp pain struck Carl as the flash of the steel blade disappeared into his abdomen.

2

A QUIET MORNING ON LAKE OLEANDER

Waylon Anderson cast a line toward the thrushes along the bank of Lake Oleander. The electric trolling motor, at the bow of the john boat, pushed the aluminum hull through the water. The morning was pleasantly warm. A blanket of clouds the evening before kept the heat in, dissipating just in time to let the morning sun continue the warming trend. A slight mugginess hung in the air, clinging like an uncomfortable suit of clothes. But Waylon didn't mind.

An orange five-gallon pail held this day's take. So far, three crappies and two bluegills fluttered their fins uselessly, as if they resigned to fate. Not the kind of haul he'd anticipated. *The bass decided to stay home this morning.*

Rounding the bend in the quiet lake, he cast his line in the direction of a log sticking up out of the water. The log always lay there, a gnarled old signpost for the anglers of the area. It marked the beginning of a much larger tree, which branched out along the bottom of the lake. His grandfather taught him as a young boy how to tie line and bait hooks at this exact spot.

"Remember to cast directly behind you in a boat like this. Not much room in here and I don't want to be put on your hook. I'd make bad bait. What kind of fish you think would eat me, Waylon?"

The memory of his grandfather made him smile. A massive man, probably six feet tall, he could do no wrong. Even now, as an adult, Waylon remembered the scent of the old man's Zippo lighter. "Smoking is a filthy habit," he told the young Waylon. "Wish I'd never picked it up."

His grandfather served in two wars, WWII and Korea. Although the family purposely never talked about it, little Waylon's overactive curiosity got the better of him. One day he asked his grandfather about the war and instantly regretted it. The look of sadness told the young boy all he needed to know. Waylon's mother said the sadness was remembering friends lost in combat.

At the sound of his lure hitting the water, a nearby turtle made an immediate escape below the watery surface. Waylon felt bad for disturbing the turtle's slumber. Something jerked at the lure under the surface. Either a fish, or the lure hooked something while he was playing the line. He knew the area well enough that it wasn't the log, so it must be something else below the mirror-like surface of the lake. He let out line, it slackened and for a moment it didn't move. The lure sunk its hook into something below the waterline. A few tricks to remove the hook from whatever it snagged onto, the lure didn't want to budge. The only remedy seemed to be to move the boat in closer.

The trolling motor made a low groan as Waylon pointed the john boat toward the log. If he wasn't careful, he'd snag the line on either the trolling motor or the engine at the stern of the boat. Nearing the log, he set the fishing pole down and plunged his hand into the ice-cold water.

The lake was spring fed, originally created by someone damming up a river that cut its way through the area. When he was young, he'd heard stories about how the lake swallowed up an entire town, the ruins of which remained at the bottom of the lake. There was also a tall tale of a lake monster which lived in its murky depths. His grandfather told him tons of stories about the lake, stories that filled young Waylon's imagination with sightings of the Oleander lake monster. In his dreams, lake people carried on a perfect existence under water. Recollections of the tall tales always brought a smile to his face. This spot, however, only plunged to a few feet deep. Retrieving the line didn't present much of a challenge.

Despite the warmth of the day, the water chilled him to the bone. Lake Oleander maintained a constant current with cold springs feeding it and water exiting in a small stream at the southernmost point. The water refreshed during the summer when you swam in the heat, and chilled to the bone when you didn't want to be wet. No one ever swam in this part of the lake, leaving it quiet for fishing.

Reaching down, he traced the line into the murky, mud-brown depths. The lead weights and the top of the lure sat only six inches below, indicating the hook was only a few more inches toward the bottom. The hook buried itself deep into something soft, like an old bag made of rubber or perhaps a discarded child's ball. The pull of the line felt spongy with a little give as he pulled. Part of the object was covered in a fine grass. Grabbing a slight spongy protrusion on one side, Waylon pulled the thing up toward the boat.

Almost losing his balance, he recoiled in horror as the object crested the surface of the dark waters. What he'd used as a handle came off, leaving the rest of the ghastly thing to plop back in the water. In his hand, the remains of a human nose, waxy and cold. Throwing his fishing pole into the water, along with the ghastly appendage, he scampered back toward the engine, tripping over one of the metal seats in his panic.

For a moment the head rolled from one side to another. One eye, hanging from the skull, lay flush against the cheek in a mangled mess of tissue. The eye sockets of the unfortunate cranium were sunken and the cloudy eyes with no pupil stared at him. Skin, the color of light brown, hung gingerly to the skull as if preparing to slither off the bones the second anyone attempted to retrieve it from the watery grave.

He recognized the head, even in its current state, as belonging to Carl Jensen. A hiker well-known on the trails in Virginia, last seen by a group of fellow hikers twenty miles south of town with a girl he'd befriended on the trail. Missing since the Monday before, the townspeople knew and participated in what befell the young man. The town stayed silent on the affair, it wasn't the first hiker to happen into town and was never seen again. It likely wouldn't be the last.

He tapped the head with the end of an oar and watched it roll over and sink back into the water. The severed remains of the young man's neck hung briefly at the surface. Something nibbled on the exposed tendons and jaggedly torn skin at the base of his neck. The sight horrified Waylon, not because it was a severed head. It was alarming that the head was seen at all.

Waylon withdrew a small flask from his pocket and took a long swig, hoping, against hope, that the whiskey would calm his frayed nerves. The elixir did its job, helping to erase the image of the fishing lure embedded in Carl Jensen's earthly remains. Either way, the day of fishing was done. He needed to find Donny. He always knew what to do.

Firing up the motor, the john boat fled the final resting place of Carl Jensen as fast as the little motor could carry it.

The churning of the water by his boat engine forced the head to bob to the surface once more. A crane swooped down into the shallow water and landed next to it. Using its elongated beak, it pecked at one of the eyes in the sockets, pulling it free for a morning snack.

3

A WELL-EARNED REST

"Honey, did you remember to pack your swimsuit?"

"Yes Mom, I packed it. Sheesh, I'm seventeen. I am perfectly capable of packing for myself."

The woman stood next to the car, giving her son an aggravated look. "Okay mister smarty pants, you don't have to get snotty with me."

Meghan Johnston had only one thing in life that meant anything. That thing just turned seventeen years old and threatened to get a full scholarship to a university far away from home. Twelve years before, his daddy left them both. A mother and a boy of five, left alone to make a way in the world. That same five-year-old, now twelve years later, berated her for being too much of a mother.

"So, mister man-of-the-house, did you remember a razor so you can shave that stupid looking thing you have growing on your chin?"

"On Earth, we call it a beard. And yes, I did."

"Good, then let's go." He'd begged to stay home. Kyle wanted nothing more than to spend time at home this summer, hanging out with friends and playing video games. A little guilt from Mom, and Kyle conceded the battle. "I'm only asking you to sacrifice a couple of days with your mother. You know, someday I'll be dead, and you are going to feel bad for not spending more time with me. Besides, the lake will have a beach and, on that beach, will likely be girls." Girls weren't the motivation she wanted to home in on; however, they always seemed to do the trick.

A few minutes later Meghan and her progeny drove through the outskirts of town, toward the wilds of Virginia. Selected destination; a resort which contacted them off a waiting list of candidates desiring a discounted rate. For the last three years they found their way onto a summer waiting list for people interested in filling up empty rooms at the last minute. Ordinarily the timing didn't work out and this year the phone call, available funds, and a week off work all coincided.

They got the room for a steal since the resort had a cancellation. The stay included a breakfast buffet and free boat rental. It had a small beach and water park. Meghan had nothing planned beyond playing board games and working on a tan while he ran off and enjoyed the lake.

The outside morphed from cityscape to countryside. Soon the forests gave way to the foothills of the Shenandoah valley. She glanced over at Kyle and tussled his hair while he read a book. He batted her hand away and said in an annoyed tone, "Mom, stop." Then went right back to reading.

A string of dead-end jobs, an abusive husband who left them, and a mortgage which sometimes threatened to overwhelm their meager resources stood out as the normal state of life. But, all of that faded when Meghan watched her rambunctious son grow up before her. Kyle had been a great kid and turned into a great man. For every bad thing or difficult situation, she'd endured, Kyle made up for all of it.

"You know, Kyle, I'm going to miss this."

"Miss what?" he asked, not taking his eyes off his book.

"Us taking trips together. Our real last chance to hang out as mom and son. After this, you're all grown up."

"Mom, I'm pretty much already there."

She laughed. Of course, he was right. "Not to me. You're always going to be my little guy."

He made a face that couldn't quite hide a tiny smirk. "That's embarrassing."

"Of course, it is. I get to embarrass you. That's my job. When you were born, the doctor said, 'Here ya go, now embarrass the hell out of him.'"

"Well, while you're busy embarrassing me, can we get something to eat? I'm starving."

"Sure, honey."

Along the roadside, two giant signs for a truck-stop called the Starlight promised the best root beer floats in the galaxy. Meghan pulled the car into the packed parking lot. Feeding Kyle became more of a challenge as he grew. A switch flipped somewhere in Kyle when he hit the age of twelve and the boy hadn't stopped eating since. On top of that, the kid perpetually needed new clothes and shoes which kept the family's funding near the breaking point.

The diner itself featured a sprawling parking lot with plenty of spaces for cars and several longer spaces for semi-trucks to pull into. The diner's booths and tables teemed with life. Every stool at the counter was appropriately topped with truckers sipping down coffee and swapping stories of the latest hauls to Poughkeepsie, Dearborn, Cleveland, or any number of other places. Many proudly showed off pictures of their family's latest achievements while others sat at tables talking to their wives on cell phones. They looked sad to Meghan. Like they'd do anything to be home at that moment rather than on a lonely piece of road somewhere.

Meghan and Kyle took seats in a booth right next to an old trucker who just put away his cell phone. He regarded them both for a moment and said, "Evening' ma'am, evening son."

"Good Evening," they said, in unison.

He went back to reading his paper and she and Kyle opened the menus the waitress set before them.

"So, Kyle," she teased, "what's your pleasure or are you just going to order one of everything?"

Kyle patted his belly for emphasis. "I saw the pot roast special on the board. It spoke to my soul."

"Pot roast is gone, sorry," the waitress said. "But Charlie was the prep-cook this morning and makes one hell of a meatloaf. Open faced meatloaf sandwich should be out of this world."

Kyle smiled. "Oh well, if Charlie made it, then who are we to argue? I'll have that and one of those famous root beer floats to go with it."

Meghan rolled her eyes. "I'll have the meatloaf sandwich and a cup of coffee."

"Alright then, be up in a couple of minutes." The waitress walked back to the window separating the kitchen from the dining area, clipping the order to the wheel, and left to make the root beer float.

Kyle studied the top of the table. Once a Formica tabletop, someone had refinished it with several layers of clear laminate coating covering a collection of local newspaper articles. He perused a story from eight years ago featuring a rash of mysterious disappearances. "Kind of an odd thing to put on a table in a restaurant."

The trucker in the booth next to them lowered the paper and eyed Kyle for a moment. "You know the story behind that news-paper article you're reading, young man?"

"No, sir, I don't."

"The man who owns this place is Fred Stephens. Navy man in Vietnam, took shrapnel and got sent home. He did alright, though. Got married and had a couple of kids. Lived here a long time. He built those tables. About ten years ago, people disappeared from town under odd circumstances. Made every paper in the state."

"This sounds like a ghost story to me," Meghan said. The old trucker's story made her a bit uncomfortable.

"You could be right," the old man said. "See, no one knows what happened to those people. They all went missing. Right under the noses of everyone in town. One day they were here and the next, just gone. Well, one of those people who went missing was Mrs. Stephens. Old Fred kept every newspaper and every bit of information on the case. At one point they made copies of the articles and made them into the tabletops in case someone passing through town might remember a small detail. Anything that will help bring his wife home."

"How many went missing?" Kyle said.

"About twenty-five total. At least one of them we think may have run off with a girlfriend."

"Sounds like kind of a far-fetched story if you ask me." Meghan said. "I mean, how can twenty-five people just go missing. Didn't they ever find any evidence of what happened to them?"

The old man took a deep sip of coffee and stared out the window toward the trees on the other side of the highway, pondering what string of words would be best to answer a difficult question. Putting the cup down and letting out a heavy sigh, he stared into Meghan's eyes, searching for answers he himself struggled with for years. "You know, there are people in this world who go on around us who are essentially non-people. Let me ask you a question. The last delivery driver who came to your house, do you remember his name? Of course, you don't. You only cared that they were there on time, were fast, and then left. The waitress who gave you coffee, do you remember her name?"

"Rose. Her name is Rose," Kyle said.

"Very good, young man. I'm impressed. Most people don't notice the little things that matter most in life. You know, I have over thirty years of trucking behind me, and I can count on one hand the number of repeat deliveries where the manager of the store even knew I'd been there before, or even my name for that matter. Many people scurry in and out of our lives and we never even notice them, not even if they go missing. We may realize a different waitress brought us our coffee. Or a different delivery driver came to our door. No one ever misses them."

"Tank, quit scaring the customers. You old crazy codger." Rose said, approaching with two plates full of food and a tall, frosty root beer float. "Excuse me, ma'am, I have your meatloaf. Fresh and hot from the oven. For the young man, his is on us tonight."

"Oh, you don't have to do that," Meghan protested.

"Ma'am, your son remembered my name. That's more than can be said for half the brain-dead fart-weasels who come through these doors most nights. He's a fine boy and really classed up the joint."

"The lady is on me," Tank said. He raised a hand to cut off Meghan's impending protest. "Before you go arguing, you'd be insulting a retired truck driver and army veteran if you refuse."

"I'd take it, sweetie," Rose said. "The Tank has never picked up a check for anyone."

Outnumbered two to one, Meghan smiled as she gave in. "Wow, thank you both. I don't know what to say." She took a whiff of the food as Rose set it in front of her.

"So, where you headed?" Rose continued. "I'm assuming you're on your way to the mountains?"

"Yep, you'd be right. We are taking a mother-son vacation for a few days."

At her use of the words "mother-son vacation", Kyle squinted at his mother and took a deep slurp of his float.

"Any place in particular, or just anywhere that strikes your fancy to stop?" Tank asked.

She dabbed her mouth with a napkin. "A place called Hideaway Resort on Lake Oleander. We got a great deal on a recent cancellation."

As Meghan took a sip of the coffee, Tank and Rose exchanged a knowing glance. Barely perceptible, yet still enough to convey a hidden meaning.

"Just be careful up that way. On the other side of the lake, there is a little town called Riapoke. I'd steer clear of it. They are not particularly friendly to strangers up that way." Tank pushed the empty coffee cup toward Rose, still standing next to their table. "Anyway, I have to go." Tank stood and slapped thirty dollars on the table, and grabbed a John Deere hat from next to his empty coffee cup. "Pleasure meeting you folks. You have a nice vacation. Just stick to the resort while you're up there and you'll be fine." Without another word, Tank walked out the door, disappearing into the late afternoon.

"That seemed a little weird-ish," Kyle said. Meghan nodded in agreement.

"Oh, that's just old Tank. Being a trucker for thirty years fries your brain. Too many pulled pork sandwiches and cups of diner coffee will do that to you. But, he's right about one thing. Not a friendly bunch of people you'll find up there in Riapoke. Just be careful is all." Her face brightened. "Say, you know. I need to get y'all some pecan pie."

"Oh geeze, no. We don't want to impose," Meghan said, putting up a hand in protest.

"No imposition, I'm about to throw it out. Besides, it's store-bought. Not the greatest pie in the world. You'd be saving me space in the trash."

For a while, they both sat in silence and ate their dinners. Meghan thought about what Tank said. It had been a strange conversation, made even stranger by Rose confirming the odd story. Maybe it was one of those local legends which pervaded the coun-tryside.

Rose wasn't kidding about the pie. It was good, but definitely store bought. The two scoops of vanilla bean ice cream it came with made up the unimpressive pie. Meghan only ate about half of the meatloaf and half a slice of pie and felt like she was about to burst. Kyle, being the typical teenage boy, finished his meal first and then the rest of her dinner. The boy was a garbage disposal with feet.

Meghan glanced over at his plate. "Are you full for once?"

"For a little while. Do you think we can get meatloaf to go?" he said.

Her eyes got as big as saucers. "Are you kidding me? Please tell me you're kidding me."

"Well, maybe I am." He shrugged his shoulders.

Rose came over to the table again. Any more coffee, Meghan?" Rose and Meghan had become fast friends when the conversation moved past Lake Oleander.

"Thanks, Rose. I think I'm good."

"Kyle, I don't think even the truck drivers ever eat that much. I don't know where you put it all. You have to keep eating though, you handsome devil you. I swear, if I was seventeen again, I'd be hanging all over you. You are just the most handsome thing in the world."

Kyle blushed at Rose's over-the-top flirtations. "Thank you, ma'am."

"And polite to boot. He's a keeper, that boy of yours." She winked at Meghan before tending to other customers.

Back in the car, Kyle fell asleep. Blessed with the ability to fall asleep anywhere and at any time, the car proved an irresistible napping place. They didn't have far to go. Still, the sun would set before they pulled into the resort. Meghan enjoyed the visit to the odd truck stop, even if it was a little longer than expected. It was a delightful place filled with delightful people and the food was pretty good.

She thought long and hard about what Tank said. The nice, yet somewhat odd, retiree made a good point. People do go through their lives in a veritable fog, never knowing who's coming and who's going. The pizza delivery guy, the last time they ordered, was a stranger to them even though there's a good chance he lived in their neighborhood. Although certain they had the same mailman for the last few years, she drew a blank on his name. The same was true of the UPS driver who worked their route. They just all faded into the background. However, if any of them failed to live up to her expectations, she'd call them out in an instant.

It wasn't that they did anything wrong. She tended to vent her frustration at the entire world, as if bringing someone else down made her feel better about herself. It would be easy for one of them to go missing, and she'd never notice.

4

STILL WATERS RUN DEEP

Waylon Anderson took a few more sips from his flask before reaching the Riapoke municipal boat ramp. The warmth of the whiskey helped shield his nerves and replenish his courage.

Nothing like that was ever supposed to happen. Asked about it in a local meeting one day they said, "Lake Oleander never exposed its dead and never would." Today, it did just that. One moment the sun cascaded down from the cloudless sky, radiating off the placid lake on a perfect day. Now the situation completely changed. Something terrible happened to Lake Oleander and by extension, the tiny town of Riapoke.

Approaching the boat ramp, he saw the normal cast of characters hanging around. A couple of boys fished from the docks as well as a couple of old men. A husband and wife, trying to launch a boat from the larger ramp, argued about the proper technique. Jack Snow, the local boat mechanic, was fixing someone's impeller in the parking lot.

Matthew Tanner, the regional conservation officer and friend of Waylon's, stood guard over all of it. Waylon and Matthew were both in their thirties. Matthew, took better care of himself than Waylon though, giving him a muscular build and the appearance of only being in his mid-twenties. With light brown hair and hazel eyes, Waylon always wondered why his friend never settled down and married. Lake Oleander was Matthew's favorite base of operation since moving back to Riapoke.

Matthew stepped forward and eyed Waylon with suspicion. Even on his worst day, Waylon handled any boat as an extension of his own body. In contrast to the usual ease and familiarity of a man whose life was spent on the water, the boat's aluminum hull bounced off the recycled composite decking with a deafening boom. Waylon could barely tie off the boat, slipping while stepping onto the dock and almost head-butting Matthew as he tried to regain his balance.

"What the hell is the matter with you, Waylon?" Matthew said, offering a hand up off the deck.

Waylon waved the officer off. "I need to speak with Donny." He lurched forward and grabbed onto the officer's arm for stability.

"Whew, Waylon, what the hell are you doing? I should arrest you for drinking while operating a boat. You are drunker than a five-dollar hooker in Singapore."

Waylon stood to his full height, four inches taller than Matthew. "Go ahead and arrest me. I'll be safer in a cell than out there." Waylon pointed over his shoulder at Lake Oleander.

"Okay, okay. Just tell me you ain't driving anywhere. I'll have someone put your boat on the trailer and you can pick it up tomorrow. Stay out of your truck or I will have to arrest you."

"Oh, don't worry about me, you're driving us. We need to talk to Donny right away."

Matthew replaced the annoyed look on his face with one of genuine concern. Something uncharacteristically worried his most unflappable friend. "Waylon, what's this all about? Have you seen a ghost or something? You're kind of scaring me a little. I don't think I've ever seen you like this."

"Just drive and I'll tell you all about it."

Matthew climbed behind the wheel of the squad truck while

Waylon slumped into the passenger seat and took out his flask and threw back another sip. "Waylon, you can't do that in here, you know that. Will you tell me what has you so rattled?"

Waylon glanced out the window at nothing and shook his head. Matthew and Waylon attended the same elementary and secondary schools together. They had been very close as kids. In high school, however, they separated into different cliques. Waylon went to hang out with the jocks of the school and Matthew became interested in law enforcement. As a result, the two grew apart. When Matthew moved back to the area, they were able to rekindle their friendship. In spite of running in different social circles, Waylon still confided in Matthew and never feared his judgment.

"Matt, out there, in the lake. I was … just casting. You know, out by the bend. The big bass stump out there. Just casting … you know. Hoping something would bite. Like I've done, I don't know, hundreds of times before."

"Okay, so what? You saw the biggest monster bass of your life? The thing had fangs, fur, and hit the surface singing Sinatra tunes?"

Tears streamed down Waylon's face. "I saw a head, Matt. A fucking head. That guy, you know the hiker that came through here a few weeks with that girl. I think his name was Carl Johnson or something."

Matthew slammed on the brakes, causing Waylon to lurch forward in his seat as the sound of screeching tires filled his ears. Matthew pulled the truck over to the side of the road. His complexion drained of color, taking on a gray pallor. The implication of what Waylon said wasn't lost on him. "You mean Carl Jensen? Are you telling me that you saw the head of Carl Jensen in the lake today? Do you even realize what you're saying, Waylon? Holy shit!"

The two men sat in silence for about a minute. Waylon reached over and handed his friend the flask of whiskey. Wordlessly, Matthew took a long drink. They sat there for a few moments more, staring at the open road.

Past the turn off which took people back into the main part of town, toward the church and a few boarded-up businesses, they'd merge with the highway. Both men shared the same thought. How far could they make it down the road before anyone noticed? From there, the road would take them to Richmond, Washington D.C., or even Pittsburgh or Philadelphia. It might just be possible to outrun the shit-storm likely on the horizon for the little town.

"We need to go see Donny," Matthew said. Hitting the accelerator, he flipped on the emergency lights. Bad news never got better with age, and this news was as bad as it could ever get.

———

DONNY SWENSON SAT BACK on his thick leather couch with a book and a nice cup of tea. A lovely evening to sit by the window and watch the rainstorm play with the trees and form puddles in the driveway. Under normal circumstances, he'd be at church, watching over the staff and answering phone calls. This rare relaxing day off hit the mark.

In the distance, a flock of geese flew lazily across the horizon. He thought about how majestically the birds flew as they headed off to parts unknown. The way they maintained a 'V' shaped pattern across the sky suggested order in a disorderly world. Like an arrowhead without the shaft released from an archer's bow. That was the right word. *Order*. Exactly the way he liked his town, the town of Riapoke.

The estate, inherited from his parents, crouched in the dead center of 250 acres of forest. All the homes on this side of town did. The home and property, if sold, would be valued at five million dollars or more. However, since moving into his parent's home in Riapoke, life became far easier. The advantages the town fell over themselves to provide made up for the difficulties in living a more rural life. Ten years ago, if anyone suggested he'd come to pretty much own the town, he'd think them nuts.

His sixteen-year-old daughter, Beth, strolled through the house.

Having found the tennis racket she'd misplaced; her current search involved a missing pair of tennis shoes.

"Daddy, have you seen my shoes?"

Shaking his head at her quest, he said, "No Darlin', you'd know if you put them away where they belonged."

She huffed at his well-rehearsed line. "Oh Daddy, you know I love you. Take it from me, that line needs to find a good retirement home."

He knew where they were. However, finding them for her wouldn't teach the headstrong teenager to put things back where they belonged. Beth needed to learn how to take on more responsibility. As the heiress to an inherited, and some newly accumulated fortune, she'd learn responsibility if it killed him.

Beth meant everything to him. She grew into the spitting image of her mother, who left him after he assumed the role of reverend at the church. She lacked his vision for the town and didn't believe in what he and The Master were trying to achieve. One night she slipped out and never returned.

The Master selected a new wife for him. A mousy woman named Helen who fulfilled the role as well as anyone could. They married in a small ceremony at the church and, although they'd never had an emotional connection, his new wife fulfilled his needs and helped raise Beth until Helen died from an unforeseen illness a year ago.

As a child, his German grandparents insisted everything in life be planned and regulated. This suited Donny well. Dinner served promptly at 6:00, and God help you if you came late. Shoes were put on for school at exactly 7:15. Not 7:14, not 7:16. Some called them control freaks; however, the beauty of order gave his life meaning.

Strict controls were part of his upbringing. He relished and stuck to them.

Days off never promised relaxation. Most of the time he spent walking around in circles, looking for something to do. His daughter eventually became irritated and sent Donny out to take a long walk, if only to give her and the house staff a few moments of peace.

In the distance, flashes of light pierced the canopy of trees with beams of red and blue. Donny never remembered Matthew ever driving his truck up the driveway with the emergency lights on.

What does that idiot want?

Donny examined his cup of tea for answers. Through careful and creative planning, and of course The Master's help, Donny managed to force all the actual law enforcement officers out of town soon after relocating to Riapoke. With a fictitious police department on the books, Donny managed a good stage show when officials from other parts of the state needed to pry into their business. Several trusted townspeople filled out the ranks of the nonexistent sheriff and deputies when it became necessary.

For the last eight years, Matthew had functioned as their one and only legitimate law enforcement official. Matthew, a handful at times, was prone to indulging his independent streak. A native son, he insisted on doing things by the book where the lives of the residents were concerned.

Until recently, he'd been trustworthy. A few details came to light recently which gave Donny second thoughts. Getting rid of Matthew would be a difficult task. Matthew had the confidence and trust of the townspeople and could challenge Donny's authority if he grew a backbone.

Donny watched the lights shine brighter and brighter until they threatened to give him a headache. The truck pulled up in front of the house. Flinging open the front door, he glared down at the man who dared intrude on this peaceful day.

From the truck, he was shocked to see that in addition to Matthew Tanner, Waylon Anderson also stumbled out, almost falling to the ground.

"Matthew, turn off those damn lights!" Donny bellowed.

He seemed to disregard the order, waving Donny off as he approached the stairs leading up to the main house.

"Damn it, Tanner, turn off those fucking lights now." Donny

didn't like being ignored. Matthew, looking annoyed, returned to the truck and flipped a switch, dousing the emergency lights. "What do you mean coming to my home with those lights on?"

"Donny, we ain't here for tea," Waylon answered. "We've got business, and it's important."

Donny let out an annoyed sigh. "You'd better be right."

Waylon had committed himself to the cause and proved a useful tool to Donny. Waylon worked for the approval of Donny and The Master. The Master loved servants like Waylon. Never needing any cajoling or prompting, a good follower who did what he was told like an obedient dog.

"Well, let's get on with it. This is my day off and I have no intention of wasting it talking to you two."

"We need to talk inside," Matthew said.

Donny glared at Matthew like he'd glare at an insolent student who'd disobeyed his teacher. "We'll talk whenever and wherever I decide we will talk, Tanner. You have no right to speak that way to your better. Remember your place."

Matthew stiffened and took a step toward Donny, who stepped back a few paces, intimidating the man. "Donny, we either talk inside ... in your office, or I'll arrest you for interfering with a police investigation. Then we can talk in my office, which is far less comfortable."

Donny waved his hand in front of his nose in an attempt to diffuse the tense situation and hide his own fear. "Jesus, Tanner, have you been drinking?"

Donny knew he owned Matthew; however, on the books Donny's only official capacity was as the town's reverend and mayor. Matthew, in theory, had the power to arrest him.

"Yes, we both have," Waylon offered. "After we're done talking, you'll do right to have a few snorts yourself."

Donny fumed at the lack of respect. He wasn't sure how to handle it. "Suit yourselves, boys. Step inside, and you can explain the liquor on your breaths. And you, Matthew, drinking on duty?"

In no mood to carry on a lengthy discussion about his commitment to ethics, Matthew pointed at the house. "Your office, now." Once again, he succeeded in intimidating Donny.

Not something Donny particularly liked, preferring to be the primary force in the room. "As you wish, Tanner. This had better be good. You're treading on thin ice today."

They proceeded through a marble entryway and walked down a dark paneled hallway. At the end a set of oak double doors stood imposing and heavy. The Swenson family crest, carved into the wood, intimidated all visitors to the space. It was an audacious thing. A shield with two falcons entwined in battle. Next to each bird, two swords crossed. The family motto was emblazoned on the bottom of the shield in a scroll. Auctoritas non veritasfacitlegem. 'Authority, not truth, makes law.'

Donny pushed open the doors. Long pieces of finely polished wood flooring gave way to several oriental rugs, a large desk, and three chairs.

Matthew and Waylon took seats as Donny closed and locked the wooden doors.

"Stand up, both of you. You come into my home, flashing lights all over creation like a bunch of idiots. You both smell of liquor. And Tanner, you asshole, ordering me around in my own house. Need I remind you of your place here? Give me one good reason that I shouldn't turn you over to The Master right now?"

Waylon shot out of the chair in response to the rebuke, fear in his eyes. Matthew got up more slowly and put both hands down flat on Donny's desk. Leaning toward the reverend, Matthew stared into Donny's eyes with a steely glare which left no doubt he wasn't in the mood for word play.

"Waylon fished Carl Jensen's head out of the lake today," Matthew said.

For a moment, no one spoke. The three men just stared at one another. Donny's mouth fell open like a man caught mid-word and failed to carry out its pronunciation to the end. The color drained from his face.

After a lengthy and awkward silence, Donny turned to the large globe next to the desk. Flipping open the secret compartment and retrieving three glasses, he filled them with bourbon. Placing two of the glasses in front of the men, he fell in the leather office chair behind the desk. "You two better sit down and have a drink."

5

SETS HER HEART AFLUTTER

Meghan questioned if they were lost at the precise moment a sign for the Hideaway Resort and Convention Center fell into the beams of the car's headlights. According to the sign, only a few scant miles of road lay between them and a good night's sleep. The prospect of rest excited her. Kyle even let a yawn or two escape before succumbing to the exhaustion of the drive and the epic amount of food he'd consumed at dinner. Pulling into the reception center's visitor parking area, eager to get their room assignment, she left Kyle sleeping in the car.

"Good Evening and welcome to the Hideaway," the perky girl behind the counter said, flashing a set of perfect, pearl white teeth. "I'm Kimberly, and it's my pleasure to help you. May I have your name please?" The enthusiastically annoying girl struck Meghan as one of those people whose highest aspirations in life peaked at professional cheerleader. Blond to a fault, expressionless eyes gave her the impression the light was still on with no one at home. She couldn't be more than a year or two older than Kyle.

"Meghan Johnston, we got in on a last-minute cancellation."

Kimberly flipped through a pile of paperwork sitting on the

registration desk. "Ah, here we go. Johnston. Right. I see there are two people in your party. Where is ... Mr. Johnston?"

Meghan made a face. "Oh no, not like that. Kyle Johnston is my son. Who is sleeping in the car."

The girl stared at Meghan with obvious disapproval at the idea of leaving a sleeping infant in the car. "Do you need a crib or anything?"

"No young lady, my son is seventeen. He'd never fit. Just the keys, please. We're both exhausted." Meghan looked at least ten years younger than most women with a seventeen-year-old son, so people assumed Kyle was a baby. However, the girl behind the registration desk struck her as dull-witted.

"Oh, I'm sorry. Is he cute?"

Meghan needed a second to process the question the girl just asked. "I'm his mother. For your sake, I'll forget you said that."

Oblivious to her faux pas, Kimberly just shrugged, flashed her perfect set of teeth and said, "Okay. Your room is on the second level, near the elevators. We have a complimentary full breakfast at six-thirty, which runs till ten. You can also reserve a boat if you want, either for the full or half day. Just don't tie up at Riapoke docks, though. They don't like strangers. They're kind of odd like that."

"You're the second person who's told me that today," Meghan mused, more to herself than Kimberly. "Well, okay, can I reserve a small boat with an outboard for the day after tomorrow?"

"Absolutely, I'll reserve one now and you can head to the docks that morning. Do you want it all day, or just for the morning?"

"Let's take it all day." Meghan picked up the room keys and turned to leave.

"Have a good night, Mrs. Johnston."

"Good night, Kimberly." The girl smiled at Meghan. Perhaps Kimberly just sounded dim-witted through the pallor of exhaustion and the long drive.

When she reached the car, Kyle woke up from his extended nap. "Hey buddy, rested and ready to take on the world?" she teased.

He stretched his long frame and let out a prolonged yawn. "Rested and ready to go back to sleep."

"We have our room. I don't think they realize they're going to go broke with you eating the complimentary breakfast." They parked the car and dragged their luggage back to the entrance. Walking into the reception area, Kimberly stood behind the counter as before, this time two other females had joined her. They giggled and turned toward each other, whispering in hushed voices like this was the hallway of a high school.

Oh God, I hope I was never that stupid as a teenager, Meghan thought.

Kyle not-so innocently flashed them a smile and the three melted in response. "Hello ladies," he said. Adopting his manliest stride, he approached the giggling trio, but Meghan caught his arm.

"Not now, Romeo, it's late and we have a lot of fun things planned tomorrow. You can schmooze the ladies another time. Good night, girls." Meghan shot them a dirty look as she scooted him away from the counter.

"Bit of a kill-joy, don't you think?" Kyle said. "I just wanted to get a name or two, and maybe their phone numbers."

Meghan growled at him. Not raising Kyle as a piece of meat for wandering eyes, he seemed to enjoy the attention a little too much. The situation reminded her of her own teenage years. Every boy with wispy hair and a cute smile turned her head too. It was too early for Kyle to make girls' heads turn. Or maybe she tried to mask the fear that her little boy was growing up faster than she imagined.

Just one more summer. Let me have my little boy for one more summer.

THE NEXT MORNING, the day seemed full of possibilities. After a long breakfast of more food than she thought even her son could eat, they took a walk, just mom and son.

The woods along the lake shore held a magical allure. They both talked of what life at the University is like, and what lay in store for him. He would be off to college soon enough and for Meghan, it all happened too quickly. For the first time, she spoke to him as an adult and he spoke to her as one as well, not as a child seeking his mother's approval.

Sunshine and warm air invigorated her. Meghan walked in silence for a short while, thinking over everything that happened to them in life. Right now, everything aligned for just this once. After a couple of hours in the woods, they returned to the resort and changed into swimwear.

The beach area lay out before them, a long stretch of sand book ended by woods on one end and the small resort harbor on the other. A generous swimming area extended into the lake, cordoned off with red and white ropes and floats letting you know how far out you were allowed to swim.

It was inevitable that either Kyle would find girls, or they would find him. The second the two of them stepped out of the hotel proper, the girls flocked to Kyle. He'd been polite, gently putting them off while he walked beside his mother.

Meghan sighed to herself at the thought of pretty young girls peeling her little boy away from her side. At least they'd hiked together that morning.

It occurred to Meghan that kids always grow up too fast in a parent's eye, no matter how old they were. She wished Kyle could stay that scared little boy, always insisting on having the closets opened and for her to chase the lobsters away who hid under the bed. She laughed to herself as she remembered the time he got the words 'lobsters' and 'monsters' mixed up, and it stuck.

"Mom, can I ask you something?"

Meghan sighed at him. "Tired of your old mother already huh?"

"Mom, you're not old and no, I'm not tired of you. But ..." His voice drifted off.

"I'm not cool enough?"

Trying to recover, he said, "No way, you're plenty cool."

She shook her head. "Go ahead, Romeo. Go find your Juliet and leave me to die on the beach, all alone."

"Okay, being a tad dramatic, Mom. Aren't you?" he said, smirking.

Meghan waved toward the beach. "Have fun, sweetie. Just be back in time for dinner. I have a table reserved. We're going to do it up right tonight."

"I will, I promise. Be back at six. I love you, Mom."

"Love you too, son." Kyle trotted off across the sand to a group of teens standing near the water's edge. While unsure what kind of trouble a group of teenagers could find at a resort like this, Kyle had always shown good judgment. Though their life had been difficult, he'd developed a good head and a strong sense of right and wrong. However, she wondered how well his level-head would stand up against the girl at the water's edge, wearing a bikini more at home in a strip club than on a beach at a family friendly resort.

"You can't keep them small forever. I guess you have to let them go sooner or later," Meghan said out loud to herself.

"I'm sorry?" a voice asked. "Did you say something?"

Meghan shielded her eyes, glancing up to see a man standing next to her. He looked straight out of a cologne commercial: Bermuda shorts, unbuttoned Hawaiian shirt, and a drink with an umbrella in it. Nowhere near the caliber of man she would consort with on a beach. She'd always prided herself on good looks and taking care of herself, but this guy fell into a whole other league.

"Oh no, sorry. My son over there has abandoned me to play with new friends. And by new friends I mean that bikini over there."

He laughed at her exasperated tone. "Well, that's okay, the bikini you just gave the stink eye to is my daughter Kelley. Don't worry he's in good hands. She's probably already planning their nuptials and naming our grandchildren."

Meghan felt the flush of embarrassment redden her cheeks. Meghan launched into damage control mode. "I'm sorry, I didn't mean to offend, I'm sure she's lovely. It's just that, one second they are running around the yard naked with a diaper on their heads and the next they are full-grown people with hormones and their own lives."

He chuckled. "Oh, don't worry yourself. To be fair, I gave your son a similar look."

Meghan laughed as well. "Since we're going to be in-laws by the end of the week, I should introduce myself. Meghan Johnston, and your new son-in-law is Kyle."

He flashed a quirky smile, which she instantly found endearing. "Well, is this seat taken? I mean, for your husband?" He gestured to the chair reserved for Kyle.

"Nope, but it's only one and no room for your ... er ... wife? Girlfriend?"

They both stared at each other in silence for a moment before bursting out into peals of laughter. "Wow, we suck at this," Meghan blurted out.

The man shook his head and smiled. "Is it that obvious? I swear I was much better at this sort of thing in my younger days. Well, let's avoid any more awkwardness and we'll cut right to the end of the conversation. I'm Mike Chase and there is no wife or girlfriend."

She motioned to the chair. "Ah, so you are a member of the jilted spouses club of divorcees international, then?"

He sat after adjusting the back. "Actually ..." his voice took on a somber tone, "widower."

"Oh, I'm sorry, I didn't mean to sound so ... well, bitter."

He brightened up a little. "No problem. It was five years ago. Never smoked a day in her life, and my wife dies of lung cancer. A tough few years. We're getting there. Kelley and I are treating ourselves this weekend. A little daddy-daughter time before she blasts off to the university."

"Kyle and I are sort of doing the same thing. I get on the resort's discount cancellation list, and they called me up to offer me this week. It's actually a pretty good deal, you should look into it. It's the only way I can afford this weekend and still feed Kyle."

He readjusted the back of the chair. "Well, we just took off on a whim. It's hard to see a little girl smile after losing her mom at the age of twelve. Having to go through puberty with just your dad is pretty much the final nail in the coffin. You can imagine how the whole menstruation conversation went."

Meghan laughed at the mental image. "You found a YouTube video to explain it, didn't you?"

"Worse ... I paid one of the assistants at my office to fill in the blanks."

They both laughed, and a comfortable silence set in. Out on the lake several boats puttered by in the warm sun gracing the early afternoon sky. She stole a glance at Mike, wondering if fate had dealt new cards for her to play with. She'd worked so hard at trying to make ends meet that life seemed to cruise by her at an alarming rate. Maybe this man was God's way of telling her it was time to get back in the game. Mike seemed like a nice guy.

Granted, he could be making up the stuff about his wife dying, but this all felt right.

"Say, Mike?" Meghan turned toward him. "I don't do this sort of thing very often, but what do you say we drink a bunch of daiquiris until we're giggling like our teenagers?"

He clapped his hands together. "Meghan, I think this could be the beginning of a beautiful friendship." He waved at the bartender behind the counter. "Enrique, bring us the best daiquiris you can make. Top shelf only! And this woman's money is no good here. Put them all on my tab."

"Yes, Mr. Chase," the bartender answered.

Meghan protested. "You don't have to do that!"

"Quite all right. Besides, tomorrow night, you can buy." He gave her a wink.

"Why do I suspect you won't let that happen?"

He laughed. After the first daiquiris were drained and the kids made occasional appearances, she discovered Mike was a lawyer. A partner in a firm specializing in corporate law. Kelley, being an overachiever, served as the captain of the debate team and an accomplished oboist in the high school orchestra. The more they talked, the more they got along. Though the tequila helped, Meghan found Mike easy to talk to.

Close to dinner time, Kyle and Kelley returned.

Kelley turned beet-red at the sight of Meghan and Mike having such a good time. "Dad, what are you doing?"

"Well, since you two hit it off, Meghan and I just sat here getting drunk and planning out a dual wedding," Mike said. "You know, the four of us get married in a civil ceremony and live on a commune in North Dakota."

"Oh my God!" She flashed an embarrassed grimace at Kyle. "Parents are so embarrassing."

"Tell me about it," Kyle added. He gave Meghan a wry smile.

"Hey, Dad, can they join us for dinner? Please say yes. Please? It'd be nice to have someone to talk to other than—"

"Your old man?" He laughed. "Go ahead, keep talking daughter, you're doing great."

Her face reddened again. "I mean, it might be nice for you to have an adult to talk to."

"Oh, I don't want to intrude," Meghan said, even though part of her wanted to intrude and Mike to insist. "It's really an imposition, and we have our own dinner reservations."

"That's easy to fix. If you're up for it, I'd love to have you over for dinner. Besides, Kelley is right, it would be so nice to have another adult to talk to. Did I fail to mention my collection of wine?"

"No, you didn't."

"Well, I have this great—"

"You had me at wine, Mike. We accept. Guess we're double dating." Meghan chuckled.

Kyle's widening eyes communicated pure horror to his mother.

"Good, everything is settled then. Let's say an hour?" Kelley said.

"Yes, Mother," Mike said, laughing at his daughter.

"What about my reservations? I should cancel them." Meghan had done enough waitressing to know how irritating unused reserved tables were.

"No problem." He motioned over to Enrique again who'd stood close by as the daiquiris flowed. "Please cancel Ms. Johnston's reservation and have them set two extra places at our table."

"Yes, Mr. Chase. Right away, sir." Enrique disappeared behind the bar.

The waiter's strange formality when dealing with Mike struck her as odd. "Exactly how often do you come here?"

"Oh, I forgot to mention. I own a small portion of this resort."

She stared at him in confused amazement. "A small portion?"

He smiled at her. "Well, half anyway."

BEFORE DINNER, Mike took them on a special tour of the inner workings of the resort to include the extensive wine cellar. Mike had a whole area dedicated to his personal collection and although Meghan was unfamiliar with most of the wines, the collection was nonetheless impressive. He admitted, though, most of the wine came from trading different bottles with friends, a hobby which was more fun than drinking the wine itself.

As tasty as dinner was, Meghan found the company even better. She suspected the dinner that had been prepared for them wasn't the same dinner being served to the rest of the resort guests. The table sat on a private loft overlooking the main dining room, with a commanding view of Lake Oleander. The fine China they ate from, was meant for special occasions and VIP visitors. Mike explained the China usually sat in a cabinet in the corner, unused by his business partner who preferred hot dogs and beer to actual human food.

At the end of the night, Mike and Kelley walked them back to their room. While Kelley and Kyle said goodnight and made arrangements to hang out the next day, Mike and Meghan stole a few moments for themselves.

"Tonight was pretty terrific," Mike said, taking Meghan's hands.

She bit her bottom lip. It had been a great evening, and she didn't want to screw it up by saying or doing something wrong. She couldn't remember a night as wonderful as this one. "Me too. I'd invite you in for a nightcap, but that would be—"

"I'd likely say yes," he said, flashing his charming smile. "You know, we've been off the dating ride for quite some time. We should take it slow. Besides, I have no idea how Kelley might react to the idea of a nightcap. She's a teenager, and she could die of embarrassment."

She smiled at him. "Embarrassment is the leading killer of teens these days. Kyle would be a goner as well. That might be a compelling reason to do it. Think of the money we would save on food bills." She snorted at the thought. "You're right, of course. Tell you what, tomorrow, let's say we do lunch? Just the two of us. We can find something for the kids to do."

"Isn't it funny how we refer to them as kids? Not kids anymore, are they?"

Meghan sighed. "I suppose you're right."

Mike leaned in and gave her a kiss on the cheek. It was a pensive kiss. He went to pull away and then surprised her by also kissing her on the lips.

"Gross you two!" Kelley shouted from down the hallway.

"Yeah, really," Kyle added. "Just how much wine did you guys have to make you guys all smoochie faced?" Kyle added his two cents to the conversation. Both Kyle and Kelley devolved into fits of uncontrolled laughter.

Meghan leaned into Mike's shoulder and laughed. The kiss, albeit awkward, was warm, welcome, and comfortable. This was her moment, her time to take a chance. "Well, kids, we just agreed to have lunch together tomorrow and if all goes well. We'll probably smooch again."

"Ewww, gross," Kelley said. Both Kyle and Kelley continued their over-the-top laughter.

Meghan hardly slept that night. Every time she found herself nodding off, thoughts of Mike intruded. So charming and so wonderfully vulnerable. The love he still carried for his late wife was very much still present. She'd have to tread carefully with a guy like that.

Although Mike didn't say so, he was well off. Running a quick search for Mike Chase on the Internet, several sites came up, most having to do with corporate law. Several of them centered on philanthropic activities. Articles about a loving wife's death brought Meghan to tears a few times. One article outlined a charity set up in her name. A wonderful woman married to an equally wonderful man.

After breakfast the next morning, they made their way down to the docks. Meghan chose a small boat with an outboard motor from the twenty available. The man in charge, calling himself Harbor Master Bill, gave them a quick tutorial and had her fill out a few forms. She listened as he gave her a well-rehearsed lecture about boater safety.

In the distance, a thin line of clouds formed. "Say, Bill. Do you think the weather is going to hold out?"

"How long do you plan on being gone?"

"Oh, just the morning. We have lunch scheduled for noon."

He handed back her license and her copy of the paperwork. "Weather will hold till then. You see anything that looks like trouble, just make your way back. The weather can turn nasty here. Doesn't seem like too much now, but Lake Oleander can be a bit of a bitch. Gets real ornery."

Meghan grimaced at the odd metaphor. "Good advice. Thanks."

They climbed into the boat, where Meghan impressed Kyle with her boating skills, backing out of the small marina. Meghan moved up to the bow, and removed her tee-shirt, exposing a bikini top while Kyle took the helm. The sun warmed her skin.

For the first time in a long while, a sense of wholeness embraced her. No pressures from work, no worrying about Kyle, no obsessing over a long since failed marriage or trying to figure out how to pay next month's mortgage. And, on top of it all, a date with the wonderful Mike Chase. With those thoughts, she drifted off to sleep.

She woke with a start to the sound of Kyle yelling something.

"What's the matter, buddy?"

"Sorry, to wake you, but the engine quit on us. It doesn't want to start."

"Let me have a look." Although not quite sure she even knew the name of any part of the motor; blue smoke coming out of the top and the pull rope hanging uselessly at the motor's side probably wasn't right. It was like the motor and the rope were refusing to cooperate with each other.

Harbor Master Bill's lecture hadn't included engine maintenance and repair. "Well, I guess we row for a while. I'll get rowing and you keep working on the engine. I thought boys, were supposed to be good at fixing these sorts of things." She glanced at her watch, which read quarter to eleven. There was plenty of time to make their lunch date. If she rowed fast, they could get back with a few minutes to spare to clean up. Missing this lunch wasn't an option.

She dropped the oars in the water with a splash and turned the boat around. Although sure they'd drifted south of the resort, their exact location wasn't entirely clear.

In the back of the boat, Kyle continued wrestling with the motor. He occasionally turned and gave her an odd smirk as she rowed.

"What Kyle? You keep staring at me."

"I never realized what a cool mom I had. Here we are, out in the middle of a lake, stranded and a little unclear of where we are, and you immediately think to jump to the oars and row. That's pretty cool. I bet the other kids don't have moms who'd think to do that."

"Thank you, I'm glad to know you don't think I'm a complete dork." Afraid of ruining the moment, she continued to row. This is the exact thing she'd hope to come out of this week, a moment which would always be uniquely theirs. A chance to connect with her son.

Meghan, I guess you did a pretty good job raising that kid of yours after all.

A loud clap of thunder took her moment of reverie away. Before falling asleep, the clouds appeared like a pencil thin suggestion of unpleasant weather on the horizon. Staring at them now, they didn't have anywhere near the time she thought they did. Not finding shelter soon meant they would be trapped out on a lake in a metal boat. A lightning magnet ensuring they'd attract any lightning in the area. The crack made her row even harder. The wind kicked up and bucked the little craft as waves grew exponentially from its previously placid demeanor.

Rain, starting as droplets, now came down in buckets as the wind drove it into them. Several inches of water accumulated at the bottom of the boat. Imagining the worst, her fear stoked an intense need to continue rowing.

Digging the ends of the oars deep into the water, Meghan propelled them as far across the lake with each stroke as possible, her muscles screaming with every pull.

"Mom," Kyle clamored over the howling wind. "Do you want me to trade off with you?"

With every stroke of the oars, Meghan let out a puff of air. "No ... thanks ... Kyle. I ... can ... manage ... for ... now."

"Okay, let me know when you want to trade off."

Edging around a bend in the lake, Kyle pointed toward something in the distance and yelled, "Mom, I see the docks!"

Thank God.

The bottom of the boat was now a soupy mess, with her tee-shirt and several items from her purse floating in a jumbled mess.

On the end of the dock, a man stood waving at them. She brushed water from her eyes, trying to identify the figure. Likely it was the harbormaster waiting to give them a tongue lashing about being out in a rainstorm. She wanted to give him a piece of her mind about sending them out into the lake with faulty equipment, but right now she was more worried about getting out of this deluge.

6

A ROUGH LANDING

Donny sat at the desk, his hands cradling an achy head. "I think I have it all now. It's hard to believe. Are you sure you saw what you think you saw? I mean, the head and all?"

Waylon worked through a second glass of bourbon. Matthew refrained from having anymore, still having to drive Waylon home. The discussion, instead of reassuring them, had actually made them all slightly more depressed.

"His nose came off in my hand, Donny!" he exclaimed. "Yes, that's exactly what I saw. And I hope to God I never see anything like that again. The head ... it looked at me." He gulped down the last of the bourbon and pushed the empty glass toward Donny. "Those dead, gray eyes stared up at me." Waylon shivered against the thought. "Barkeep, another please."

"I think you've had more than enough. Matthew, I think you should take Brother Waylon home. You're okay to drive right?"

"Yeah, I'm fine. Waylon, why don't you wait outside a second, I need to ask Donny something." Waylon, remembering his place, stood up and stumbled out of the room.

"What's on your mind, Deacon?" Donny asked after the door

closed behind Waylon. It was clear he had already anticipated and feared the grave question troubling Matthew.

"Do you think this is part of the prophecy? I mean, we all know the stories. We're trained on them since our selection. Is this the prophecy?"

Donny leaned back in the huge leather chair, rubbing a whiskery chin while examining the trees dancing in the wind outside the huge bay window. The pair sat in silence for a moment. Matthew held his breath in anticipation of an answer he wasn't sure he wanted to hear.

"Deacon Matthew, I don't know. I'm not sure anyone knows. That is a good question for The Master. I'm going to ask him, but you know how these things work. We'll either get a concrete answer or more questions. I have to tell you, out of all the things I was prepared to deal with today, this wasn't one of them."

Matthew shook his head. "Me neither. Well, Donny, have a good rest of your day. Sorry to spring this on you like we did. I had a duty to report it right away."

"You did well Matthew. That idiot Waylon would've screwed it up, left to his own devices. You're a good brother to him." He leaned forward, lowering his voice. "Keep an eye on him, make sure no one else finds out about this. If he gets out of line, you know what you have to do. I authorize you to take matters into your own hands."

They locked eyes for a brief moment, and then Matthew nodded resignedly. "I understand. Hopefully it won't come to that. But, I'll do what needs to be done."

"That's why you are a deacon. Go with the Master's grace, Brother Matthew."

"Go with the Master's grace, Brother Donny."

Matthew walked out of Donny's office, closing the heavy wooden doors behind him. He took a moment to admire them. The first time he'd seen them was when he had been commissioned as a deacon. The intricate workmanship suggested the artist was a master craftsman.

All the more private ceremonies were held here. In addition to the Reverend's house, the office also served as the church's main office when no one was at the sanctuary.

Matthew found Waylon slouching in one of the hallway chairs, staring at a spot on the floor. "C'mon Waylon, time to get you home."

Waylon stood wordlessly; his gaze still fixed to an undefined spot on the floor. To Matthew, Waylon appeared frailer than just an hour before, as if being in Donny's office shaved a few years off his life.

Matthew knew part of Waylon's down-trodden look was due, in part, to his continued battle with his illness. The sickness advanced quicker than anyone thought possible. Not even Donny knew the extent of the sickness. The stress took a heavy toll on him.

Waylon turned to face Matthew as his friend started the engine. "Matt, what happens now? I mean, for real?"

Matthew hadn't gone by Matt in years. He'd always been Matthew to anyone who knew him. Matt was the name Waylon used when they were kids. The use of the name reminded him of a time on the playground, where Waylon sat under the oak tree trying to stop a nosebleed Eric Wickerman gave him. Waylon balled like a five-year-old. He'd asked him the exact same question then, "Matt, what happens now?"

As kids, what to do was always black-and-white. Mathew found Eric Wickerman and beat the shit out of the boy until Eric promised not to pick on the much-smaller Waylon ever again. Today, Matthew wished the answer was as simple as tracking down Eric and beating him up again. Times were simpler then. "I don't know buddy."

"That's what I thought. Do you think this is the prophecy?"

Matthew put the truck in drive and navigated the long, winding driveway back to the main road. He thought about the question his friend had asked. Even as kids, Waylon turned to Matthew for guidance when life fell out of alignment. As adults, given the right stresses, they fell into their traditional roles as leader and follower.

"I've got to tell you, Waylon, I have no idea."

Matthew came back to the city by choice. After finishing the state law enforcement academy, Riapoke made the perfect home base. The town municipal and religious leadership, one and the same, pulled strings to get him assigned to the region permanently. Matthew grew up here and knew the people. He'd do anything for them, and they would do anything for him.

Although familiar with the goings-on of the community and managing to stay in touch with the people, he knew little about the Church of the Master before returning home. The reverend had come to town three years before his return and took everyone by storm. Neighbors who'd never seen the inside of the church transformed into the most devout fanatics. Donny, a local boy who'd moved away in his college years, was welcomed back as a prodigal son after his parents died.

Donny Swenson had a gift for preaching and knew how to get people to see things his way. Radiating charisma, the man worked crowds into a frenzy, and soon Matthew understood what many others did. When he lacked in substance, he could always compensate with charisma.

Different from his conservative Baptist upbringing, Matthew enjoyed the services, becoming more and more involved in the church over time. They'd introduced a training program for both children and adults. He liked this approach and it helped him become more involved. Matthew received a commission as a deacon and was handed a key to the church. He also learned the awful truth of the organization he was oath-bound to support. At that point, it was too late to back out.

"Matthew, what are you thinking about?" Waylon asked, disturbing his reverie.

Matthew sighed. "I was thinking about when I moved back to this town. You remember when I arrested you for being drunk on your old boat? Boy, you sure were lit that day."

"I do. I never thanked you for that."

"Thanked me for what? I arrested you."

A congenial note tinged Waylon's voice. "True, you arrested me.

You also treated me like a person, not just another drunk off the street."

Waylon had his fair share of problems with alcohol over the years. Although he'd gotten drunk on a regular basis, rarely did it harm anyone or anything beyond his own liver. Matthew took it upon himself to take care of him, to be the older brother Waylon didn't have. As the years went on, the drinking increased.

Waylon confided in Matthew his terrible news. Drinking, for him, was the only defense against the pain of the cancer, incurable and aggressive, taking over his body.

"You're not a bad guy, Waylon. You just need help every once in a while. Well, here you go, safe and sound." Matthew brought the truck to a stop in front of his apartment building. "Remember, stay away from your truck. I don't want to see you down at The Oyster tonight. I find you down there, I'll put you in lock-up until tomorrow. Got it? I don't care if you drink at home. But sure as shit, stay home."

"Okay, Matt. I will. Thanks for taking care of me ... again." Matthew watched as Waylon stepped out of the truck and headed up the stairs to the apartment. His friend looked old, moving slower than he'd ever seen before, he guessed that little boy who held a bleeding nose in the playground now had a life measured only in a few weeks or months if he was lucky.

The Oyster Bar was the only place in town open past ten. On top of making a mean corned beef sandwich, they also served liquor to the local residents until the town's unofficial curfew. Waylon was a regular. Despite his friend's frail state, and assurances, Matthew knew he'd have to check later to make sure Waylon resisted the temptation.

A sudden drenching rain made the streets vanish until the wipers caught up with the onslaught. Lost in thought, the darkness overtaking the sky impressed itself upon him and complimented his melancholy mood. He hadn't remembered any bad weather in today's forecast, though this time of the year it was hard to predict impending storms with any certainty.

Expecting chaos to ensue, Matthew drove to the ramp. Surprisingly, things moved a lot more smoothly with the storm than without it. A couple of people waited patiently to get boats on trailers and the sudden downpour didn't bother anyone. He watched as the last group just finished ratcheting a pontoon onto a trailer. As soon as it was secure, they would pull it out of the water to finish the rest of the work in the parking lot.

Parked in the corner, he continued to observe the dissipating boating population of Riapoke. Matthew watched each boater drain their boat's bilge at the lake rather than just drive off with water still accumulated, a ticket-able offense with the rise of the zebra mussel; an invasive crustacean which traveled from one lake to another in the bilge water of boats. They likely only behaved themselves because he was watching them, like a strict parent insisting they clean their rooms or eat their broccoli.

The moment the final trailer pulled off the boat ramp, the worst of the rainstorm hit. He could barely make out the light at the end of the dock. The unenviable task of checking the grounds to make sure no one remained out on the lake fell to him. Right now the idea of getting out of the truck was absurd, the noise of the rain pelting the roof of the cab was almost deafening. Steeling himself and taking a deep breath, he pulled a green raincoat and rubber hat out of the center console, hoping they would keep the worst of it away.

Matthew had made mistakes in his life. However, his dedication to the residents of Riapoke wasn't one of the things he regretted. He'd learned to ignore the world outside of town. Within the city lines, however, he made sure all was as well as possible. Stepping out of the truck, a six-inch deep hole in the parking lot swallowed Matthew's boot, soaking through to his bare skin.

Damn it, I need better boots.

As he approached the docks, he was relieved to find them empty. A flash of lightning passed overhead. The rain, draining off the main road, formed an appreciable river in the center of the parking lot which sliced its way down the boat ramp and into the lake.

Casting a cautious glance toward the sky, he stepped out onto the dock. While the planking was recycled, non-conductive building material, the frame underneath was aluminum and could carry the electric charge from a lightning strike with terrifying efficiency. Any more lightning, and he'd abandon this task until conditions were less dangerous.

A small, yet powerful light sat on an eight-foot pole at the end of the pier. Installed to help late night boaters, without it the boat ramp sat in complete darkness which posed a hazard. The light was set to activate with a timer or if a sensor in the parking lot sensed rain.

As a boy, he remembered standing on the end of the dock, skipping rocks across the lake. The lake had been a huge part of his life, almost like a family member. As the rain pummeled his hat and raincoat, he quietly worried about the implications of Waylon's find. Carl Jensen was one of several dozen unfortunate souls calling the lake their final resting place. The population of Riapoke had long since collectively sworn this fact to secrecy.

This bothered him. As a sworn officer, under oath to uphold the law, he should be the one to speak for the innocent. By the time the terrible secret of the town of Riapoke took hold of him, the web had proved inescapable. If Matthew were to turn his back on Riapoke, which he would do in an instant, his family would suffer the consequences. He had to protect his mother, father and sister, who were still within The Master's reach. They were the only things tying him to Riapoke and the awful secrets it held.

As a deacon, the prophecy The Master foretold became his secret to bear.

One who had given of themselves for all and should remain hidden, would be found at the water's edge. A stranger brings upheaval, while a native son betrays. A mother's courage refuses to abandon a task as she represents a false offering. A son saves that which he cannot live without, and Riapoke sees its own end.

While many residents spent countless hours attempting to decipher it, the cryptic meaning of the message eluded them. Even The

Master himself remained unclear on what it meant, only that it was something they must always be on guard for.

Off in the distance, just past where the waves formed a solid mass of gray, something caught his eye. At first, the form wasn't clear. A mass of shadows solidified, and a boat emerged from the chaotic downpour. Its passengers trying to make it to the dock. A woman rowed in the center of the craft while a man, seated aft, worked the motor, trying to steer them. It would be comical if the rain and the waves weren't threatening to sink the boat.

They needed help, and quick. Matthew waved his arms at them to get their attention, while searching the dock for the rescue rope.

7

THE PENITENT MAN

Donny navigated the roads toward the church. The day, beginning as nice as it had, took a turn for the worse. News like this couldn't wait, and The Master may provide direction. Reflexively, he breathed into his hand, catching a whiff of bourbon. The Master hated it when people came smelling of booze. While encouraging underlings to drink as much as they pleased to keep them compliant, the higher up you went in the order the more sobriety was demanded.

The Master issued a standing order that he was to be immediately informed of any strange events. Everyone from deacon on up knew the prophecy. They read a copy of the proclamation while the original parchment sat under glass, protected as a foundational document of their faith. In many ways, it served as a central tenet of Riapoke's religion. To keep their way of life meant teaching vigilance for the fulfillment of the prophecy. The events stood as a final warning before it all came crashing down around them. Missing the signs also meant missing the opportunity to forestall the town's demise.

Donny's car turned into the parking lot of the sprawling church complex. Centered on one-hundred-fifty acres of pine forest, it dominated the area. In addition to a huge sanctuary, a bell tower rose one-hundred feet into the air. Two wings extended out on either side of the sanctuary, each standing two stories tall. One wing serving as church offices and meeting rooms. The other served as an education wing and storage area. In the back of the church a large pond with a fountain in the middle made up a contemplation garden. Its parking lot, huge compared to most churches, had parking for over five hundred cars. The church was far larger than a congregation of this size would ever need.

The building's enormous size was never planned with the size of a congregation in mind. The church was constructed so large to cover the evil lurking underneath. It had to keep prying eyes away from The Master's inner sanctum. It also ensured those never destined to leave his lair from ever being able to escape.

Legend spoke of the Powhatan Indians finding the cave. Exploring the hole in the earth they found springs of fire protruding from the walls. Following the cave to its terminus, they met The Master. He told them of time before time. The god-like being spoke of love and loss, of formation and destruction, and many stories captured in legends and ancient tales told around the campfire.

He foretold their ultimate demise and the epoch which saw the end of the Native American dominance on this continent and subsequent enslavement to the white man. Years later, the stories were handed down to the descendants of those early cave explorers.

The cave sat forgotten for many years. Future explorers would discover the cave and The Master. By then, the tone had changed. Presenting himself as the only true God, he instructed them to serve him alone, so he could keep them safe. Those explorers built a house at the entrance to the cave. Those early buildings became larger structures. Now it stood in its present form, a brick and mortar church building. Complete with an altar, a secondary, and rarely used cave entrance, remained hidden directly under the floor of the sanctuary. The main entrance to the cave was accessible behind a door in the pastor's office.

Waiting at a light that stubbornly turned red just before he reached the intersection, Donny wondered about the early Indians. Why did they never ask The Master to ensure their survival? The Master could do anything, including protecting them. Either they chose not to ask for those things, or their fate was already written in stone.

The rain continued its assault as he drove the short distance to church. The weather station had suggested the rain would give way to beautiful blue skies later that morning, which fit his mood in some ways. The rain was cleansing, and yet destructive at the same time. The prophecy, although confusing and nebulous, could be interpreted the same way. Both cleansing and destructive at the same time.

"I must stop over analyzing this," Donny said to no one. "The Master will know how to handle things." No one, in the history of their order, had ever come across anything like this.

He pulled into the church parking lot. The space reserved for the reverend featured its own carport, which kept him from getting soaked during a rainstorm, right before preaching. A three-foot area of space remained uncovered where the carport ended, and the large awning covering the front of the building began. That point always felt symbolic. One side represented the church and everything serving The Master, the other side represented everything he could control and his home. The gap stood as a chasm between plausible deniability and oftentimes terrifying knowledge.

The questions ran deep, and he hoped The Master would make it all clear. Sometimes, gaining a little knowledge can be just as frightening as the lack of it.

Leaping across the short expanse, Donny repressed the trepidation which always came with entering the church. A short walk up the stairs brought him face to face with the heavy wooden doors. Carved years ago by a master craftsman, the man's name was now lost in time. The artistry that went into the doors was so great, in fact, The Master determined the man should be sacrificed as a tribute. A little unusual, since tributes were usually nobodies passing through town to other destinations.

The Master told them, years ago, that every tribute should be someone on the fringes of society, those no one would miss. Someone who's starting point was as unknown as their ending point. This way they would add their own unknown journey to his. Plus, such people would be far less likely to have anyone looking for them.

Donny remembered the man who carved the doors as being different from the others. He didn't beg or even protest when presented to The Master. The artisan, upon being presented as a tribute, said, "I've lived my life as a good Christian and I'll die as one. This thing, this monster, will surely exist long after you're all gone. I ask you, what of your own souls when this is over?"

With that final question, The Master reached out with one razor sharp claw and cut the man in half. Looking down at the slain body, he said, "And I ask you, what did your Christian God do for you? Where is your Jesus now? Not here. It's me, it will always be me. Let this be a lesson to my followers. Through me, you shall be saved. Without me, this shall be your fate."

That moment never sat right with Donny. It wasn't that he doubted anything The Master did that day, but he'd stood in awe as the man maintained his beliefs even in the face of imminent death. How this man, standing on death's door, remained so calm intrigued him. Every time Donny stood in the presence of The Master, it terrified him. While The Master bestowed amazing graces upon people, it could destroy those same people if they fell out of line.

In the beginning, The Master took whatever hearts Donny arranged for him. More recently, he'd demanded the actual victims be brought and presented to him in a ritual sacrifice. The rituals had taken on more formality as well. The Master had become increasingly angry at the victims. The change concerned Donny, not enough to make him question what he saw as the unfailing wisdom of The Master, but the change in his demeanor was worrisome.

8

THE BITTER RESCUE

Matthew almost stumbled into the water after tripping on something laying across the dock. The town was forced to install a rescue rope at the end of every pier by the state, after a rash of accidental drownings. Suddenly their installation seemed less ridiculous.

He coiled the rope around his arm and assessed how long a throw to make to reach the besieged boat. The two people still struggled to make it to shore. It would be close. In the short time the rain started its ferocious assault, the wind gusted to hurricane force levels, churning the water into an angry froth. The woman rowed the boat but made little headway as the wind blew them farther from the shoreline. The man in the back, trying to steer the craft with the motor, shouted something, but the words were lost in the howling wind.

Matthew had to make the throw count. Once the rope took flight, if he missed his mark, it'd fall into the water short of his mark. The way the small boat was floundering, he wouldn't have time to reel the rope back in for a second try. Everything hinged on his aim being dead on.

THE WIND BUFFETED the little craft. A sudden gust blew across its hull, sending the port side of the boat dipping into the water like an oddly shaped soup ladle. The lake flooded in at an alarming rate before Meghan shifted her weight to bring the lip of the boat up out of the water. The craft, now carrying excess weight, took on an even more sluggish demeanor.

Toward the docks, she saw a man standing under a light. He picked something up and looked as if he were going to throw it at them. Behind her, Kyle yelled something. Even his deep baritone voice got lost in the howling wind. The bottom of the boat now filled with water halfway up the side. If they took on anymore, the boat would likely disappear beneath them.

Digging deep and pulling on the oars with all her might, Meghan's flagging strength finally gave out. She berated herself for not putting Kyle on the oars in the first place, as he surely had far more stamina than she. Meghan was in great shape and crushed any exercise. Even the strongest of her cross-fit class would've found this a challenge.

As if responding to projected fears, the boat struck something beneath the water, and both grabbed anything they could think of to stay inside the crippled watercraft. They were still too far from shore to hit a rock, Meghan reasoned. A log or other floating debris the more likely culprit.

The boat listed again to port. As it did, the corner of the boat disappeared under the roiling surface of the water. With the craft swamped now, Meghan tried to yell for Kyle. The wind and the rain swallowed her voice as soon as it left her lips. She felt terrifyingly alone.

Oh my God. I've killed us both. I'm going to die, and my dear sweet child will die with me. How could I be so foolish? Why didn't I stay awake? I could've seen the storm coming and we would have started back earlier. We'll drown.

Meghan was shaken from her personal moment of panic by an

arm sweeping around her chest. The Eagle Scout in Kyle took over. She was shocked at how strong his grasp was and how he'd reacted on instinct. Beneath her, she felt his legs kicking against the water.

"Hang on, Mom, I've got you! Just don't fight me!" he screamed, kicking against the torrent of waves and wind.

Going limp in her son's arms, Meghan watched as the boat slipped under the waves. Suddenly, something large made a splash in the water. It took a moment to make the thing out, but relief washed over her when she saw it was a rope.

Meghan clasped her fingers around their miraculous lifeline, her numb joints crying out in protest. Gripping with every ounce of remaining strength, she held on for dear life.

The rope went taut as she felt the person on the other end of the rope pulling them back from the brink of drowning. Behind them, items from their boat bobbed in the water, standing testament to the tragedy of their ill-fated excursion.

The lake bottom startled her as her feet connected with the cement of the end of the boat ramp. She made a movement to stand up and Kyle yelled, "Not yet, Mom, a few more feet and we'll be alright." She had to let him drive this train.

"What the hell were you two thinking?" a man's voice shouted. It didn't sound anything like Harbor Master Bill.

Steadying herself, she ascended the small incline of the ramp. Looking around for the first time, she realized they weren't at the resort.

Kyle stood on the dock, panting. "Our motor quit, and the boat became overwhelmed in the storm."

Meghan, now joining Kyle, searched the man for any indication of who he was and why he was out here or maybe where they even were. The man was a police officer, the words conservation officer over the right breast pocket of his raincoat gave him away. She offered, "It was an accident."

"Well, I hope so. Nobody in their right mind would do something like that on purpose. Let's get you two out of the rain for now."

A few moments later the officer let them into his truck and handed them two towels from his emergency kit.

Meghan shivered against the cool of the faux leather seats, still dressed in her bikini top and cut off shorts. Kyle was none the worse for wear, except for being soaked to the bone. Meghan sat in silence, drying her hair and trying to make sense of how they got there ... wherever there was. Looking out of the window at the lake, items from the boat flowed down the natural currents of the lake, the boat's hull nowhere to be found.

Finally, able to catch her breath and sort out how close they came to their demise, she turned toward her rescuer. "I didn't get the chance to thank you, officer, for saving us. Had you not shown up when you did, we'd have been goners."

He glanced up, eyeing her in the rear-view mirror. "I don't know about that. The kid did a good job saving you both. Quick thinking on his part got you most of the way. Could've brought you both in safe on his own, I imagine. The rope only helped out a little."

She looked over at Kyle, sitting in the passenger seat next to the officer, she smiled at him. "I know, he's a pretty great kid." Kyle likely saved them both. The officer's throw might have come up short if Kyle hadn't closed the gap with his strong swimming.

"Welcome to Riapoke. Not the way most people get here, though. Funny how things work."

Kyle cocked his head to the side, narrowing his eyes in an inquisitive stare. "You mean we aren't back at the resort?"

The officer shook his head. "Nope, you are on the other side of the lake. I can have you back there in twenty minutes by boat or about forty minutes by car once the weather lets up. We don't have anything to do with them. We try to keep to ourselves around here."

She nodded, remembering what she'd heard about the locals. "Well, sorry about all of this. Is there somewhere we can rent a car to get back?" Since her purse sat at the bottom of the lake, she'd have to get the credit card company to authorize a rental car. It seemed to her there should be a system in place for just such an emergency. "Oh, and a cell phone, I need to make a call. Mine is currently with the boat, wherever that is." Under normal conditions, Meghan would have thought the officer's roaming stare was directed at her exposed cleavage. However, right now she guessed her appearance presented a less than appealing vision of beauty.

He shook his head at her through the rear-view mirror. "Ma'am, I don't think you understand the situation. You see, I'm the conservation officer for this district. You just brought a boat out into hazardous conditions and then you sunk it. Now the lake is polluted with gas and oil. Now you tell me you dumped your phone in the lake which contains mercury and other bad things. You're not going anywhere."

"You mean I have to pay a fine?" Meghan asked. Incensed that he'd have the gall to give her a ticket under these circumstances, this whole thing sounded ridiculous. "I didn't know the storm was going to come up that fast. And the motor died. We would have made it out of there if the motor hadn't quit." She'd managed to keep her ire down, but only barely.

He shook his head. "I'm afraid it isn't going to be so easy. I must place you under arrest for negligent pollution of a state-controlled body of water. The law is the law. I know you're having a bad day, but I have no choice. The state code mandates I take you into custody until we can get this all figured out."

Her mind swam with dozens of scenarios, and all of them bad. She envisioned herself trapped in this little town for all eternity, only being let outside to collect trash along the side of the road.

This is a joke, someone had to be pulling her leg. His treatment of her as public enemy number one was unfair for having the bad fortune of being caught in a torrential rainstorm. Arresting someone for sinking a boat is the dumbest thing she'd ever heard.

A knot thrust its way into her throat, and tears stung her eyes. What about Kyle? He was only doing what she'd told him to do and he'd saved their lives. Through sobs, she said, "My son ... he didn't do anything. He's innocent."

The officer, uncomfortable with her emotional display, let out a heavy sigh and rolled his eyes. "Oh ... come on now, lady. Geeze, don't cry. I hate seeing people cry. That's the last thing I need today. Look, you didn't murder anyone. A night in our fair town and a fine will be the worst that'll come of this. I'll take you to see the judge and chances are he'll just slap you on the wrist and tell you to be more careful next time. I'm not even charging the kid with anything and I'll even pick up chicken from the deli for you two if you have to stay at the jail. But, please stop crying."

In most situations, Meghan was unflappable. More likely to get angry than tearful, the reality of their harrowing brush with death overwhelmed all her senses. They'd only wanted a nice day out on the water, followed by a nice lunch with a handsome man who'd showed an interest in her. Instead, they almost drowned, and in the process managed to sink a boat they'd likely be paying off for years to come. Mike would be well within his rights to never speak to her again. Hot tears streamed down her cheeks.

A contrite look crossed the officer's face. "Look, lady. I'm sorry, what is your name?"

Kyle spoke up, looking a little annoyed. "Her name is Meghan Johnston and my name is Kyle Johnston. When my mom is upset, it's usually best to just let her relax a little. Do we need a lawyer or anything?"

Matthew took a deep breath. "I'm Matthew Tanner. This is my district, and I'm about the only law enforcement in this little town. I saw what happened. I know it wasn't on purpose. So, let's take a deep breath here. Ma'am, may I call you Meghan?"

As she nodded her assent, he handed her a small packet of tissues. "Okay, I'm going to tell the judge there were extenuating circumstances and the boat was at the mercy of Mother Nature. Like I said, he'll make you board in the house tonight. Way more comfortable than a real jail. Then he'll let you go in the morning. No problem."

Meghan dabbed at her eyes. Maybe the situation wasn't as bad as her frazzled imagination had conjured up. The rain even let up a little. The officer indicated they'd be likely free to go in the morning. Glancing over the top of the seat, the digital clock next to the radio read 12:30. Mike probably thought she'd stood him up by then.

The officer jumped out of the truck, telling them to stay put. Walking over to a little shelter built for fishermen to clean their catch of the day, Meghan watched him pull out his cell phone. He had an intense discussion with the person on the other end of the line, although he was too far away for them to make out the conversation.

She leaned back on the faux leather bench style seat and closed her eyes for a moment, willing herself to calm down. From the front of the vehicle, Kyle turned toward her.

"Don't worry, Mom, it'll be alright. So we spend a night in this one-horse town, no biggie. At the least, we'll have a great story to tell our friends back home. I mean, went on vacation and got arrested as environmental criminals. Far more interesting than coming back with a bad sunburn."

Meghan let out a giggle at his ridiculous recap of the situation. Kyle always knew how to make her laugh and bring much-needed perspective. A sense of humor was the one good thing he'd gotten from his deadbeat father. Thankfully, Kyle's morals and sense of right and wrong all came from her.

The door to the truck opened and shut again. "Alright folks, here's the story. I just talked to the judge, and he's out of town for the week. However, our city commissioner Donny Swenson will be able to sort out the fine. Don't worry about a thing. He'll take good care of you. You're lucky. Donny is also the pastor of our local church, a fair-minded man. The cooking at his place is pretty good. You'll be in for a treat at dinner, better than the deli chicken."

He started the truck as Meghan watched the waves fall over themselves out on the lake. The rain slowed to a drizzle, and the wind had calmed significantly. Things weren't so bad. They'd talk to this Donny guy and be on their way by lunchtime tomorrow. Kyle was right, she sometimes worked herself up over nothing.

9

THE DANGERS OF BOATING

Mike Chase paced the floor of the owner's suite.

He shouldn't be this nervous about a lunch date. After all, he'd spent a good portion of the previous day with Meghan at the beach, and they'd enjoyed a lovely dinner. They hit it off and even though liquor had possibly clouded his judgment, they had chemistry. Now if only he could only avoid screwing the whole thing up.

Putting one tie down and then picking up another, the man staring back in the mirror judged both unfavorably. The image scowled back at him, displeased with every decision he'd made that morning.

He felt someone watching him from afar and turned toward the door. Kelley stared with amusement and shook her head, laughing at the comedy-of-one playing out in the room.

He winked at his daughter. The way she smiled and leaned against the door frame presented an almost perfect copy of Mike's wife. She was the spitting image of her mother in every way, a stunningly beautiful girl with a head on her shoulders that would give anyone a run for their money. His heart ached that his wife wasn't here to see the woman their daughter had grown into.

Kelley and Kyle hit it off, but only as friends she assured her father. In her words, they weren't each other's type in 'that way'. She could see them becoming good friends, though. The previous day she thought of about a dozen girls she knew who'd fall head-over-heels for him if they had the chance.

The last thing in the world Mike wanted to do was put his daughter in the uncomfortable position of dating a boy while he dated that same boy's mother. But he was letting his imagination run a little wild.

"Dad! Oh, earth to Daddy. Come-in Daddy! You okay in there? You're sweating bullets. Heck, you might need another shower before your date."

"That obvious?"

She giggled. "Uh, yeah. So, tell me, are you interviewing her for a job or trying to sell her life insurance?"

He frowned at Kelley, having no idea what she meant.

"The ties, Dad. Seriously, this is lunch, not a business meeting. Give the ties a rest and relax. We keep the jacket and pants, and we bling you up a little." Kelley crossed the room, taking the ties away from him and throwing them on the bed. Opening up a small travel jewelry box, she pulled out a pair of cufflinks, a gold watch, and a necklace which was her mother's favorite.

After a few minor adjustments, she turned him toward the mirror and brushed off the shoulders of his coat. Kelley was right, of course. The tie came across as too stuffy for lunch. His daughter gave great dating advice. The irony, of course, was that her own father was the present recipient of that advice.

Kelley admired her handiwork. "Perfect. You clean up pretty well, Mr. Chase. You know that? Now remember, I want you home by eleven. No later, tomorrow's a workday." She laughed at her own motherly tone.

Staring at himself in the mirror, a sadness overcame Mike. After her mother died, he'd thrown himself into work and single malt scotch, a mistake that almost cost them everything. Kelley intervened when he needed saving. They both cried a lot back then. The psychologists called the phenomenon a 'delayed grieving process'.

Mike Chase hadn't even talked to any women, in a romantic sense, until yesterday. It felt like he'd hit the jackpot with Meghan. Unlike the type-A women he met in his profession, Meghan was genuine and charming. Talking to her came easy, almost like talking to his wife. "Kelley, I don't know about any of this. What if I blow it or say something stupid? What if I found out we don't connect, and it was the drinks last night? What if—"

She snapped her fingers at him. "Hey, head case ... let's get with the program." Kelley put her hands on her hips and smiled lovingly at him. "Dad, I think it's time we talked."

He rolled his eyes. "Sweetie, I think I know how it all works. Remember, a flying stork didn't deliver you. Things happened between me and mom."

"Ewww ... gross. No! God! What I meant was that you and I had a rough patch after Mom died. We sorta got lost, and I didn't know how to get back."

He shook his head. "Yeah, I'm so sorry about that. I should've been there for you, and I wasn't. You were there for me though." Mike smiled at her. "My daughter came back for me."

"Dad, we came back for each other. When you saw what I needed, you put the cork in the bottle and saved both of us." She gave him a warm hug. "I love you, Daddy. You're the best daddy in the whole world. Don't forget that. So, I give you permission. I'm letting you go. You're all grown up now."

"You mean, like, to lunch?"

"No, silly, I mean if you want to date and bring women home and introduce them to me, you should. I don't want you to hold back because of me. You need ... no strike that ... you deserve happiness too."

He wiped away a tear forming in the corner of his eye. "Oh, sweetie, thank you. That means more to me than you can know. But ... it isn't that easy. Your mother was the only woman in this world that I loved in that way. I don't even know if I can do this. It feels so alien to me."

She rolled her eyes and grabbed his hands. "Daddy, what's not easy? Kyle and I had tons of time to talk, and it sounds like you're both in the same boat. So, you two can be nervous together. Go ahead, give it a try and I'll bet you will have a great time." She leaned forward, adopting a more serious tone. "Dad, I know what you are thinking. I would bet that Mom would want this for you too. Time for you to find your happiness again."

He stared at the reflection in the mirror, linking his arm in hers. "Kelley, my daughter, I think I already have that."

She straightened up and stepped back from him. "Good. Now, go get the girl. Remember, standard rules apply. If you have her in here, please put a tie on the doorknob or something. I don't want to walk into the proverbial beast with two backs."

"Kelley, I'm not sure if I'm more shocked that you know about the tie thing or the reference to the beast with two backs." He glanced down at his watch. "Oh, wow, time to get moving. I need to hustle to meet her at the restaurant."

Down in the restaurant, Mike scanned the main part of the dining room. Not seeing Meghan anywhere, he took a seat.

Kelley and Kyle planned to hang out by the pool and meet other teens in the game room. Kyle seemed like a nice, level-headed kid, and it made Mike happy to see Kelley making new friends and having fun. This week, his daughter of old had emerged.

The sommelier brought up a bottle of white wine from the cellar and put it on ice that morning. The wine stood out as the perfect balance to the fish special being prepared for lunch. Meghan mentioned a fondness for fish and white wine, so he'd made a calculated guess. The kitchen staff prepared anything he asked for and even things he didn't expect. Owning a resort did have its perks.

He glanced at his watch again. The big hand sunk a few ticks past noon. He shrugged. Being fashionably late wasn't the worst thing in the world, he reasoned; it was the people who insisted everything run on schedule all the time that annoyed him the most.

At twenty past the hour, Mike resigned himself to the realization that he'd been stood up. His first at-bat in the dating game, and the pitcher hadn't even thrown the ball. He ran through every word of their conversation the day before, searching for anything he might have said that could have offended her. Draining the wine glass, Mike stood to leave when his phone rang. The caller ID read, Kelley.

"Hey sweetie, what's up?" Not wanting to admit he'd been stood up.

"Dad, is Kyle with you guys?" There was a surprising tinge of concern in her voice.

His heart rate raced. The urgency in her voice suggested something was very wrong. "No, Meghan never showed. Why?" He winced at his confession, feeling the sting yet again.

"Come down to the boathouse right away. This might be an emergency. I think something may have happened to them."

He jumped up from the table and ran out the side door. The rain reflected his sudden worry, pelting him even harder. The parking lot in the distance gushed over its curbs with rainwater. Beyond that, Lake Oleander roiled in an angry gray mass.

He sprinted across the yard, and the docks, entering the boathouse. Bill stood by in his rain slicker, along with Kelley and a couple of her friends.

Kelley spoke excitedly. "Bill, tell my Dad what you told us."

"This morning, that lady and her son took one of the boats out," he obliged.

"Yeah, they told me they were going out, so what?"

"Mike, that's the thing. They haven't come back."

"We got worried when Kyle didn't show," Kelley added. "We called up to the room and no one answered. Ricky saw them take a boat this morning, so we went over to the big picture window and saw one boat still out. That's when we ran down here, and Bill told us it was their boat."

Mike's heart fell through the floor. His date was apparently in mortal danger. His eyes darted out the door, onto the lake. It was stunning how quick the visibility vanished to only a few feet from the dock. Anyone stuck out on this lake was in serious danger. Lake Oleander wasn't wide, but it was spring fed. Its notoriously cold water could induce hypothermia, even in the heat of summer.

Mike turned to Ricky. "You were right to worry. Do you remember which direction they headed?"

A skinny boy in the back spoke up. "Yes, sir. They headed toward The Trough."

Mike nodded. The Trough was a local euphemism for where Lake Oleander reached the southern end of its curve.

"We have to go search for them, Bill," Mike said. He fought a pitched battle to keep his stomach under control.

The old man threw up his hands, exasperated. "Mike, there's no way. Then we'd have two boats missing in this. We have to wait until the storm stops. Why don't you call the police over in Riapoke? Let them know to look-out for them."

"That's part of what I'm afraid of ... them ending up over in Riapoke." Mike had heard the stories over the years and met a few of the residents. Rumors abound of people finding their way into town and vanishing without a trace. "We can't just sit here and do nothing, Bill. We have to go after them."

"Dad, no," Kelley petitioned. "The rain is too much. You have to wait until this storm blows over. You know that's true."

Bill moved the window shades out of the way and scanned the surface of the lake. The early afternoon had taken on more of a dusky grey. "Sorry Mike, we don't have a choice. To go out in this would be suicidal. We need to hold off for better weather."

As if to drive home his point, a large log floated by, looking like an alligator who'd made his way too far north and took up residence in the lakes of Virginia. An unseen current pushed it along to an unknown destination, waves fiercely lapping over it.

While changing into thicker, more practical clothes, Mike called the authorities in Riapoke. Apparently, the local conservation officer, who had jurisdiction, was out on another weather-related call and wasn't expected back for some time. The dispatcher assured him people had survived worse, and he should try to relax until someone contacted him. Mike said, "Okay, thank you," and hung up the phone, not feeling very assured. In his heart, he wanted to reach through the phone and slap the dispatcher for being so dismissive of Meghan and her son.

An hour after learning they hadn't returned, Mike watched Bill place a few items into the boat they'd need to mount a rescue operation. What Mike understood about the law, he lacked in the understanding of lake shore living. Every few minutes Bill told him to move out of the way, muttering to himself, "It'd be easier if you just stayed in the office while I did this." Mike finally got the message.

Not meaning to be in the way, he reluctantly backed off, but not far. He willed Bill to finish so they could get underway. Finding Meghan and her son were the top priority. Part of him knew the situation carried a strange gravity, not unlike a detective investigating a missing persons case. The longer they lingered at the dock, the less chance they had of bringing Meghan and Kyle back safely.

Finally, Bill indicated all was ready.

"What do I do, Bill?"

"You sit there with these binoculars. Scan the water for any sign of the boat, or ..." Bill hesitated to finish his statement.

"Or what?"

"I'd rather not say. Just keep your eyes peeled for anything out of the ordinary."

Mike's expression grew somber. "Oh," he said, finally understanding Bill's macabre meaning.

They headed south along the shore, in the direction the skinny teen indicated. In the absence of better information, it was a reasonable direction to start their search. The lake widened out in spots but ran North and South and formed a huge U, if viewed from the air. Getting lost on the water and ending up on the other side of the lake wasn't unheard-of.

Lake Oleander took its name from a flower that never grew there. Legend says someone once tried to plant oleanders and failed. Yet the name of the lake stuck. Given the rash of unusual disappearances around the lake the past fifty years, the name association with the flower was appropriate. Oleander plants could be deadly.

Bill continued to scan the horizon while Mike stood on the bow with the binoculars. Twice Bill had to yell at Mike to sit down. After a rainstorm, logs and large sticks lingered just under the surface. One jolt from hitting a good-sized piece of timber, and he'd take a swim.

They made their way around the U-shaped bend in the lake and headed back North. The city of Riapoke lay on the exact opposite side of the lake from the resort. About the only built up features of the lake shore were the city of Riapoke and the Hideaway. A few houses butted up along the water's edge, but they were fewer on the Riapoke side, owing to highway accessibility. The mix of deciduous and conifer trees along the waterway sat unbroken except for a few homemade piers jutting out into the water in a few places. Once there was a restaurant near the trough which did alright for a few years but closed during the recession. The building stood crumbling and abandoned.

The city, for its part, did little to dispel the negative rumors surrounding it. It wasn't so long ago that people visited Riapoke on a regular basis, and even though the townspeople still maintained a cold detachment, they were friendly to visitors.

That was ten years before the one, and only, church in town effectively cut Riapoke off from the rest of the world. Parishioners were forced to obey a strict oath of conduct, which included swearing to stay within the boundaries of Riapoke unless permitted to leave. From what Mike understood, few ever made such a request.

He hated the idea of waltzing up there and asking someone if any strangers were swimming for their lives on their side of the lake.

10

KILLING A FRIEND

Inside his church office, Donny opened the door leading to the cave where The Master lived. He was reminded of the awesome responsibility of being The Master's voice in the community. It gave him power over the entire town, but that power was limited and revocable by The Master at any moment.

Making his way down the stairs hewn into the rock by unknown hands, the walls came to life as flames shot up, lighting his way. Instead of providing heat, the unearthly flames provided light and little else. The flames didn't even produce smoke. Once he ran his hand through one of the flames. Instead of being hot, the flame was ice-cold.

At the bottom of the staircase, he used a large key to open the metal door leading to The Master's inner sanctum.

"Oh, great and merciful Master," he chanted. "I come before you as a pilgrim in the wilderness. I come in search of the way, the truth, and the light. I beseech thee to—"

The Master walked out from around the altar with no fanfare. He took the form of a lion, causing Donny's voice to catch in his throat. In years past, he'd appeared as a seductively dressed woman, a man, even a child. Most of the time, he preferred to take the form of a demon, with leathery wings.

"That's enough, high priest. We have much to discuss and very little time to discuss it."

Donny reflexively backed away, trying to mask his fear. "Yes … yes, master. I needed to speak with you right away. Something has happened, and I thought it wise to inform you immediately."

The Master laid down on the floor, examining one of his paws. "Do you not know me so well? Do you think I'm so ignorant that I don't already know what is written in the stars? I know it all. I know how it ends. Even now, I know there is one making her way to you, who brought the instrument of our destruction."

"So, the prophecy is true?" Donny backed up, leaning against the wall for support. The news hit him like a thousand-pound weight suddenly dropped onto his shoulders.

"Prophecies are interesting things. They are written on parchment by men who make judgments about the most likely outcome. They are unable to take into account what happens when someone works against fate, shaping it differently. Even a curse can only last for so long before it weakens and is cast aside like a child's toy. You ask me if the prophecy is true. Yes, high priest, the prophecy is true."

The cold dampness of the wall leached through Donny's shirt. Trying to keep a healthy distance between himself and The Master, the room felt smaller than usual. "But Master, if it's a prophecy, how do we keep it from coming to pass?"

The Master trotted up to Donny, staring intently into the eyes of the surprised cleric. "You have no faith in our ways. Sadly, you have no faith in yourself either, high priest. When this all unravels because of your disbelief, I shall make sure yours is the first soul I take. On this day, you must sharpen your resolve and follow my instructions carefully. Mark my words, the woman spoken of in the prophecy will come to you by the time the sun surrenders its last rays. You are to bring her before me as the final tribute. Make sure the woman's son meets your daughter. They are destined to wed. Their children will continue and expand my reign."

Donny searched The Master's eyes, not daring to divert his gaze, or risk death. The warmth of the beast's breath tickled the hairs on the side of his face. He wished he'd brought the amulet with him. It protected the wearer from any supernatural harm, including The Master. The source of the magic was unclear; however, it was strong enough The Master forbade its use except for the most formal ceremonies.

He willed his heart rate to return to normal. As it did, The Master seemed to calm as well. The immense cat turned away from Donny and paced the floor.

"Good," The Master said. "You're learning to control your own fear, something you must do in the coming days if you want to survive. Other than myself, you are the only other person who can know this truth. We are all in grave danger. Strengthen your heart high priest, what I ask of you is no easy task. However, I would not put this yoke on your shoulders if I didn't believe you could complete your mission." Sitting on his haunches again, the enormous cat held up one of its immense paws. "What safeguards have you put in place? I am most concerned about this information getting out and I fear Brother Matthew may not be as loyal as he needs to be. Brother Waylon, while faithful, also lacks the ability to control his tongue."

Donny almost forgot the purpose of the visit. The Master already knew how much and how little either of the men knew. "Master, Matthew and Waylon have a strong bond. I told Matthew to keep an eye on Waylon and to ensure no one else knew about today's events. If word spreads, there will be panic in the streets of Riapoke and nothing I can say will bring the situation back under control."

"For now, don't concern yourself with this. Hear my edict and follow closely. I think you erred in your handling of Waylon. Alcohol has clouded his judgment and he can no longer be trusted. Tell Matthew to kill him tonight and leave the body at the house by the lake. I don't want that fool running his mouth off to the townspeople. I suspect he is our betrayer."

"But Waylon didn't do anything to deserve—" Donny's voice dried up as The Master eyed him. One of the large cat's paws spread out in front, displaying dagger-like claws.

"Oh no, please," The Master said. "Don't let me stop you. I love it when my high priest argues with me about the rules and mandates I put forth."

"I'm sorry Master. I forgot my place. Please, I beg of you. Forgive me. I'll take care of it right away." Donny fell to his knees in a supplicating gesture.

"Do you know why I chose this form? I wanted to appear as something you both revered and feared. Strong and threatening, and at the same time beautiful and commanding." In a puff of vapor, The Master changed from a lion into his regular form of a large demon with black wings. "In this body, you fear me. You see me as a grotesque figure because your culture doesn't believe in such things. When you see that which you don't believe exists, you fear it. You have lost touch with what it means to have gods and demons walking among you." With another puff of vapor, the demon form was replaced with that of a sultry woman he'd seen before. "And in this form, you neither fear me nor respect me. You see me as something to protect. A young woman who needs a strong man."

He morphed into the huge lion again. "Be clear. No matter what the form, you are here to obey and respect my commandments. Do you understand me?"

"Yes, Master. I understand."

"Are you sure you're certain?"

"Yes Master, Waylon will die tonight. If not by Matthew's hand, then by my own."

"Good. Nothing is written in the tablets of time, there is still a chance we'll prevail. Leave me now, as the woman will be at your house shortly. She cannot call out of town until she is in a cell. Whatever you have to tell her, you tell her. Until the woman is dead and her son is one of us, the town will remain without any means of communication with the outside world." The Master turned from Donny and walked back into the darkness of the cave. More than once, Donny had wondered what world extended past that dark portal. Today, however, he found the urge to leave the cave far out weighed any other curiosity.

A few minutes later, Donny maneuvered his car along the tree-lined highway. The house was close enough to the church, only a few minutes away by car. Even in that short period of time, his mind raced with questions. What would this woman look like? Why did Beth have anything to do with this?

The time spent with The Master overwhelmed his nerves. Even with the car's heater running at full blast, the air felt icy. Terrified of the unknown, Donny wanted nothing to do with any of this. The idea of picking up his daughter and just driving out of town crossed his mind. They could make it beyond The Master's reach.

He dismissed the idea as soon as it entered his conscious mind. The Master is a God and there would be no place he could go, no distance he could travel which would put them far enough away from The Master's eternal reach. At this point Donny, and his family, were fully vested in the town of Riapoke and this woman and her son. He'd have to see this through till the end.

Beth was his pride and joy. How might the boy react to her? Is he a threat to her? The Master wouldn't deliberately put Beth in danger, would he? He might, unintentionally. The Master didn't see individuals, only the greater good. Both their fates may already be written in stone.

Poor Waylon didn't deserve to die. However, not following through, wasn't an option. The terrifying image of The Master's enormous paw played in his mind.

He pulled out his phone and dialed. "Matthew, this is Donny."

"Hello, Reverend. What can I do for you?" came the voice from the other end.

Donny hesitated for a moment. "I need you to kill Waylon. It isn't an order from me, but from The Master himself. I want to be clear on that. You are to take him out to the house by the lake. Make it quick. Do you understand?"

A pause on the end of the line suggested Matthew was stunned by the request. Donny knew Waylon and Matthew enjoyed a close bond as children, so asking this was like asking Matthew to kill his own brother.

"Are you sure about this?" Matthews' shaky voice replied.

"Yes, I just came from the lair. I don't want to discuss it, just do it. Call me back when you're done."

Matthew let out a prolonged sigh. "All right, reverend. I hate this, but I'll do it. In the meantime, I have two people I'm bringing in to see you. They need sentencing."

Donny's breath caught in his throat. Are these the people The Master referred to? "A woman and a boy?"

"Yes, how did you know?" Matthew asked.

Donny felt a headache coming on, throbbing at his temples. "I just do. Bring them to the house."

A moment of silence passed between them and Matthew sighed again. This time the sigh sounded even more despondent than before.

"Matthew, for what it's worth, I asked The Master to spare his life," Donny said.

"Thank you for that," Matthew replied. "I'll see you in about ten minutes."

Donny made a quick phone call to the house staff to ensure two guest bedrooms were prepared. Not the same as a true jail, but it served the same purpose. Especially since his security team locked and unlock doors at his discretion.

He hit another button on his cell phone and the voice of a young woman answered. "Yes, Daddy?"

"Elizabeth, what are you doing right now?" He only called her Elizabeth when he needed her to do something. The rest of the time she went by Beth.

"I was headed to the beach with Terry and Wendy. Why?"

"I need you to stay home, okay sweetie?"

"But Daddy, I want to go hang out. Terry leaves for college in a week and—"

Donny tamped down a flash of rage. He knew that the more he

pushed her, the more likely his obstinate daughter would disobey. "I understand sweetie. However, I need you home tonight and tomorrow. The Master has a task for you and you're going to enjoy it very much. We have a visitor for you to entertain." Donny remembered the words of The Master that his daughter and this boy were compatible.

From childhood, Elizabeth had been taught how to defend herself and manipulate those around her. She had been trained for the day she'd take over his role with the congregation. Something went wrong along the line, though, and now that hormones had reared their ugly heads, Donny worried Beth was becoming psychotic. Her frequent display of poor decision-making skills and fits of uncontrolled rage worried him. Regardless, he still thought of her mostly as his little girl.

He heard a huff at the end of the line. "Of course, Daddy. I'll stay home."

"That's my princess. I'll be home in a few. Wear something cute. I think you are going to like this guest."

"Gross, Dad. You are being all creepy."

"Okay ... I'll stop. Love you, pumpkin." As he ended the call, the possibility of jeopardizing his daughter crept up again in Donny's mind. The Master must have a plan, even if Donny couldn't see it. Still, he couldn't shake the feeling this situation bothered The Master. The Master always relied on fear to ensure people stayed in line. With Donny, there was always a line of reason and discussion open. This time, The Master gave him the impression fear played a big part in his decision-making. It bothered Donny.

He pulled into the driveway and walked hurriedly up the stairs to the house. The housekeeper, Shelly, was busily putting away washed linens.

"Shelly, is everything prepared for our two guests?"

Without discussion, she nodded, "Yes, sir. Am I correct in assuming they'll be staying for dinner?"

"Yes, that's right."

Donny poured himself a double scotch from his liquor cabinet.

He almost never drank this late in the day, but his conversation with The Master had left his nerves in shreds. Outside the house, headlights from an approaching vehicle caught his eye.

"Elizabeth, please come here." Donny shouted down the hallway.

"Yes, Daddy," his daughter answered.

Beth came into the room and although being less than thrilled about being told what to wear that evening, she did as she was told. Elizabeth had to follow his instructions to the letter if this whole thing stood a chance of working out. If The Master's understood this situation correctly, Beth and the boy must grow close in order to stave off the fulfillment of the prophecy.

He stood at the window and watched the three exit the truck. Matthew exited the driver's side, and the boy climbed out the other. Matthew then let a woman, presumably the boy's mother, out the rear. From his vantage point, they painted an odd scene. The woman, who didn't look like she could have a son that old, was dressed in a bikini top and cut-off jeans. The boy wore a t-shirt and a pair of swim trunks. By the prophecy, this petite woman and her handsome son potentially spelled ruin for their way of life. Donny didn't see it. He'd have to rely on the wisdom of The Master to see them through.

11

THE LONG ROAD TO RIAPOKE

Having found nothing in the lake to indicate anything happened to Meghan and her son, Mike and Bill continued toward Riapoke. Mike hated dragging Bill into this mess, but they should be safe enough if they stuck together. Bill, bred from farm stock, was a formidable man. Spending a career as a merchant marine sailor, he knew how to handle himself. Mike, however, was incapable of frightening anyone. Though he had taken good care of himself and outside of a few karate classes as a boy, fighting wasn't his style.

As they made the turn in the lake, the docks of Riapoke lay ominously in the distance. Scanning the surface of the water, he trained his binoculars on something that made his heart sink. In the middle of the lake a red boat cushion bobbed aimlessly. It could have come from anywhere. A knot in the pit of the stomach told Mike a different story.

"Looks like a cushion floating up there," Bill said. The older man's eyesight was still as good as ever.

"Yeah," Mike said. He said a short prayer that it didn't belong to the resort.

Using a gaffing hook to catch the cushion, it hung in the air, confirming Mike's suspicion. 'Property of Hideaway Resort' was emblazoned in yellow letters across the top. Under those words, written by hand in indelible marker, was the number 21. The same number as the boat Meghan and Kyle borrowed that morning. They made it at least this far. No other explanation fit.

Circling the boat around, a few other disturbing items bobbed up and down. A bottle of suntan lotion, a half-empty bottle of water, and a bag of snacks floated together as if clinging to dear life.

"Bill, I think we need to get closer to Riapoke."

Bill frowned disapprovingly. "Not sure I like that idea."

Mike knew Bill lived in the area, since before Mike bought his half of the resort from a retiring former owner. Bill constantly warned people away from Riapoke, citing the rumors and innuendo surrounding the small town. Even as an adult, it shaped his opinion of the place.

"Bill, I'm not going to tell you that you have to come with me, but I sure as hell don't want to go alone."

The bow section of the hull hit something just below the surface of the water. A grating sound assaulted their ears as the boat moved forward. Mike grabbed one of the oars and pushed it under the surface to feel what lay beneath.

"I can feel it, but it is a few feet down and I can't see what it is. Bill, back us up a bit."

Bill reversed the boat's engine and the hull scraped again on whatever it was. Without hesitation, Mike jumped into the cold waters of the lake, popping to the surface a few seconds later.

"What has gotten into you, Mike?" Bill stood from his captain's chair.

"Give me a minute." Mike disappeared again, legs dangling in the air before disappearing below the water line. A few moments later he breached the surface again. "Bill, throw me a rope!"

Not questioning Mike's sudden irrational behavior, he threw one of the bow lines to his boss. Catching the rope, Mike descended again. It was a good twenty seconds before he surfaced. "Get me out of this water, I'm freezing my ass off!"

"Damn fool, you ought to know better than to jump in like that.

You're going to freeze to death." Bill put a blanket around Mike after pulling him up on the deck. "What in tarnation were you doing anyway?"

"I found something, Bill. Something big and aluminum. I think it's a boat. Let's attach the rope to the bow eye and pull it up."

"There are tons of junk in the bottom of this lake. It could be just about anything. Who knows, you may have found the hood of someone's car or a piece of an old aluminum pier."

Mike shook his head, "No way, this is the hull of a boat. I felt along its edge, and the fore section of the hull is sitting upright with the aft on the bottom. I am pretty sure we can get the thing up and have a look at it. The metal moved easily enough when I pulled on it."

"Could be an old boat someone sank years ago," Bill offered as he pulled on the rope. A fishing boat going down in the waters of Lake Oleander would have made the news on both sides of the lake. It had been years since anything like that happened.

A wave of panic hit Mike as the tip of the bow broke the surface. He couldn't see the registration numbers on the side of the boat. His gut spoke volumes on the subject.

"Hold her there, Mike, I'll grab the gaffing hook." Grabbing the side of the boat with the long-hooked pole typically used for fishing, Bill reeled in the side of the hull and rolled the craft over on its side. As soon as the sides of the boats met, Mike ran another rope through the oar sockets and secured it.

Mike scanned the bow. The boat belonged to the resort. More precisely, this was the boat Meghan and Kyle left in. A chill ran up his spine as the number 21 crested the water's surface.

The resort boats were indestructible under normal circumstances. If this one had sunk, then something unexpected happened. As Bill worked feverishly to get water out of the stricken boat, Mike examined the piers of Riapoke. "Maybe they made it over there?"

"They could swim that distance, even in a storm like this. The water is pretty cold, though. They could've just as easily been swept somewhere else. Anytime in the water would have made them hypothermic," Bill retorted.

Mike hated the thought of Meghan and Kyle stranded in that town. That was the most palatable outcome, given the raft of acceptable alternatives. Still, even the slowest swimmer should have been able to cross that distance.

"Bill, let's head into town," Mike said.

Bill shook his head. "Are you sure that's such a good idea? I'll go in with you, as there's no way I'd let you go alone, but they haven't been missing that long. We should go back to the resort and call the police again. Going into town can be dangerous."

Mike winced at the suggestion. "I know, and I have a bad feeling about all of this, but I have to do something. I won't force you to go, but I'd sure feel better if you did."

Bill started the engine and edged the throttle forward, slowly dragging the water-logged boat along with them. "Well, it'd give us the chance to bring the boat up out of the water. We'll need to get that home anyway. Alright then, let's go. We'll take this slow and stay together."

Dragging the boat made their progress slow, which gave Mike time to think about the situation. Tales he'd heard sounded like rumors to keep kids from going into town and starting trouble. Just rumors. However, enough circumstantial evidence existed to give him pause.

As an adult, tales of monsters roaming the woods were shoved aside as childish fantasies. What couldn't be dismissed, however, were the very real instances of missing people. In some cases, Riapoke was the last place the person was reported being seen, or in a couple of cases, persons. The lawyer in him couldn't let that strange coincidence just skulk away unnoticed.

The town and the local magistrate accepted the official findings that the people went missing in the mountains and were presumed dead. Victims all shared one startling commonality. They were mostly loners with no family or friends around to inquire about them. With no one asking questions the authorities had no reason to check the validity of the official findings. Over the last ten years, there were many such cases reported. Mike suspected the number was far higher than the number reported with people just vanishing without a trace and no official report being made.

The boat's hull made a dull thud as it bounced up against the side of the wooden dock, bringing Mike out of his inner dialog. Mike jumped up on the platform and tied their boat in a knot solid enough to hold the boat, but easy enough to remove if they found themselves in need of making a hasty escape from town.

Bill jumped in the crippled boat and started bailing water.

"Looks like it was just swamped, no real damage. Let's get the boat bailed out, and we can get out of here. The battery is water resistant, but not waterproof. It could still have enough juice to run the bilge."

"Let's leave that for now. I want to find out what happened to Meghan and Kyle. I'd like to bring them back with us, if they are hole up in this town somewhere."

Bill, huffing and puffing from the exertion of bailing out the boat, panted, "Just give me one sec." After a minute, Bill flipped a switch, and the electric whir of the bilge pump pierced the after-noon quiet. Bill grunted in approval.

Mike found himself reassured at the sounds of water being shot out of the side of the boat. "You are a wizard on the water. Now, let's see if we can't find our missing guests."

Bill stepped up onto the dock. "I think we just got lucky that the battery had enough juice to work the pump. Let's hope our luck holds." Bill pointed toward the lights of town. "Ever actually visited Riapoke?"

"Nope, you?"

Bill frowned. "Always been a peculiar place. Really insular people. It got worse after the new pastor took over. I think the name is Swenson. Once, many years ago, I came here for a funeral. An old friend of mine passed away who'd moved to Riapoke to live with family. He only lived about six years after moving here. The towns-people treated me nice enough, but kinda weird at the same time."

Mike walked down the dock toward shore. "What made it weird?"

"You know how you go to places like funerals and weddings and people talk, kids will play outside, people cry, and that kind of thing?" He let the rhetorical question sink in before continuing. "Well, no one did that. As a matter of fact, everything seemed staged. And no one talked to me. The only person to talk to me was my friend's sister, and she limited the conversation to his last days. There was this man who kept following us around. I tried to shake him, but it only brought him closer."

Mike laughed nervously. "Well, everyone grieves in their own way."

Bill said, "No Mike, no one grieves like that. Reminded me of stories I'd heard of North Korea or something. Everything felt rehearsed by an unseen central authority. Everyone acted exactly as expected. At one point I asked someone a question, and they struggled for an answer like they had no idea what preordained reply was appropriate. Like I'd gone off script or something."

"Way to add to the creep factor, Bill."

Bill nodded his head. "Good. I am glad you get it. That means you understand what I'm driving at. We need to tread carefully. These people aren't normal, not by a long shot. Going into town could be the last decision we ever make. Are you sure you want to do this? Not too late to turn back, you know?"

"Bill, I can't describe it. I just have to find those two. Aside from that, how bad can it be? There are two of us and if we go slow and stay quiet, we might be able to get in, find them, and get out. No muss, no fuss."

Although it was the middle of the afternoon, the streets lay deserted, the rainy day evidently driving everyone inside. From the parking lot of the boat launch, several buildings loomed up a rise about a half mile away.

The town of Riapoke once abutted the lake. It was rebuilt farther away after repeated flooding. One of the state offices responsible for the waterways' management had given them money to create an enhanced wetland to accommodate additional spill-ways for water when the weather turned wet. The majority of the buildings sat at a natural crest at the top of a small rise. The remains of the old town sat rotting in the woods just off the boat ramp's access road.

Bill shrugged his shoulders in a clear gesture of disapproval. Mike got the impression Bill's angst ran deeper than he was letting on.

The storm, while intense, worked itself out and had moved out of the area. The trees sat oddly quiet, as if the birds themselves remained under a celestial gag order. Wind, which had whipped so furiously earlier, died down to a light breeze. Gray skies overhead pressed the sky toward an early twilight. Mike wondered to himself if it was better to wait it out until nightfall before poking around the town. Yet, snooping around at night would be hard to explain, should they be caught. Desperate to break the uncomfortable silence, Mike asked, "So, Bill, how long have you worked for the resort?"

Bill thought about it for a few seconds. "Let me see ... I started about three years before you got here. I worked the front desk for a couple of years and then became head maintenance man, chief bottle washer, and master of all the rental gear."

"Still like it?"

Bill harrumphed, his voice deepening. "Mike, these are the kinds of conversations you have with someone before you fire them. Oh, sorry, I forgot. Rather, eliminated a superfluous position in a matrixed organization. I believe that's what you people call it."

Mike laughed. "You're funny. No, Bill, as far as I'm concerned you can stay at the resort until the buildings fall down. I just hate the silence. This place is creepy enough."

"It earned its reputation. You know about the murders—sorry, disappearances. But not much about the good people of Riapoke. I've been here long enough to know a little about them. The place is more like a cult compound than a town. The whole shebang is run by Reverend Donny Swenson. He's the head honcho of everything around here. He's in charge of the police, fire department, garbage, even controls the local school board."

"Chief bottle washer too?" Mike asked.

Bill chuckled. "You're catching on. Yep, if it happens in Riapoke, it's because he had a hand in it. Most of the people around here are afraid of him. He commands them to come to church, pay taxes, and personally approves of everything. Even to the point where marriages are reportedly arranged, and all pregnancies must be approved. That's right, you can't even have a baby in Riapoke without his permission."

"Creepy," Mike said. "How do you know all this?"

"About eight years ago, before you bought your share of the resort, a twelve-year-old boy found his way to The Hideaway. Kid was confused, half-starved, clothes all torn, filthy from head to toe like he'd spent a few days in the woods.

"Of course, we fed the kid, clothed him. The boy stayed in one of the rooms to recuperate. Some staff volunteered to keep an eye on him."

Mike and Bill had eclipsed half of the distance between the pier and the town's main street. The idea of a child of twelve stumbling through the deep woods surrounding them, desperately seeking help, sent ice through his veins. His thoughts flashed back to Kelley. "So, what happened to him?"

"We got him talking. His name was Ethan Slater. Mother and father were killed by someone ... or something. When we asked for a description, he froze up on us. Whatever it was, it terrified him. He described it as a demon or a ghost.

"We asked Ethan how he managed to escape. He told us he'd run out the back door of the church and got lost in the woods. He followed the lake until he showed up here. You should have seen that boy plead with us not to let them take him back to town."

Mike kicked a branch off the road and into the ditch. "What happened to him."

Bill grimaced. "We did the only thing we could do. Legally, we had to call the police, and they sent an officer from Riapoke."

Mike interrupted him, "But, that's exactly what you should've done in that situation."

"They came with papers and a magistrate's order to take him into custody. I had no choice. About a week later, I called the police station in Riapoke to find out what happened to the kid. The guy I talked to said no one had heard of Ethan Slater. No family with that last name lived there." Bill fell silent.

Mike was afraid of his next question but felt compelled to ask. "So, I'm guessing you don't believe their version of the story?"

"They killed that boy, Mike. As I live and breathe, I know in my heart they killed Ethan. We should've protected him, and we failed. If you'd only seen the terror in that boy's eyes when the police took him away, then you'd think twice about what we're doing."

12

FOUR FOR DINNER

Meghan and Kyle stepped out into the light rain. The conservation officer held a raincoat over the top of their heads to keep the rain off, failing to keep them dry. Meghan wondered how many square feet the house covered. At least 4,000 square feet or more, it may be the largest house she'd ever seen. The sheer size was impressive and more than a bit intimidating.

A figure stood in the window looking down at them. Possibly the authority who'd stand in judgment of them.

The conservation officer broke the silence. "Watch yourselves on the steps, you two. Wouldn't want either of you slipping and falling."

To Meghan, Matthew didn't come across as a mean person, just a guy doing a job. She was glad he'd had an extra jacket to wear on the ride over. The temperatures fell substantially from the warm humidity of the morning. Although her bikini and shorts no longer soaked through, they still retained the dampness of the lake water. The promise of warmer and drier clothing was welcome.

The officer knocked on the door, and after a couple of moments, it opened. In front of them stood a short woman wearing an apron. "Good evening, please come in."

"Thank you, Shelly. Reverend Swenson is expecting us." Matthew said to the woman.

Shelly motioned to the chairs in the attached dining room. "I know, he'll join us shortly. Please, have a seat."

"Thank you, Mrs. Swenson," Kyle said.

Shelly looked perplexed. "Oh, I'm not—"

A door closed along a hallway that led to the back of the house. "Oh God, she's not my wife. She's convinced she is sometimes. Shelly is my assistant, maid, nanny, cook, occasional errand person, and trusted adviser."

The man stood just inside the living room entryway leading from a hallway that ended at the open door of an office. The reverend stood tall, well over six feet. Brown hair, in need of a haircut, cascaded down his head and tapered off at his temples. Meghan made out specks of gray hair, intelligent looking eyes, and a few wrinkles. They were about the same age, or close to it.

Matthew patted Meghan on the shoulder and whispered, "Reverend Swenson."

"That'll be all Matthew," the reverend said. "You have an errand to run for me, I believe."

"Yes, sir. I do." Matthew took the coat off of Meghan's shoulders and turned toward the door with a nod at both Meghan and Kyle. "You're in good hands. I'll call in the morning."

The reverend gave the conservation officer a stern look. "Wait, Matthew, aren't you forgetting something?"

"Oh, yeah." Matthew reached into his pocket and pulled out the arrest papers he'd filled out in the parking lot of the boat landing.

As he handed them over, Meghan stole a quick glance at the papers. Meghan's name was scribbled on the line 'Defendant'. It made her feel like a common criminal. Would something like this show up on a permanent record? What about work? They had an arrest policy that stated anyone charged with a crime would be terminated immediately. And what would any of this mean for Kyle?

"Thank you, Matthew," the reverend said. "Now, head off to take care of that other business. Give me a call when it is done."

Matthew winced in pain as Donny spoke to him. Not physical pain, but mental. To Meghan, it looked like whatever Matthew was reminded of made him uncomfortable. She watched as he quietly made his exit, closing the door behind him.

"Now, let's see who we have here," Donny said, putting on a pair of reading glasses. "I am going to go out on a limb and say, young man, that you aren't Meghan. You'd make an ugly Meghan, my good lad."

Kyle cast his mother a nervous glance and the reverend an uncomfortable grin.

"Come on kid, you have to get used to the 'bad dad' jokes if you are going to stay with us tonight. I have a ton of them. You can smile, can't you?"

Kyle let out a nervous laugh. "Who, may I ask, are you, Sir?"

"The name is Reverend Donny Swenson. I'm also the fill-in judge while he's out fly-fishing in Alaska." Donny stood mute for a moment while reading the papers. "Meghan Johnston, you are charged with a pretty serious offense. Since it took place off our shoreline, our own conservation officer has jurisdiction. According to our state laws, I could lock you up for about six months."

Meghan started crying anew. Terrified of what might happen to Kyle in this situation, she'd be unable to protect him. They'd lose the house if she lost her job. The idea of being the only mother at the university crashing on her kid's sofa flashed through her mind. "I know, Sir. I didn't have any control of the situation. Believe me, if I could've saved the boat, I would have. It all happened so fast. And I just didn't —"

Kyle put his arm around her. "Sir, a lot of this is my fault. I got lost and didn't know how to get back. The engine stalled and I—"

"Relax, you two. The law is pretty clear. However, the law is also flexible in matters like this too. How about Mr. Johnston? Wasn't he on the boat with you? We don't have to go out looking for another person, do we?"

Meghan shook her head. "No, he's long since out of our lives."

"Sorry to hear that. Hate to see the American family torn apart. I'm a widower myself. How about anyone else we need to call? Any close family who'd be worried?"

Meghan wiped her tears with the tissue Shelly handed her. "No, Sir."

Reverend Swenson smiled at them and moved to the roaring fireplace in the corner of the living room and threw in the arrest paperwork. "Well, that takes care of that matter."

Kyle watched the man in amazement. "You're dismissing the charges?"

"Well, neither one of you looks like a hardened criminal. Really, if the roles were reversed, I doubt I would have fared any better. There is a condition though, and it's not negotiable. You have to stay here tonight. The bridge out of town took damage in the storm, and we have no way to get you home by boat until morning. This part of the lake isn't safe with all the debris jarred loose in the storm. So, you'll stay here as my guests."

"How about a cell phone? Can I call the resort and let them know where we are?"

The reverend shook his head. "Sorry, cell towers went down a little while ago too. We just are having no luck today. The storm hit us pretty hard. You're lucky Matthew saw you out there. That's the price we pay for being so remote." He straightened up. "Tomorrow the weather is supposed to improve, and we can get you out of here after breakfast. The municipal department is already fixing the bridge. Heck, I'll have Matthew take you back to the resort himself."

Meghan thought about Mike, sitting there at lunch, waiting for someone who'd never arrive. He was probably thinking the worst right about now. He'd mentioned having to go back to the city tomorrow. With no way to reach him, he'd never know the truth. What if he hated her now?

At least she wasn't going to face six months in jail. With any luck, she'd be back in her own room at the resort in the morning. On balance, the situation worked out far better than it could have.

"Ehhem ..." A voice from the corner of the room broke the momentary silence.

"Oh forgive me." The reverend shook his head. "Where are my manners? I forgot to introduce my daughter, Elizabeth."

Elizabeth moved forward, sidling up next to Kyle. She tried to grab his hand, and he pulled it away. A full foot shorter than he; it was obvious the proximity intimidated him. "It's nice to meet you ... Kyle," she cooed.

Taking a step back, his face went a deep shade of red. "Nice to meet you as well." Kyle moved toward and just slightly behind his mother for protection from the overeager Elizabeth.

"In the meantime," —Shelly spoke up— "Meghan, let me get you dry clothes. I have things that'll fit you from when I was younger and thinner. A little out of date, but certainly a lot drier."

The idea of dry clothes sounded pretty good to Meghan right now. "That would be superb."

"Great," Shelly said. "While you two take showers, I'll get the clothes. We'll get you settled."

"And then we'll all sit down and have a nice dinner," the reverend said.

"I don't want to put you out. I feel awful about all of this. I'm sure this isn't exactly the way you wanted to spend this evening."

He held up a hand. "I'll hear nothing of it. The powers that be ordain that our paths cross, and I'd be a terrible minister if I didn't offer my hospitality. I've been blessed in this life, and it's my highest honor to share it with you, if only for one evening."

Kyle spoke up. "Thank you reverend. I know my Mom and I are anxious to get back to the resort in the morning." He glanced over at Elizabeth who stared up to him, with a doe eyed gaze. "Under the circumstances, it's nice that you offered to let us make the best of a bad situation."

"Polite boy, isn't he?" The reverend gave a paternal and at the same time condescending nod toward Kyle. "Meghan, you should be proud."

Missing his condescending look, Meghan sighed and smiled at

her son. "Reverend, you don't know the half of it."

"Please, call me Donny. Most everyone does. While you are getting settled, Shelly and Elizabeth will give you the grand tour. I have a ton of work to attend to, so I'll see you at dinner." Donny turned and disappeared into the office, closing the doors behind him. The door locked, snapping shut with an odd metallic formality.

Shelly gave Meghan and Kyle a tour of the house. All the while, Elizabeth hung off Kyle at every step. He rebuffed her attempts to take his hand, smiling in relief when he was able to close a door between them.

Meghan took her shower first. Returning to her room, she found the softest bath towel she'd ever felt. The soft terrycloth texture stood out in sharp contrast to the cold terror that had been Lake Oleander. The shower helped, but when she closed her eyes she could still feel the cold murky water around her, threatening to engulf them. She sat down on the bed thinking through everything that happened. Kyle was correct in his assessment that this would make a great story.

A rap on the door disturbed her moment of self-reflection. Meghan answered, "Who is it?"

"It's Shelly, dear, may I come in?"

She hiked up the bath towel, covering herself. "Sure, come in."

Shelly entered with a pile of clothes in her arms. She laid them down on the bed with a maternal smile. "Here you go. I think I found everything you'll need to be comfortable for tonight. We even found clothes that I think will fit Kyle. He's a tough one, long and skinny."

Meghan leafed through the clothes. They weren't perfect, but they'd suffice until the morning. It beat changing into an orange jumpsuit and sleeping behind bars. "Hey, Shelly, can I ask you something?"

Shelly was more gray than brunette and wore reading glasses that gave her the look of a librarian. She was at least ten years older than Meghan. "Sure, anything."

"The reverend seems like a nice enough guy. Is he always this cordial to guests? I mean, he seems like he is going out of his way for us."

She patted Meghan on the hand. "Oh, that's just the reverend's way. Yes, he's just that nice to everyone. He believes in treating all guests as if they were The Master himself."

"The Master?" Meghan asked.

Shelly's cheeks suddenly flushed, as if she'd said something she shouldn't have. "I mean God himself," she stuttered. "That's what I meant. Treats everyone as if God himself had come to his door, and the good reverend must take them in. A genuine, kindhearted man. Don't worry about a thing." Shelly stood and left the room without another word.

The Master? She'd heard God referred to by many names, but never The Master. While her family had always gone to church, they weren't as steeped in religious teaching as they probably should be. Shelly's exit also seemed odd. Some might call it hurried, as if she suddenly developed a fear of Meghan.

She put on the clean tee-shirt and pants. The dry material energized her. Being stuck in a cold lake and almost drowning made one appreciate dry clothing and a warm shower that much more. Not as good as her own stuff, back at the resort, but shipwrecked beggars facing felony charges couldn't be choosers.

She attempted to bring her untamed locks under control when there was another soft rap on the door. "Yes?"

"It's me, Mom," came Kyle's voice.

"Come on in."

He poked his head into the room, a tired grin on his face. "How are you doing?"

"You need a haircut." She brushed the hair out of his eyes and tried combing his hair. "I guess I'm doing okay. Not perfect. We are the mighty Johnston party of two, and we can make it through anything. Mike will forgive us for missing lunch."

"You mean you, Mom. It was your date." He gently batted away her attempts at making him look more presentable.

Assessing her son's clothing, Meghan let a giggle escape. They gave him a pair of jeans, three sizes too big. A belt, pulled tight, held them up at the waist. He wore a white tee-shirt with a polo shirt over the top, also three sizes too big. A little more preppy than normal, in a strangely discombobulated way.

"Who brought you your clothes, Mom?"

She looked confused. "Kind of an odd question. Shelly did. Why do you ask?"

"I'm not sure what to make of it. Elizabeth brought these in. She just ... walked in on me. No knocking or anything. And I mean, Elizabeth walked in on me ... all of me. That girl gives me the creeps."

Meghan found it hard not to laugh at her ferociously blushing son. "Ah, well. You have an admirer."

"More like a stalker. Be serious, will you? This whole place seems weird, doesn't it?"

"Okay, a little odd maybe. I'm sure walking in on you was just an accident. What's the matter, don't want the cute girl seeing your wee-wee?"

Kyle shook his head. "That's your takeaway from that?" Kyle sounded frustrated. "I'm not sure it was an accident. It felt more like it was planned. Maybe she stood by the door and waited for that exact moment to come in. She stared at me, Mom, not a normal stare, it was creepy and leering. And that's another thing, I know I locked that door. I'm sure of it."

"So, she stared. Was it like a serial killer or like a crazy cat lady you accidentally made eye contact with?"

He frowned. "Neither. Maybe both at the same time, I guess. She's just weird. I want to get out of here as soon as possible. Promise me?"

She straightened the collar of the borrowed polo shirt. "Okay, Mr. Fraidy-cat, we'll get out of here first thing in the morning. After I patch things up with Mike, we'll have a quiet lunch together and forget all about this mess. Don't forget, the way this whole thing turned out could have been far worse."

Another rap on the door interrupted their conversation. "Come in," Meghan said.

Shelly appeared. "Oh good, you're both here. Dinner is served. The reverend requests you both join him." She locked eyes with Meghan for a moment before casting her glance to the floor and shuffled out of the room.

Down the hall from the bedrooms, a large dining room furnished with white linens, fine china, and crystal stemware lay out as if the President was expected for dinner. The sight promised food, and a good meal at that. It could've also been the oppressive hunger overwhelming her from not eating since breakfast. Kyle, naturally, sat down at a place and prepared to dive into the food.

The reverend held up a hand, a clear instruction to everyone to curtail their enthusiasm for the moment. He said, "I'm not sure what your faith beliefs are, but in this house, we always say grace before dinner."

Kyle stood back up and moved away from the food. Elizabeth motioned to the chair next to what he gathered was her usual place. "You can sit next to me, Kyle."

Meghan thought the way she patted the chair was a bit over the top. Her boy might be onto something with his suspicions. Elizabeth was taken with the handsome boy staying the night. The disturbing vibe Kyle mentioned earlier radiated off the girl. Elizabeth was too eager, and it clearly made him uncomfortable. Then again, it could be chalked up to raging hormones and her sheltered life.

"Yes, Kyle, sit next to Elizabeth," Shelly said, placing another large silver serving dish down on the center of the table.

Kyle did as instructed. While he sat down, he shot his mother a glance which bordered on terror.

Shelly removed the dome-shaped cover, revealing the largest roast Meghan had ever seen. Perfectly cooked. Brown with only a hint of pink, the juice flowed from the meat. Other covers on large silver serving dishes were removed to reveal potatoes and cooked carrots. So much food that even Kyle would've had a hard time finishing it all.

The reverend folded his hands and bowed his head in prayer,

and the others followed suit. "Dearest Master ...", the reverend paused uncomfortably like he didn't know how to continue his prayer. He restarted, "Dearest master of all things. Let us bow down before you and pay homage. You give us all good things in life. You bring us safety from the outside world and new friends in the guise of strangers. I ask your continued blessings over this town and all who inhabit it. I ask for your continued guidance as we go through this time of turmoil and trouble. May you continually bless us and allow us to serve you. Amen."

Kyle added, "In Jesus name we pray, Amen."

Meghan glanced up at her boy, proud that he still remembered to add that little postscript he'd learned in Sunday school. Glancing over at the reverend, she was surprised to see a flash of anger cross his face. Shelly looked shocked too. What had Kyle said to elicit such a reaction? What kind of religion did these people practice?

After the plates made their way around the table, and the meal began in earnest, the conversation devolved into the more mundane. Meghan and the reverend talked about what she did for a living. Elizabeth and Kyle talked about school and their plans for the future.

The reverend asked, "So, how long are you planning on staying at the Hideaway? I understand it's a nice resort. Sadly, my duties here in town make it hard for me to get away much. Although, as you can see, I have my own little resort right here."

Meghan swallowed a mouthful of food and said, "Every year, toward the end of the season, I put our names on a bunch of resort waiting lists, hoping to score a cheap vacation. This year, we were lucky enough to get one. It worked out pretty well. At least until today ... and the boat. But we did get to meet you nice folks."

He smiled at her. "A wise man once said, strangers are only friends we haven't met yet."

Kyle spoke up. "Ned Flanders said that, I think."

Meghan laughed, but their hosts said nothing. Elizabeth was the first to break the uncomfortable silence. "No, that was William Butler Yeats. Who's Ned Flanders?"

Kyle stared around the table in momentary confusion. "You know, *The Simpson's*. From television?"

The reverend glowered at Kyle, reminding Meghan of the way her father looked when poor grades came home from school. "We don't indulge in television watching in this house. It's a foul habit breeding ignorance."

Kyle recoiled at the man's sudden rebuke.

Meghan jumped in to save him. "I wholeheartedly agree, television has gone downhill over the years. Either you're watching trashy television shows or news stories that are filled with bad news. The reality is that nothing educational is even available for today's youth." As if to drive home her point, she smiled at Elizabeth. "Better to stay away from television."

The reverend stared at them. There was no mistaking how uncomfortable the present situation made him, despite his willingness to open the house to the strangers and dine with them.

Dinner finished in an uneasy silence. Meghan tried to think of a way to excuse Kyle and herself when Reverend Swenson remarked, "Only one thing left to do."

Shelly reappeared with a platter holding five small shot glasses, placing two orange colored ones in front of Elizabeth and Kyle. She then placed a glass, filled with a green liquid, in front of Meghan before handing similar ones to the reverend and taking one for herself.

He stood up from his chair and held up his glass. "It is tradition, in this house, that when we have guests who darken our door, we always extend to them the warmest of wishes and hospitality. Fate brought you to us and in some ways, you'll leave your mark on us. For that, we are eternally grateful. For the children, Shelly has brought mango juice, a special juice from a special fruit. Its tastefulness and nutritional value are known far and wide. It is my way of giving you the best in life before you travel out into the world."

Meghan held up the shot glass. "And for us?"

He smiled at the interruption. "My German Oma und Opa would haunt me if I neglected to offer my guests a taste of the home country. Sour-apple Schnapps." He smiled and raised his glass to his guests. "Prost!"

With that, Shelly collected the dishes and disappeared into the kitchen. Donny then excused himself abruptly, disappearing behind the enormous wooden door of his office. Meghan only caught a brief glimpse of the room beyond. It looked like a sumptuously appointed room, dripping with oak and leather.

For a moment, Kyle and Meghan stared at each other across the dinner table. No one had even said good night to them or anything. Shrugging off the awkwardness, they returned to Meghan's room, unclear on whether the impromptu dinner party had actually come to an end. They spoke in hushed tones so as not to be overheard.

"That was the strangest dinner party I've ever attended," Meghan said.

Kyle affixed her with a look of pure relief. "You're telling me. You know Elizabeth kept a hand on my thigh the entire dinner? I think in some countries, we'd now be legally married."

Meghan laughed as he once again turned beet red. "Do you want me to say something like, 'Keep your damn hands off my little boy. You're giving him cooties?'"

"You're embarrassing. No, don't do that. I just want to go to sleep and get the heck out of this place. Maybe the hotel will understand and give us a night for free and you can schmooze your new boyfriend."

She laughed at the obvious jab. A sudden, inexplicable exhaustion overwhelmed her. Eyes heavy, she gave Kyle a hug and closed the door. Stretching out on the bed, thinking of a moment to rest, dinner made her tired.

She tried to get up. Her arms and legs felt like lead weights threatening to pull her down through the mattress. The room spun around like a carousel sent out of control. Something was terribly wrong, and Meghan lacked even the strength to lift her head from the pillow or make a sound to alert a would-be rescuer.

Managing a last-ditch effort to move toward the door, she slipped off the side of the bed and crashed onto the floor.

13

ATTEMPTED MURDER

Mike and Bill stayed low to the ground to avoid being seen. The last thing they needed was to attract any attention to themselves. Bill led them farther off the main road, deeper into the woods. They knew that eventually, someone might see the boats tied up at the dock and go looking for them, so speed was of the essence. Running parallel to the road and in between the wetlands and the lake, ran a smaller dirt path.

"Where do you think this goes?" Mike asked.

"No telling," Bill replied. "It looks like an old forestry road or something. Maybe an old driveway to someone's property before they moved the buildings out of here. It looks pretty overgrown."

A foul stench in the air swept over them, assailing their nostrils. Mike couldn't place the smell, but then it triggered a memory from his childhood. As a family, they'd go to their uncle's house in Kentucky and the garage had that same distinct odor. It was the unmistakable smell of rotting meat from when they cleaned deer carcasses from his hunting expeditions. The skin hung from rafters in the garage until it was ready for tanning.

In front of them lay a good-sized house. Pieces of siding were missing, and the lawn was littered with rotted and rusted pieces of construction materials. Mike and Bill stepped gingerly around an old bathtub laying in the grass to avoid making any unnecessary noise. A voice up ahead stopped them in their tracks.

"I just didn't think this would happen so soon, Matt. You know? At the most I thought I had another month before we had to do ... this. Can't you hide me for a little while longer. I just wasn't ready for this right now."

Another voice spoke up. "I'm sorry Waylon, you know I'd give anything to not have to do this, and you also know I have no choice in the matter. The simple fact that I'm standing here, right in front of you, is because we're friends. You have a right to know that I take this personally. I'll never forget you. This is the best I can do for you now. You'll be in a better place in a moment."

Bill motioned to Mike to crouch behind the bathtub. They peered around the end of it, toward the house.

"Take care of my mom, Matt," the first voice begged, breaking with emotion. "She's getting on in years and needs someone to watch after her."

The second voice responded, not with hostility but a note of tenderness. "I will, buddy. You have my solemn promise. I'll make sure of it."

"Thank you, Matthew. Can I have a minute ... I mean, just a minute? Should call mama and say goodbye to her. No, wait. Matthew, I just want a moment to—" A thunderous shot broke the stillness of the forest. Mike understood what he'd heard. The loud noise was immediately followed by the sound of something heavy making a dull thud against a wooden floor of the house like a sack of potatoes being dropped.

"Sorry Waylon," the single voice said with a hint of regret. "Now you're at peace. This is the best I can do for you right now."

Mike laid flat to the ground, sharing a worried glance at Bill. His eyebrows knitted together, over eyes as wide as saucers. There was no mistaking what just happened. Some commotion coming from the house sounded like the body of the unfortunate soul being dragged further inside.

A few more minutes passed, and an engine started. A large truck backed onto the road. Mike peered through a crack in the old tub and identified a light bar and the shield from a police department on the back of the vehicle. The driver was either a police officer or had some association with a law enforcement agency. It lurched forward and disappeared around a bend in the driveway.

Letting out a sigh of relief, Mike climbed to his feet. "What the fuck was that, Bill? I mean, what did we just hear?"

"I think we just witnessed a man being killed." Bill rose to his feet and brushed the dirt from his clothes. "I've only seen one other person killed in my lifetime and I swore it was the last. Mike, what the hell did we get into?"

Had they just listened to an execution? Mike's mind spun with a flurry of thoughts. Yes, it sounded like someone being killed; but who, and why? Without moving in for a closer inspection, they couldn't answer either of those questions. Perhaps there was a perfectly logical explanation for all of this.

Mike put his hand on Bill's shoulder. "We have to check this out."

Bill shook his head vigorously. "Mike, this is too much. We need to get the proper authorities out here. This is way beyond us."

"I agree. Although, we need to find out if what we think we heard is what we really heard. We don't even know if that guy is dead. We have to check, if only to make sure we don't leave an injured man to die."

Bill reluctantly nodded his ascent. "Okay, we go up there and peek in the windows and see what we can see. Then we get out of here."

The two men advanced on the little building. The smell stung at their nostrils like the scent tried to drill its way in. A breeze, which should have felt refreshing, blew at them from the direction of the house, bringing the obnoxious odor along for the ride.

The house sat still in front of them, like a huge monument to unseen horrors. Its sagging wood and decrepit countenance speaking volumes about the irrationality of entering it. The wooden floorboards issued a stubborn squeak against their footfalls as they advanced, threatening to give away their presence to anyone within earshot.

Mike made a mental note of the number of flies they encountered as they got closer. A few at first, then the numbers became intolerable as the flies amounted to a great gray swarm. No amount of swatting made a difference. At the door, the smell and the flies became too much to handle as Mike's stomach screamed its objections.

The two peered into the dark recesses of the house from the doorway. No one moved inside the dilapidated structure. Still, they stepped inside cautiously.

"I feel something wet, I—," Bill said, stopping mid-sentence.

Mike heard a loud thud as Bill fell to the floor like a ton of bricks. "Crap, Bill are you okay?" Mike activated the flashlight app on the cell phone. Sweeping the beam toward where Bill had fallen, he caught sight of something on the wall which made his heart stop.

"Yeah, I'm okay Mike," Bill grumbled. "Just fell down. Help me up."

"Bill, look." Mike felt like it was someone else talking. Things like this didn't happen to him. His beam of light trained on two tables pushed up against the walls. Tied down, in frightening poses, were human remains in different stages of decomposition. On the floor, at the base of one table, an arm lay on the ground, congealed in its own dried blood. It looked like an animal had been gnawing at the arm as a few of the digits had been bitten down to the bone. In front of each table, holes, like makeshift drains, gave way to the cellar below.

Bill, regaining his feet, joined Mike. "What the hell is this place?"

Mike remembered reading about a case like this in law school, a case so horrifying it had turned him from criminal to corporate law. A serial killer took each of his victims and tied them to tables in a basement. After allowing each to die of starvation, he sodomized the corpses and then chopped them into little bits. "It reminds me of a kill room of sorts. We need to get the fuck out of here. Get back to the resort and call the FBI. This is way beyond what we came here for. This is ... I'm not even sure what to call it."

Bill nodded in agreement with Mike's sudden change of heart. Pulling out his own cell phone, he used his light to sweep the sides of the room. Bodies, and body parts, lay stacked in strange arrangements everywhere like piles of wood or maybe an odd art exhibit. Some were nothing more than mutilated corpses. Flies buzzed and rats climbed everywhere in the room, feeding on the human buffet.

Lines of blood on the wall above the tables told a gruesome story. The lines were traced in finger-like patterns, indicating they were made by the victims clawing for some sort of escape or perhaps relief from whatever was happening to them. Some of the people strapped to the tables were alive while they were being tortured to death. These people weren't just simply cut apart here, this room is where these people died in the most gruesome manner possible.

"Let's get the hell out of here," Bill said. Putting his phone away, he turned from the door and let out a sudden yelp.

"What happened?" Mike cried in alarm.

"Something's got my leg!"

Mike swept the beam of light around and fought down a wave of nausea. The outstretched hand of one of the bodies lay on the floor, its fingers wrapped around Bill's pant leg. "I'll get it, wait." Mike reached down, gingerly prying the fingers holding onto Bill. To his surprise, they were warm and flexible, with no sign of rigor mortis in the joints.

"This one is still warm, Bill. This may be the victim we just heard get shot. Let's turn him over and search for identification."

They pulled the body outside, under the fading light of the afternoon and far from the plague of flies. Certainly, the smell was better too.

Flipping the corpse over, they saw the gunshot wound, fresh and still leaking a considerable amount of blood. Mike searched the unfortunate man's pockets while Bill checked their path to make sure a wallet or some other identification hadn't fallen out.

And then the corpse spoke, "Please, help me."

Mike fell backwards at the shock of hearing the man speak. "Holy crap! Bill, this guy is still alive."

"Hel ... Help ... me. Please, help me," he weakly whimpered.

Mike tried to find something to shove in the guy's wound to stop the bleeding. "Just hang on there, buddy." Ripping off his button-down shirt and wadding it up to make an impromptu bandage. The man winced in pain as he applied pressure.

"What happened?" Bill asked.

"Maaath ... Maaaatt." The man went silent. For a moment, Mike thought he'd seen a flash of fear in the man's eyes. "Ssss someone shot me." It took the man forever to get even one word out. Each word more labored than the one before it.

Mike stood up. "Bill, wait here. I'm going to go back inside and see if I can find a first aid kit or anything to work with. This guy isn't going to make it if we don't do something quick." Without waiting for an answer, Mike ran a few paces back into the house. He ignored the grotesque display and checked the remaining rooms. In the back, he found a dated kitchen.

Disparate to the other rooms, this one was clean, almost sterile. There was an old-style pump which emptied into a sink and a stove set up in the corner, fed by a small green propane canister. A large table stood in the middle which had a small candle in the center.

He threw open the cupboards. The first one contained a complete set of dining utensils. They were arranged on the top of a stack of dishes. A cup and linen tablecloth sat next to silverware. The way the linen laid out so neatly in the cupboard would be creepy even in a regular house. The rest of the cupboards contained some spices and more linen cloth, but little else of consequence.

He filled a pot with water and grabbed one of the cloths. Mike prayed it'd be enough to stop the bleeding. Their options were limited. If they couldn't stem the tide of blood, they'd never get the man out alive. Mike ran through his life-saving skills, learned in Boy Scouts, and cursed himself for not paying better attention.

Upon exiting, he saw Bill holding the man's head and shoulders, talking quietly to him and holding the now blood-soaked shirt to the gunshot wound. Mike handed the towel to Bill. "Switch those out. We'll have to try to get him back to the boat. Do you have any cell phone signal out here?"

Bill answered without glancing at his phone. "Nope, nothing."

The man, groggy, but still conscious, spoke up. "Outside phones ... blocked. No signals, no calls outside town."

"What's your name?" Mike asked.

"Waylon ... And ..." He winced in pain, biting back the next word.

Bill said, "Don't try to talk. Just relax for now." He turned toward mike. "We need to get him back to the resort and call the police."

Waylon grabbed Mike by the arm with a surprisingly strong grip for someone suffering a gunshot wound. His eyes bulged with terror. "No, No police. No hospital. You need to leave. They'll kill you too."

"I think he's right," Bill said. "We need to put distance between ourselves and this place. We need to get back to the boat and back to the resort."

"No, we can't just leave him here. He comes with us, as long as there is a chance we can save him." They weren't that far away from the dock. Carrying another man would slow them down. In a perfect world, Mike knew they should build a stretcher. This situation didn't fit the standard of a perfect world.

They found an old ball of twine laying on the porch and secured Waylon's bandages as best they could. The dying man asked for water and Mike knew they tell you not to give a patient in his condition water, but he gave it to him anyway. It was only a matter of time before the blood loss would make any further first aid unnecessary. A little water likely didn't matter at this point. Waylon needed a hospital, and no amount of first aid would alter that reality.

Picking their way through the bushes and brambles proved more difficult than expected. The weight of Waylon and the approaching dusk added to their abysmal progress.

Mike slowed as something caught his attention. Blue and red

lights danced through the trees and leaves up ahead. In the clearing of the boat ramp, people were standing around. "Bill, wait."

Bill looked over Mike's shoulder. "What do you suppose is going on down there?"

"Not sure, but it can't be good. Let's put him down." They gently set Waylon on the ground. As they did, a little groan escaped. At the very least, he was still alive. "Stay here with him, I'm going up to have a look."

Bill protested, "Wait Mike, why don't I go down there and you stay here with him?"

"No, I've got it. Just keep the cloth on his wound." Not waiting for a response, Mike carefully picked his way through the woods. Hiding behind trees, he timed his movements to avoid the lights of arriving vehicles. Stopping short of the boat ramp parking lot, Mike hunkered down behind a small dirt pile at the end of the lot. It made an effective berm between the boat ramp and the forest.

Several people milled around, close enough that Mike could make out their conversation. Mainly they spoke of the two strange boats sitting at the docks. "I'm not sure where those boats came from," one of them said. "As soon as I saw them, I called Matthew. He said he'd never seen them before either. Looks like they may have come over from the resort."

"You ever been to that resort?" asked a second man.

"Oh, no way. The Master would never allow such a thing. Besides, why leave Riapoke? Nothing outside of this town we need."

"I don't know about that. I'm always curious."

The first man laughed. "You know what they say about curiosity and the cat right? Except you don't have nine lives, my friend. You'd be best to keep that curiosity to yourself."

Just then, a uniformed man walked up from the docks and pulled out a cell phone.

Interesting, Mike thought. His cell phone works, but ours won't? He was reminded of what Waylon had said.

Before dialing, he spoke to the crowd. "You people need to go home. Thank you for calling it in. I'll deal with the boats."

"Matthew," the second man said. "Did you figure out anything about the boats, like maybe where they came from?"

The man in the uniform shook his head. "Nothing yet, it's kind of a mystery. You folks get on home now. I'll take these boats to my yard, and we can sort out ownership in the morning. Probably just busted lines from the storm, and they washed ashore from another part of the lake. Have a good night."

The dejected mob, expecting more intrigue, moved back up the road toward their vehicles. The officer sat down on the dirt pile at the end of the parking lot. It was the same pile of dirt Mike used as a convenient hiding place and observation area.

"Donny? Yeah, it's Matthew. Say, I'm down at the docks right now. Got a call from Fred Taylor earlier. Found a couple of boats tied up to the dock with no owner around. They're both from the resort, and I'd swear the second boat here is the same one that woman and the kid sunk earlier."

Mike's heart sank as Matthew spoke those words. The officer had to be referring to Meghan and Kyle. Mike wanted nothing more than to jump up and explain that these were the people they were looking for. Only the question of the officer's reaction kept him from doing so. There was also the matter of him being covered in Waylon's blood. It might prove difficult to explain. This could be the same officer who shot Waylon earlier and wouldn't think twice about shooting them as well.

Matthew spoke again. "Okay, I'm going to take the boats over to my office and lock them up in storage. I'm sure the owners will turn up sometime. We should play it safe until we know what they want. They may have come here looking for the woman and the kid."

He paused for a few moments, listening to whomever spoke on the other side of the line. Then let out a long sigh. "Between you and me, Donny, that was the hardest thing you've ever asked me to do. But, I did it. I want you to let The Master know of my devotion."

After another brief pause, he said, "Thank you. Tomorrow we'll send in a crew to prepare the body. What? Oh, I left him at the workhouse like you asked. No, I'm sure no one saw it. I'll fill out a death certificate in the morning. Donny, Waylon also asked if we would take care of his mother. I don't think that's an unreasonable request." After a few moments, Matthew said, "Okay, great. I think Waylon would be happy to know that. I have official things to take care of. I'll call you tomorrow, late morning. May The Master of understanding grant you peace, Reverend."

Mike watched in stunned silence as Matthew stood up from the pile of dirt and walked back toward his truck. This was definitely the officer who shot Waylon. They had little time to do what they needed to do. If the officer had left Waylon for dead, someone he knew and called a friend, then he'd likely kill both him and Bill with little or no remorse. Worst of all, they'd likely think nothing of killing Meghan and Kyle. He needed to find them before this police officer had that chance.

14

I WANT MOMMY

Swimming through semi-consciousness, Meghan struggled to make sense of the sequence of events. Sleep should never come on as easily as it had. She didn't remember changing clothes or even getting under the covers.

The outside world felt different from the air-conditioned room she'd fallen asleep in. Opening her eyes, the world around her felt strikingly unfamiliar. Along the walls an eerie light pierced the darkness from flames which seemed to have no beginning or end. It could have been the effect of her still groggy mind, but the lighting reminded her of the fake flames from a cheap gas fireplace. It cast an eerie, unnatural glow.

The air felt oppressively humid, and yet cool at the same time. In the distance, a steady dripping noise interrupted the otherwise crypt-like quiet of the space. To Meghan, it sounded like a small bead of water continually formed at the tip of a stalactite and then dropped into a pool of water at an unseen base. The sound brought back memories of the trip they made to Luray Caverns when Kyle was little.

She sat up, adjusting her eyes to the dim lighting. She sat upon a granite stone which sat in the middle of the room. Rather than separate from it, the rock rose up from the floor to roughly the size of a dinner table. Meghan swung her legs to the side and tried to stand. The room swirled around her, and she had to use the rock for support as she made her way toward what looked like a door.

Risking another step forward, Meghan was rewarded with a successful movement of her legs. She made progress toward the iron door that stood open on the other side of the room one step at a time.

Within a foot of reaching the opening, the iron bars slammed shut, cutting off her exit. Meghan stumbled backwards and fell to the floor. She sat up and rubbed her elbow which she hurt in the fall.

From the hallway a deep voice laughed. "I really must apologize, Mrs. Johnston. I was having a little fun at your expense. I didn't mean to frighten you just now."

"Who the hell are you and what are you doing?" Meghan wanted to sound braver, but her question came out as a high-pitched squeak.

The reverend stepped around the corner and stood outside the bars. "Surprise. Don't worry, Meghan, your stay here with me won't be long. Just long enough for me to do what I have to do."

"What are you going to do to me?" The enormity of the situation crashed down like a ton of bricks. Donny, the reverend, must have put drugs in her food last night. That didn't make any sense, though, as they all ate the same things. Everything came out of the same serving dishes or pitchers.

Meghan ran through the events of the evening before. The only thing anyone ate that was separate were the schnapps at the end. Glasses were poured in the kitchen, away from prying eyes. Shelly carefully offered one particular glass to her over the others, handing it to Meghan.

"This wasn't our deal," Meghan said. "You were going to make me spend a night in your house and then let me go. Where's my son?" She wanted badly to cry, but choked down the impulse. Losing control of her emotions would get her nowhere.

The reverend laughed. "You still think this is about that silly little boating thing? I didn't take you as being that naive. You have the good fortune of being hosted by our little burg's own deity. You see, those of us living here in Riapoke owe everything to The Master. He provides, grants favors, loves us, and punishes those who need punishing. All he asks is that a few of his needs are met. And that, Meghan Johnston, is why I have to keep you here. You don't know it yet, but you are very ... very important."

"What do you want from me?"

The reverend looked confused for a moment. "Me? No, not me. You should be asking what The Master wants with you."

Meghan paused. She'd have to play the reverend's sick game to get out of this situation. "Very well then, what does he want?"

"Isn't that obvious? Your soul."

Meghan stepped back from the bars and leaned on the block. Half expecting him to laugh and step back, revealing the cameras of a practical joke TV show. He just stared back at her, face as blank as the walls of the cave which now made up her prison.

"Don't worry, when the time comes, I'll make it quick and painless. Understand this though. When we're sent a tribute for The Master, we are obliged to make sure they are taken. I just have one little thing to take care of first, a little loose end to clear up. Your son needs a good reason to want to stay in Riapoke." Seeing the horrified expression on Meghan's face, the reverend added, "Don't fret, my dear. Unlike you, your son isn't a tribute. Well, he is, but a tribute of a different sort. He's going to add his own DNA to this primordial pool of ours. In a way, you'll never leave Riapoke. At least, genetically."

At his words, Meghan lost her last grip on her composure. "What the hell are you talking about?"

"Kyle is a fine boy. He'll make a fine addition to my family. My new son-in-law will have the honor of fathering a whole new blood line of high priests. You should be honored. Future generations will look upon you as the mother of our world. The boy is to wed my daughter."

She spit at him, launching a gob of mucus which landed on his face. "You're insane! He'll never agree to that! He'll insist on seeing me."

Donny wiped the spit from his face without comment. "Oh, I'm counting on it. In the morning we'll begin the process of inducting him into our little family. Pretty soon he will be surrounded by the loving people of Riapoke who'll run to his aid to find his poor lost mother. We'll be there to hold his hand, every step of the way."

The remaining wall holding back Meghan's anger finally failed in a dramatic flourish of anger. "You leave Kyle alone, you son-of-a-bitch!"

The reverend remained infuriatingly calm. "Temper, temper, Mrs. Johnston. The Master wants you good and pliable for his needs, not full of anger and hate. Don't worry, there'll be plenty of time to develop a proper appreciation for the special situation you're in."

————

KYLE REGARDED the clock on the nightstand for a moment. Almost eight in the morning. After the excitement of the day before, a good night's sleep certainly was welcome. Going to bed with a full stomach always helped him sleep. He let out a big yawn and stretched.

He woke up with one singular thought. They needed to get out of this strange house, and away from these strange people as soon as possible. Besides, his mother was sweet on that Mike guy. Nice enough man, for sure, Kyle saw it in his mother's eyes at dinner. Kelley indicated her father was taken with Meghan as well. Kelley knew everyone at the resort and dragged him around for introductions. She even introduced him to a couple of girls Kyle wanted to know better.

Down on the driveway, the same squad truck which brought them here the day before sat at idle.

Maybe the officer returned to take them back to the Resort? That'd be nice. We'll be on our way just as soon as I'm dressed.

Much to his surprise, his clothes, dried and folded, lay at the foot of the bed. Shelly must have washed them the night before. Dressing and stepping into the hallway, the house sat silent and empty.

"Mom?" Kyle asked. He peered around the corner of the open door, expecting to find her staring at herself in the mirror, on the lookout for gray hairs. To his disappointment, the room stood empty. The bed sheets lay flat and unrumpled, like no one slept in it at all. The clothes she'd worn the day before weren't there either. She must have put them on and gotten ready to go and was now downstairs waiting.

Moving to the window, he observed Elizabeth and Shelly down on the walkway next to the driveway, talking to the conservation officer. Shelly had a peculiar expression on her face, and Elizabeth had mascara running down her cheeks. Kyle felt a sudden pang of worry for his mother. He needed to get down there and find out what was going on.

He took a deep breath and descended the stairs. Approaching the three, Elizabeth and Shelly suddenly fell quiet.

"Good morning," Kyle said, nonchalantly.

The officer stepped forward, gabbing Kyle by the shoulder and wrenching his arm behind him, pushing Kyle over the hood of the truck as he did. "You're not going to think so."

"Hey, what the hell!" Kyle exclaimed as a pair of steel handcuffs closed around his wrists.

The officer spoke up. "I can't believe I am saying this. Kyle Johnston, I'm arresting you for the rape of Elizabeth Swanson."

"Wait, what?" Kyle shouted out in disbelief.

"That's right, you monster. My father treated you like a son, and you did this to me!" Elizabeth shouted. "You know what you did."

Kyle became enraged. "I didn't do anything to her! I was in my room all night. I didn't do this. Where is my mother?"

"You were all over my little girl last night," Shelly yelled. "I saw him, Matthew. He's a monster!" She spat on the ground at Kyle's feet.

"Me? No, I didn't do anything. She was all over me. I didn't do anything to her, I swear!"

"Oh yeah? Then what the hell is this?" The officer pulled something out of Kyle's pocket. A pair of pink panties.

"Those are mine." Elizabeth strode forward and tried to slap Kyle, but Matthew easily pushed her away, sparing Kyle. "You sick bastard. Are those a trophy? You pervert! He defiled me!"

"Stay back, Elizabeth." The officer turned Kyle around to face him. "Care to explain?"

"He's a pervert, that's all the explanation you need," Elizabeth screamed.

"Shelly," Matthew directed. "Take Elizabeth inside for now. I'll be back later to take her statement."

Shelly spat again on the ground at Kyle's feet. "Come on, love, let's get you inside." Shelly put an arm around Elizabeth's shoulders and directed her upstairs.

"I don't know how they got there." Kyle stammered. "Someone put those in my pocket while I slept." He yelled after Elizabeth. "You brought me my clothes last night. You came barging in the room after my shower. I want my mother and a lawyer. You can't do this to me!"

The officer pushed Kyle into the back of the squad truck. "Son, I'd serve you best to keep your mouth shut. You're in a lot of trouble here. Rape is a felony offense, and I doubt the judge will sentence you as a minor."

"What? No. Officer Tanner, you have to believe me. I didn't do this."

Matthew got into the front of the truck and started the engine. Turning around briefly, he made eye contact with Kyle. "Look, Kyle, like I told you before. The best thing you can do is keep your mouth shut. Until we get this mess straightened out, you are going to sit in my jail."

Kyle stared out the window at the trees as they started down the driveway. He'd come close to crying the other night when his mother became so worried about being arrested. Right now, though, Kyle felt more pissed off than terrified. He desperately wanted to know where his mother was. Did she even know what was happening? How did this happen?

15

BREAKING AND ENTERING

As Waylon's blood continued to trickle from his body, his speech became more and more random and nonsensical. Waylon continued talking about the hellish nightmare of the town's existence. He spoke at length about the whole thing being run by the town's reverend and something called, The Master.

In his few moments of clarity, Waylon strongly advised against going into town. Although the warning was stern enough, Mike had his doubts of the ailing man's reliability. Waylon hadn't heard of Meghan or Kyle.

Bill helped fill in the gaps in Waylon's memory, from his visit to Riapoke many years ago. Waylon suggested the police station was the most logical place to check. If they weren't there, the town's only church might be the next best place to look. He speculated that the appearance of Meghan and her son could be connected to his experience on the lake and the discovery of a severed head. Bill dismissed a lot of it as the ravings of a man whose life was slipping away.

According to a local legend, Waylon said, a body entombed in the lake would remain at the bottom. If a corpse surfaced, it was an ominous sign signaling catastrophic change. Every Riapoke resident had been trained to seek out these signs and report them.

Bill woke Mike up at around 3:00 am. Waylon's situation had gone from bad to worse as his breathing became labored and ragged. Fifteen minutes later, Waylon took in one final strained breath and let it out in a long, slow sigh. Waylon Anderson passed into whatever version of an afterlife awaited him.

Mike managed, somehow, to sleep after Waylon passed away. He woke, surprised to see the sun's rays piercing the tree line. The night before was difficult for all of them.

At first, he and Bill considered leaving the body at the impromptu camp. However, as Bill pointed out, the conservation officer might notice if his friend's body went missing. Their search for Meghan and Kyle could become infinitely more difficult if the entire town were suddenly hunting for them. Neither relished the idea of going back to that place.

In the early morning light, they fashioned a small stretcher, it was easier to carry Waylon's body this way than trying to carry the dead weight back to the slaughterhouse. Even so, the task still took twenty grueling minutes. A small bead of blood leaked off the end of the tarp they'd re-purposed as a stretcher. It stood out as an ominous sign of things to come.

Mike knew turning back no longer presented an option. If even part of what Waylon had said was true, they were running out of time. Finding Meghan and Kyle was their top priority.

Silly, though, as I barely know the woman, Mike thought.

Mike felt compelled to save her, as if his wife directed the chance meeting and even now drove him to do all he could to rescue this woman and her son.

"How should we leave the body?" Bill asked.

Mike looked puzzled. "What do you mean?"

"Well, we just can't dump the body randomly. We need to make sure we leave him exactly as we found him. Then again, I don't know how often people come out here anymore."

Mike gave Bill a puzzled look. "You've been here before?" It seemed Bill's comment came from a place of surprising familiarity.

"That's not what I meant. Based on the piles of garbage lying around, I'm guessing people don't come out here too often. Even so, we should cover our tracks as well as we can."

Bill's logic was sound. Trying to remember exactly how they'd found Waylon proved difficult, trying to view the memories of the day before through the stress-stained lens of recent events. Neither one of them remembered what position they'd found the unfortunate man in, so they reached a compromise based on their best recollections. Leaving Waylon just laying there felt wrong. However, the choices at this point were limited. They dumped the makeshift stretcher into an old root cellar under the house which looked unused for many years.

Heading back toward town, they tried to find a fresh set of clothes to change into, perhaps from someone's clothesline. Mike doubted anyone would simply wave hello and then ignore two blood-covered strangers walking through the center of town. They kept to the woods as much as possible, only peering into the clearings at the homes and businesses in the distance. Their attempts to wash the blood from their clothes proved futile as they were soiled past the point where simple water stood any chance of cleaning them.

Mike thought about their next moves. Walking into town would likely result in them ending up like Waylon, or worse. The dead man's suggestion to check the police station sounded like their best plan of action. Failing that, checking the church offered the second-best destination. The downside of the plan was that in either place, they would stand out like sore thumbs. They had to wait and slip into these places when they knew no one would be around.

Mike remembered his ethics class from law school and one case where a lawyer bent the rules a bit to win a case. This situation far surpassed a simple bending of a rule and ventured into a course of action likely to get him disbarred. However, lives hung in the balance and time was slipping away. Mike could always justify his actions after he saved Meghan and Kyle.

They needed a good vantage point to watch the police station until they were sure the building was clear of people for the night. Mike wished Waylon talked a little longer. Details like how many police officers were in town suddenly took on extreme importance. Would they have to avoid one, two, fifty? They had no way of knowing.

Approaching an opening in the wood line, they spied an abandoned storefront, an old clothier with a sign reading 'Closed'. The darkened dirty windows and the rotting wooden sign out front gave the welcome impression that it had been many years since the sign on the door last read 'Open'.

Bill looked at Mike. "Sad, the plight of small-town cults in America. The economy mustn't be doing too hot."

Although the joke was a little flat, Mike chuckled nervously. "Do you think there is an alarm system on that building?"

"Doubt it," Bill said, shaking his head. "It looks like that place hasn't been touched in a while. The windows don't even look like they have sensors on them. Should be easy enough to get inside. But I have to ask you, are you prepared to do this?"

"Bill, after everything we have seen and heard, why would you even ask me that?"

"Just checking," Bill answered. "This road looks pretty deserted. We can run across it and hope no one notices. You go first, make for the alleyway and hide behind something. Once you are safely away and I don't hear an angry mob coming after you, I'll go next."

"Gee, thanks, Bill. You're all heart," Mike said, flatly.

Mike stared down both directions of the roadway for any signs of life. Thankfully, the road remained clear. A simple two-lane highway; to him, it might as well be the width of a football field. Once he broke cover, there was no turning back. If anyone spotted them, it could spell the end.

Dredging up as much courage as possible, Mike took the first step onto the pavement. Legs, knees, and feet worked against him as cramps sprang up in both of his calves. Propelling his tired body forward, Mike risked a brief glance to the left to see a pair of head-lights turn onto the roadway, coming toward him. Still over a half mile away, depending on speed, that distance would quickly be eclipsed.

It didn't even feel like himself disappearing into the darkened shadows being cast across the alleyway next to the building. The image played out in his mind as a film based on his life. Ducking behind a row of garbage cans, he scanned the rest of the alley for movement. The area looked clear enough, except for a cat looking for dinner.

Down the alley, in the street, a flash of color caught his attention as the car drove by at an alarmingly slow speed. Or maybe it was just his overtaxed imagination. Someone, sitting behind the wheel, talked on a cell phone. They didn't seem to have spotted him. Mike let out a sigh of relief. They'd gotten lucky.

Waiting behind a cluster of metal garbage cans for what seemed like hours, several cars and trucks crossed in front of him in both directions. No sign of Bill, indicating he'd either been delayed by vehicles crossing the road or worse, spotted by one of them.

Hoping to hell no one grabbed the older, slower man, Mike felt the oppressive weight of going it alone if Bill were out of the equa-tion. Bill provided his direction and his only link to the outside world if their plan went south. The distinct possibility of leaving Kelley without her remaining parent loomed in front of him.

A cold reality gripped him. Bill's words rang true, they shouldn't have come. Mike wondered what his daughter was thinking right now. Likely worried because Dad had gone missing the night before and hadn't come home as expected. How did they let this situation get so out of control?

Perhaps his worry about Meghan overrode common sense. Concern for a woman he barely knew, may have put him in mortal danger.

Mike's heart rate climbed to an unhealthy level as time ticked away and Bill failed to appear in the alley. Older or not, it shouldn't have taken him this long to cross the street. Was this all a huge mistake? If it was, it had the potential for making him pay with his life. Worse yet, he gambled with Meghan, Kyle, and now Bill's lives as well.

Two more cars drove by. Mike concluded that something went terribly wrong. Bill must have been captured. Creeping back up the alley and glancing out across the street, the woods showed now sign of the burly former seaman. While possible the older man still waited out there, the road stood clear of vehicles, nothing should keep him on the other side of the road.

Mike returned to the back of the store. There was only one thing to do at this point, he would have to press on alone. Prying off a badly worn piece of plywood covering a broken store window, he climbed inside. Time to reformulate the plan. The reality of having three people to rescue set in.

The store sat as empty as Bill figured it'd be. It reeked of dust and disuse. He made a quick search of the place, finding an old shirt with the store's logo on it. He sighed in relief as he changed out of his bloody undershirt.

Thank heavens for small victories, he thought.

The floor of the store looked like a marketing firm had installed the floor as fliers and newspaper ads littered the entire space. Based on the dates of the newspapers, the place had been closed for at least ten years. Many of the ads, he noticed, were for a tent revival led by one Reverend Swenson.

On the counter, next to an old cash register, lay a small receipt book, a Yellow Pages, and a pencil, dutifully waiting for business that never came. Flipping open the antiquated phone book, a relic from a time before smartphones automatically found the phone number of any business, Mike found an old city map showing the layout of a younger version of Riapoke. Although browned and brittle, and discolored from a water leak, the streets and major landmarks were clearly legible. A blue badge symbol marked the location of the police station. Similarly, a cross depicted the location of the local church. He tore the map out and put it in his pocket.

Now, armed with a cleaner shirt and an old map of the town, Mike steeled himself for what came next. It was time to find Bill, Meghan, and Kyle.

16

THE ENEMY OF MY ENEMY IS NOT MY FRIEND

Kyle paid close attention to the sequence of roads they drove down. If the opportunity presented itself, memory of the roads could help to escape the situation. Still, sitting tight, offered the most logical course of action for the moment. Once the officer looked at the panties and analyzed them, he'd realize Kyle didn't rape Elizabeth. He just hoped he wasn't being framed.

Sitting in silence the squad truck turned the corner down another road, a large building loomed in front of them. It rose from the green trees and the serene park-like setting, as if commanding even the forests attention. Although there were no religious symbols on the building, it had the air of a church.

Matthew turned to Kyle, and with a growl said, "Stay here. Not that you have any choice at the moment."

Kyle said, "Geeze, and I was about to run out for coffee. Where's here, anyway?"

Matthew answered, "We're at the church. I need to check in and then we can be on our way."

Kyle watched Matthew walk up to the door, where he was greeted by the reverend. There was no way Kyle would voluntarily talk to that man right now. Surprisingly, the reverend and Matthew only shared a couple of words and then separated. Donny disappeared inside the building and Matthew turned back toward the truck. An odd reaction to the officer telling him that Elizabeth accused a house guest of rape and the officer was taking the boy to jail. The reverend should be ready to kill Kyle with his bare hands.

Matthew walked back toward the squad truck. Irritation and confusion played out across his face at whatever the reverend said. The officer slid back behind the steering wheel of the truck, slamming the door with a clang of steel. "Well, you're a lucky teen."

Kyle lifted his handcuffed wrists and said, "Really? Because I'm pretty familiar with luck and this doesn't seem lucky to me."

The officer ignored his flippant remark. "Reverend Swenson says he's sure Beth is making the whole thing up as a plea for attention. He's not going to press charges; however, he wants to talk to you after I'm done."

A sudden sense of relief overtook Kyle. "Thank God, someone has some sense around here."

"Don't get too cocky, lad. You're still going to spend time in jail. Regardless of what the good reverend says, I want to analyze these panties and confirm Elizabeth is lying. The law is still the law, and I have procedures to follow."

Kyle sat back in the seat. "Fine, proceed away. There's no way you are going to find any evidence of rape. I told you, I didn't do it."

"Kyle, that is a good attitude to have. And, if he's right, and you didn't do it, I'll be the first one to apologize. However, that leaves the question of what kind of attention she is trying to get."

Kyle leaned forward in the seat. "Maybe the answer is as simple as she's bat-shit crazy?"

"Watch the language, kid." Matthew tried to hide a smirk and failed. "Although, you might be onto something."

Kyle kept a close eye on the road signs as they made their way through town. There were plenty of reasons to worry about the course of this investigation. He'd seen plenty of stories on television about people who were wrongly accused and convicted. An escape plan would be a good thing to have in his back pocket. Although, this situation might work itself out after all.

———

MIKE FOUND the police station just where the map indicated. Off the main road and across the street from a deli. There were only a few cars transiting this little town and even fewer people walking around, making his movements a little easier. The depressed little town gave the impression that time, and economics passed the once thriving streets.

The rear of the police station opened to a large parking lot. In it were three squad cars of a bygone era. The aged beasts looked like someone periodically wiped the cobwebs off of them and repainted the shield of the town, so they were more like static displays rather than functioning law enforcement tools.

The rusted front gate lurched open, disrupting thoughts of how best to approach the building. A squad truck he instantly recognized from the boat launch pulled in. Mike watched with horror as the conservation officer stepped out of the driver's seat and opened the back door to let out Kyle, who wore a pair of shiny handcuffs.

Stifling the urge to yell out to the boy, this situation plunged from bad to worse. Mike played with the idea of waltzing into the police station as an attorney and demand an immediate release. After what happened to Waylon, Mike suspected such a brazen act might get everyone killed. Sticking to the original plan made the most sense. Besides, he didn't exactly look like an attorney at the moment. Not to mention, he certainly didn't smell like one.

He caught a slight movement out of the corner of his eye. Mike froze in place, watching a shadow move behind the fence. At first, the shadow looked vaguely bear shaped. It came out of the wood line and morphed into a man. Stubby fingers grabbed the chain-link fence and, in a move impossible for such a large frame, deftly hoisted himself up and over. In the half-light of the back yard, the figure landed with a thud on the other side of the fence before ducking behind a rusted shipping crate.

The man's dark shadow morphed again into the more familiar Harbor Master Bill as he moved into the light. Mike exhaled in relief at seeing the bear-like man again. Although, what happened to him still remained a mystery.

Skulking out from behind the storage crates, the old sailor knelt behind one of the ancient squad cars. Bill had no way to know Kyle sat inside the police station.

Mike wanted to shout out to Bill to have him wait while he had a chance to get into the yard. However, the door to the station opened and the officer walked out. He grabbed something out of the squad truck, stepped out of the gate, crossed the street and disappeared into a small coffee shop.

Mike turned back toward Bill and caught sight of him entering the police station. He rushed out of the bushes to join him. If anyone else was inside the station beside Kyle, the older man surely would be at a disadvantage.

Running across the parking lot, as fast as possible, he tried to remain low to avoid any people passing by, he ducked under the awning at the back of the station. Grumbling about bad luck as the door handle refused to move, a very serious looking cipher lock stood in between him and Bill.

How the heck did Bill get in? There was no way he could guess the code.

From inside the station, shouting erupted. Mike couldn't tell who was shouting at whom, but whatever was happening wasn't going well.

He tried yanking on the door handle; however, the door simply refused to budge. Restraining himself with a calming breath, he tried pressing numbers in sequence which didn't work either. The worn buttons on the old cipher were the one and the three. These two buttons likely were the most frequently used. Since ciphers were normally four digits in length, Mike started trying random combinations. Desperation set in as attempt after attempt only produced failure with the obstinately locked metal door.

Without warning, the impenetrable door flew open, knocking Mike to the ground. From inside the police station, Kyle rolled through the door as if he were thrown through a window in an old western. Behind him, Bill walked out holding a gun.

Mike barked, "Bill, what the hell are you doing?"

Bill smiled at him. "How convenient is this? Now I have everyone together in one place. The brat kid, and the hero from the resort. The reverend was dead on when he thought there was no way Matt was going turn you lose."

Mike glanced over at Kyle, whose face was red. A small abrasion below his right eye indicated someone had been less than gentle with the boy. Otherwise, the gangly teen appeared no worse for the wear.

"Bill, what's going on? Why do you have that gun?" Mike made a move to stand up.

"Slow it down there Mike. I don't want to shoot you in broad daylight. I suppose it doesn't matter though. The reverend will make sure to cover my tracks. He always has."

"Bill, you mean ... you're one of them?"

Bill laughed, a hearty laugh that would be almost jovial if it were coming from a man not pointing a gun at them. "You really are dense, you know that? I suppose I can't be too hard on you. Funny how things happen. You see, it's probably a good thing The Hideaway never checked my employment application that closely. If they had, they'd notice most of it was made up. I was in the service, that's true, discharged for beating my lieutenant half to death. I spent a little time in the brig and then they returned me to my last known residence. Wanna take a guess where that might have been?"

Kyle spit on the ground in front of Bill, "Assholesville?"

"You're funny kid, I like you. You've got spunk. Watch your mouth or I'll slap you around a little more. They sent me back to my native home of Riapoke. Guess what I found? Reverend Swenson and his little demon. He tried to control me and I beat the shit out of Donny for his efforts. You can say we reached an agreement. I was allowed to live out of town and they supplement my income in exchange for keeping an eye on the resort." Bill leaned against the wall of the building and glared down at the two.

"I'll put it another way. I'm a spy. The reverend needed someone on the outside to make sure no one got in or any crazy ideas of coming over for a visit. Keeping an eye on the other side of the lake is just one of the many things I do for the assholes of Riapoke. They pay me and I don't have to take part in any of The Master's nonsense.

"Yep, the good cultists of Riapoke. Once you get past the ritual sacrifices and that torture chamber down by the lake, this place ain't half bad. The bodies they dump in the lake make for nice sized bass. I think they like the eyes. Still, it's been five years since I last came to town. Good thing too, Waylon might have recognized me if I'd hung around more often. Now get up Kyle and stand over there with him."

Kyle stood up and joined Mike.

"Let's all go back inside for a minute," Bill said, using his gun to gesture toward the door. "I need to call someone. The reverend will be so pleased about this, seeing how we have mommy all tied up. We were so worried about how I'd find Mike again and you delivered yourself to me. Thank The Master, as they say here in this backward little hellhole."

Bill kept his gun trained on Mike and Kyle as they marched into the station. Mike's brain raced through all possible options. How is it that Bill had duped him over and over again? Suddenly, his reluctance to come here made sense. The signposts were all there. Bill was trying to buy the reverend time.

"How did you even—"

"'Get away', I think are the words you're looking for. I have a cell phone which bypasses the cellular block on this place. I just had to get time away from you to make a phone call. The car you saw was actually sent to pick us up. When you disappeared into the alley, I decided to just head straight to the station. Don't worry, Mike, your part in all this will soon be over."

With Bill's gun pointed straight at them, Mike couldn't risk a fight. Bill not only had the advantage in terms of strength and size, he might pull the trigger and injure Kyle, or worse. Gambling with the boy's life wasn't an option.

Bill motioned for them to get inside the cell. "Going to lock you up for a bit while I make a few phone calls. I'm sure the good people of Riapoke will be happy to reward me handsomely for my hard work. I gotta hand it to you, Mike. I did everything in my power to slow you down, even stop you. Guess I failed in that regard. For the record, if you had decided to return to the resort, there was no way I would have let you make it there alive."

"How did you know about Kyle and Meghan?" Mike said, following the boy into the cell.

Bill stepped toward the cell door to close it. "Shortly after these two were picked up by the conservation officer, I got a call from Donny. While you changed your clothes, I got my marching orders. That's when I put the brakes on our rescue mission. Yep, Mike, you sure are one tenacious son-of-a-bitch."

As Bill moved to shut the cell door, all three were all startled by the sound of the front door of the station creaking open. Walking in, hands full of food boxes, was conservation officer Matthew Chase. "Sorry Kyle, they were out of French fries, so I got you chips instead—"

No one moved. Matthew's eyes flew open wide, processing the two additional people in the office, one of whom held a gun. Bill stared back at Matthew, contemplating his next move. Kyle watched Mike, silently imploring for direction. Then Bill turned the weapon from Mike toward Matthew.

The trained officer dropped the food, while simultaneously drawing his weapon. Bill was faster to aim his weapon on Matthew. However, Matthew had more training in such situations. In an explosion of gunfire, both guns went off. One bullet found its mark and the other bored harmlessly into the back wall.

In the explosion, Mike pushed Kyle to the cell floor, using his body as a shield. Mike peered back to see Bill grasp at his chest and fall backward into a shelf full of books. Sliding down to the floor, the stricken man grabbed at a chair, pulling it down with him as his gun skittered to a halt a few feet away.

Bill stared up at the ceiling and said, "I don't know how ... I just ... what happened. It's cold." With that, his hands fell to his sides into a growing pool of his own blood.

Keeping his own weapon pointed at Mike and Kyle, Matthew picked up Bill's gun off the floor and put it in the drawer of a desk. "Alright, you two, come out of there. Actually, scratch that. Kyle, you stay there. Other guy, you come out slowly, whoever you are."

Mike edged out of the cell, his hands high in the air, his eyes intently focused on the business end of the gun which he knew had already killed two people. "Just take it easy, my name is Mike. I always pay close attention to anyone with a gun."

"Good man. Thinking like that will keep you alive. Turn around. I need to make sure you're not armed."

Mike did as instructed. Matthew patted him down for weapons. Satisfied with the search, he motioned toward the second cell. "So far, so good. Get in that cell and close the door. Kyle come out of there, I want to deal with you first."

Mike stepped in the cell, closing the door behind him. It latched with a metallic click.

Kyle was visibly shaken by the dead body now laying in his way. Gingerly, he stepped over it, while trying to do his best to avoid looking at the slain man. Risking a glance downward, he made a repugnant face. "What about the harbor master there?"

"Oh, that's what he was? Well, we'll deal with him later." Matthew sighed in exasperation. "He's not going anywhere. I object to people pointing weapons at me. Kyle, get out of your clothes."

"I'm sorry, what?" Kyle asked, dubious of the order.

Matthew glared at him. "Look, do you want to be cleared of the rape charge or not?"

Mike spoke up, "Kyle, don't say anything. Rape charge? I'm this boy's lawyer and I represent—"

"Look, Counselor, if that is what you really are," the last of Matthew's patience had run out. "I don't think you understand the situation. I just shot a man, and I already have a lot on my plate. I am beyond done with today. Let me do what I have to do to clear this kid of the charge. It may be the easiest thing to clear up right now. So, shut the hell up and let me do my job." He turned back to Kyle. "Can we all agree that for the next few minutes everyone can just stay quiet?"

Kyle and Mike nodded in almost perfect unison.

Matthew took a deep breath and let it out slowly. "Thank you. Counselor, I have little interest in sending this boy to prison. I just need to make sure he didn't do what he was accused of. To be honest, I'm already convinced he didn't do anything."

Fearing making the situation worse, Mike decided to let the officer call the shots for now. Sorting out the legal ramifications of this situation could come later.

Kyle did as he was told and Matthew handed him an emergency blanket to cover himself with. "I only need the underwear."

"What are you going to do with them?" Kyle asked.

"If this were a big city, I'd send these off to a fancy laboratory and they'd analyze them for me. But, right now, I can only do what I can with what I've got. While it isn't fool-proof, I can eliminate you as a suspect. At least good enough for me. The reverend thinks Beth was lying, and something smells fishy about all of this."

Matthew retrieved a kit from one of the cupboards and opened it up. "Your body produces a thing called acid phosphatase enzymes. It's found in your semen. I have a simple chemical that can tell me in a few minutes if there is any present or not. So, no acid phosphatase, no sexual activity. Now, I can't completely rule you out because if you took your underwear off then it won't show. But, a negative on hers and yours calls the rape charge into question. As I said, I have other reasons to doubt Elizabeth's story, but this will seal the deal in my head."

For a couple of minutes, Kyle watched the officer test the pieces of clothing. "Well kid, congratulations. I don't think I have any reason to charge you with a felony. You're free to go, but I wouldn't advise it. As for you," he said, looking at Mike, "I want to know what the hell you're doing here. Also, can anyone explain who that is?" Matthew pointed to the still body of Bill on the ground in a pool of blood.

Mike was unsure what to say. On the one hand, the officer could be a bloodthirsty, cold-blooded killer. However, if he'd wanted to kill them, he would have already pulled the trigger. Since that hadn't happened yet, there must have been a good reason.

"Well," Mike began, "Officer Tanner, It all started when we took a boat out to find Kyle and his mother ..."

Matthew listened in silence, only interrupting once or twice to ask questions. While Mike recounted the story, Matthew pulled a body bag from an evidence kit and had Kyle help put Bill's body inside it. He stared at the dead man's face, searching for any recollection after Mike mentioned that Bill said he was a native. Shrugging his shoulders, he zippered up the body bag unceremoniously.

Mike came to the end of his retelling of his part in events leading up to this moment. The three of them sat in silence. Matthew stood up and crossed over to the cell door. "Thanks for being straight with me. I suppose I owe you the same. First thing, call me Matthew. Almost no one calls me Officer Tanner." Unlocking the cell door, Matthew motioned to the table and chairs in the center of the room.

Kyle and Mike sat down and Matthew walked over to the coffee pot and started making coffee. For a moment, he stopped scooping grounds into the filter and stared off into the distance. "Yes, I killed Waylon. There is something you need to know." A tear slipped from his eye. "Waylon Anderson, a good friend, was dead in a month."

Matthew let a sigh slip as he remembered happier times. "Yes, I killed my friend. He'd asked me to end his life when the pain became too much for him to bear. The medicine was too expensive, and his mother needed the money for other medications. His pain had become almost unmanageable."

Mike sat in stunned silence as Matthew recounted his side of the story. His lawyer instincts told him Matthew was telling the truth. The pain on the officer's face was too genuine to be made up. Shooting his friend didn't come easy and Matthew's narrative of a mercy killing was plausible; given what they'd witnessed in the forest when he thought no one was looking. Mike remembered Matthew uttering the words, now the pain is over.

"So, why did the reverend want Waylon dead?" Kyle asked.

Matthew leaned back against the wall, watching the last few drips fall into the coffee carafe. "Okay, so that is where this gets complicated."

"Thank heavens for that," Mike said. "The simplicity of this situation was too boring for my tastes."

Matthew smiled at Mike's attempt at levity. Pouring three cups of coffee, he continued his story. "You see, Waylon found something in the lake that was never supposed to be found. There is a belief that dates back from the Powhatan tribe that says a body thrown into Lake Oleander shall never surface. There's a prophecy that one of Riapoke's own will turn their back on its people and two strangers will come to town to bring it all to an end. The reverend thinks that Meghan and Kyle are the ones."

Kyle jumped out of his seat at the thought. He hadn't thought about his mother since Bill smacked him around the room. "You know where my mother is?"

"I do," Matthew said. "She's in great danger. We need to proceed carefully."

"We?" Mike said. "Aren't you one of them?"

Matthew leaned forward, cradling his coffee cup in his hands. Standing up from his chair, he crossed the room to the coffee maker. "I used to be, until I was forced to kill my friend." Pouring himself more and then refilling Kyle and Mike's cups.

Mike's lawyer's intuition again told him Matthew was being honest. Matthew appeared more and more like an ally in what was to come. "What changed?"

"I guess I started to ask myself why?" Matthew said. "I mean, why would it be that a reverend should be all powerful over the town? The reverend is a cruel man. I became a deacon in the church to try to protect the people. That's when they let me into some of the church's darker secrets. If you can call it a church." He sat down heavily in his chair. "Really, it is more of a cult, built around the Reverend Swenson and the one they call, The Master."

Kyle took another sip of coffee. "Who is The Master?"

"Evil incarnate," Matthew said. "I've only been in his presence one time, the day I became a deacon. It must be sustained by the hearts of the recently deceased as a sort of sacrificial offering. The town normally feeds it people wandering through town. You know, hikers, campers, travelers who wander too close. People no one will miss if they vanish without a trace."

"Like the news stories I read in the diner on the way to the resort," Kyle said.

"The diner on the interstate. Yes," Matthew nodded.

Mike thought over their situation. There was something about Matthew's story. Like an incomplete jigsaw puzzle with a few key pieces missing. "Matthew, I have to ask you. Why didn't you try to stop this? As a law enforcement officer, you should've been the first one to say something."

Matthew got up from the table and motioned for Mike to help him. They picked up both ends of the bag containing Bill's lifeless corpse and lugged it over to a small chest freezer. Barely large enough to hold the big man's remains, it doubled as Riapoke's morgue when they needed one.

"We all have skeletons in our closet, counselor," Matthew said with sudden intensity. "Mine are disturbing enough to make me keep my big mouth shut. At first, ignoring the occasional disappearance of some hiker or hippie down from the mountains came easy. I never participated in the actual killing, as a law enforcement officer they wanted to preserve my plausible deniability. The weight of it all became too much to bear. Killing Waylon was the last straw. If he'd been healthy, I would have gotten him out of town somehow. Now, I just want to see that dam church burned to the ground."

"Last question," Mike huffed, setting his end of the body bag down in the corner of the freezer. "Why are you helping us? I mean, you could have just shot us and left us for dead, but you didn't."

"Kyle and his mother are the ones spoken of in the prophecy. If I can see that, then Donny and The Master can as well. You'll need help, and by helping you I can save the people of this town. There will be a ton to atone for after this is all over. The three of us were brought together for a reason, and I suspect it is to ensure this madness ends."

As the body landed in the bottom of the chest freezer with a dull thud, Mike shot a glance at Kyle. "We need a plan."

17

A FAMILY CHOOSES

The rock walls were only interrupted by a set of metal bars cemented into the rock. The lights from the flames rising out of the walls gave the only light. Hoping to get the rust on the metal bars to give, Meghan shook them, with little effect. There had to be a way out of this nightmare.

Pacing up and down the ancient cell, she searched for anything that might help her, but only found dried up rat droppings and a few abandoned wooden boxes discarded in one corner. Searching their contents, she found them empty and decrepit with age.

Her thoughts drifted to Kyle. What was he doing right now? Was he safe? What were these crazy people planning to do with him?

Her eyes welled up with tears, as she remembered her own mother's words the day Kyle was born. "Your whole life just became secondary to his. Everything you do, from this point forward, is about him. Don't screw it up."

What would Mom think if she saw me now?

From somewhere inside the cave, something metallic clicked. To Meghan, it sounded like a key actuating a door lock.

She wiped the tears away and straightened her clothing. Donny may have temporary control over her freedom, but it would be a cold day in Hell before he'd take her self-respect.

Footsteps came from far off. The rhythmic footfalls were reminiscent of someone descending a flight of stairs. The reverend appeared out of the darkness.

"Approach the bars, Meghan." He said, motioning her toward him.

"What if I refuse?" she said, staring into his eyes.

He frowned at her. "Suit yourself. I thought after you had spent all that time in this cell, you'd want to use a real bathroom, and maybe take a shower."

A real bathroom would provide an opportunity to see more of the surroundings, she reasoned. Plus, she did have to go. Still a little reluctant, she approached the door.

"Good girl. Put your hands through the bars."

He pulled out a pair of handcuffs and put them on her. "In case you get any ideas, the outer door to my office is solid steel and it has a cypher on it. Cooperate, and you'll have as much time in that bathroom as you wish. I have provided all the things necessary for a proper shower."

"Why are you being so nice to me all of a sudden?" The words sounded catty as they came out of her mouth. She thought about apologizing, and then reasoned that under the circumstances she had a right to be catty. Hell, she had a right to claw his eyes out.

He opened the door and ushered Meghan out of the cell and pointed up the stairs toward an unknown destination. She trudged up them one by one. The surrounding walls were as moist as those of her cell. The condensation was oppressive and clung to the inside of her lungs with every breath.

Stealing a glance into every room, several appeared to be outfitted as cells and others for storage. One room was unlit, its metal door hung open and slumped to one side. It connected to the frame with one hinge, the other having rusted away years ago.

At the top of the stairs they approached a solid metal door with a wheel in the center. It reminded Meghan of the doors she saw inside submarines in old movies her dad used to watch. Bypassing the wheel, the reverend pushed a key into a lock and the door swung open, exposing another wooden door. It reminded Meghan of a silly old cartoon where a dopey looking hunter opened one door only to find another door, and then another, and another. Reaching inside, and pushing it open, artificial light flooded the stairway from the other side, momentarily burning her eyes.

He motioned inside the room. "After you Meghan, my dear."

The office was lavishly appointed. Dark oak panels and leather covered the chairs. It reminded her of the judge's office where she finalized her divorce. To her right a huge oak desk dominated the room. The legs were gnarled, and the tabletop was of one solid piece of wood. At either corner of the desk, lion's heads stood out intricately carved.

On the back wall, behind the desk, stood volumes of books having to do with faith and religion. There were several versions of the Bible, a Koran, the Torah, and several other titles which were unfamiliar to her. The left side of the room featured two doors. One of them more substantial than the other, having a metal lock which required a code to open.

The lack of windows in the office bothered her. Meghan never realized how important windows were to a room until they weren't there. This room was obviously meant to be private. A sanctuary against the world outside.

What prompts a man to need a shield from the outside world?

"You'll find everything you need in there," Donny said. "I also took the liberty of bringing a fresh change of clothes for you." He pointed toward the other door in the room. "I'm going to take the handcuffs off, if you promise you won't try anything stupid. Do we have a deal?"

She wanted to wrap her hands around his throat and squeeze until he stopped moving. However, Donny was physically stronger than her so strangling him was not an option. Plus, she was on his turf, placing the odds clearly in his favor. "Fine, I promise."

Turning the brass handle of the door, it swung open, revealing a small white tiled bathroom, fashionably out of place, given the dark wood theme of the office. A simple bathroom of porcelain and linoleum, the fixtures made it more at home in 1985 than in 2017. On the commode lay a pair of pants, shirt, underwear, towel, and washcloth. Shelly must have written down her sizes at the house to prepare for this moment. Meghan shuddered at the thought that this plan had been so well thought out.

Closing the door, she searched for a lock, but there wasn't one. There wasn't even anything else in the room to prop the door shut if she showered.

A red light blinked in the corner of the room, catching her eye. "What the hell?" She waited a few more moments and then another blink from the corner. Looking more closely, she focused on a small black dot, the size of a bug. Then the light flashed again. The room had a video camera. He'd be watching the whole time. A wave of nausea overcame Meghan, and she shot the camera glare that she hoped would kill anyone watching from the other side.

The sick bastard likes watching.

Before she could say something scathing, Donny's voice crackled to life over an intercom system. "You didn't think you'd be unsupervised, did you?"

"You're a pervert!" Meghan's face ran red with anger. Even if she had to skip the comfort of a real toilet and a shower, there was no way she'd undress in front of him.

"Meghan, I'm hurt. I'm not a pervert. I'm just paranoid. If you open the shower door, you can hang the floor mat over it, and I'll be unable to see you, save for your legs and head. The vanity blocks the view. I will certainly admit to other vices; however, watching women shower or use the toilet isn't one of them. I have a daughter, for Pete's sake."

Giving the video camera a dubious scowl and grabbing the mat from the floor, Meghan flung it over the shower door. It seemed to shield the camera's view sufficiently. Scanning the rest of the room for other cameras, no other black dots peered out from the walls.

She could hold off going to the bathroom until after the shower, and maybe steam would obscure the room enough.

Lingering in the shower, in no particular hurry to return to the rock-hewn cell. The heat from the warm shower penetrated her sore bones and muscles. No matter how hot she made the water, it never reached the right temperature to squeeze out the penetrating cold of incarceration.

Shutting off the water, the room steamed over to shield her from the intrusion of the camera. Meghan used the toilet and washed her hands.

As she stepped out of the bathroom, Donny stood up from the desk. "Good, my turn."

"You're just going to leave me here?" It had to be a set up. Perhaps she was going to be killed while escaping.

He pointed to the door. "That way is locked, only I know the code, and only two others have keys. And the other way leads back into the cave. You're welcome to go back to your cell. Going down there, unsupervised, can be incredibly dangerous. There are things down there you can't even imagine. However, you can certainly go if you wish."

He disappeared into the bathroom, leaving Meghan alone. Examining her surroundings, she scanned for anything that might help her escape. On the desk was a letter opener, pens, a small pair of scissors, and a few pieces of loose-leaf paper. She grabbed the letter opener, hiding it in her waistband and covered the handle with her shirt.

Her mind raced for anything else to help someone who might be looking for her. If there were windows to break, she would. In the bathroom, the sounds of the reverend finishing up his urination meant time was running out.

Her mind raced to an episode of a crime show where the victim left DNA clues around a crime scene before her murder to help solve the case after the fact.

The water from the sink turned on as Donny washed his hands.

Thinking of her own demise felt counterproductive. Cutting a few locks of hair off and sprinkling it on the floor would ensure DNA evidence remained all over. Before she could act, the door to the bathroom opened, ending her chance to leave a clue behind.

"Well, now that we've taken care of our business, don't you admit that you feel better?" He said, drying his hands on a towel from the bathroom.

"I'd be a whole a lot better if you just let me go."

He smiled at her. "Better for you, not so much for me."

"Why? No one has to know. It will stay between us."

"That's where you are wrong, you see—" His words were cut off by a knock on the door. "Who is it?"

"Henry Sheffield, sir," a nervous voice answered.

"Sorry, Meghan, I have business to attend to. Actually, this could be good for you to be a part of. All you have to do is watch." Donny crossed the room and input a code which unlocked the door. With his hand over the lock, Meghan didn't have a chance to see the code. "Well, come in, Henry"

A thin man in his mid-forties entered the room as Donny slammed the door shut behind him. He eyed Meghan standing near the bathroom door. "I'm sorry I'm a little late reverend. I was busy closing the shop and came as fast as I could."

Meghan saw fear in the man's eyes. Her experience so far indicated he was right to be scared. In stark contrast, the reverend remained perfectly calm and collected.

"Not a problem, Henry. Nothing to apologize for. How are Carol and the kids?"

The man shot another glance at Meghan, which screamed out a silent plea for help. "Fine, sir, everyone is just fine."

"Good, I'm glad. Now, down to business. I need you to explain something to me. A little bird told me that you and your wife are up to no good. I certainly hope that isn't true. Is it?" Reverend Swenson leaned back. Henry watched the man, unsure what to say.

"Sir, I just tried to ..." Henry's voice trailed off, the man looking like a caged rat about to be fed to a boa constrictor. "I mean, with the way things have been going around here, I just thought it would be a good idea—"

"You thought what?" the reverend interrupted. "Maybe having a little nest egg was a good idea? You know The Master loves all and is a benevolent soul, Henry. But, siphoning money off the registers at the store to plan your escape from town is just ... well, it's sacrilegious. What have we done to offend? Doesn't The Master provide everything you and your family need? Everything you have is because of him."

Sweat appeared on Henry's forehead and his skin took on a pale, sickly complexion. "Reverend, surely you understand," he stammered. "I just want what's best for my family. All we want is to leave town and never come back. Can't you just let us go? I promise, you'll never set eyes on us again."

An awkward silence filled the room. The reverend sized up Henry like he considered how best to deal with him. Henry shrunk in the chair, his shoulders hunched forward as he tried to melt into the seat cushions.

The reverend burst out in a fit of laughter. "Henry, relax. I'm not going to do anything to you. As a matter of fact, after we are done here, I don't care what you do. I just want to show you first, before you go, what your impact on this little town has been. Then, if you want to leave, you certainly may. No problems." The reverend stood up from his desk and motioned toward the door that Meghan knew led to the cave. "Just a few minutes of your time and then you can decide what's best for you and your family."

He put his hand around Henry's shoulders and ushered the man through the door and down the stairs. Henry appeared far more composed than before. The reverend's words had definitely placated the man. Although still hesitant, he went as instructed.

The reverend spoke in a gentle, soothing tone. "Henry, you and Carol have made huge contributions to this town. I remember when you asked for approval to conceive those two boys. But, at the time, we only approved one child and then The Master saw fit to give you twins. What a joyous occasion that was. Do you remember?

"Then you wanted to take over the hardware store when The Master called Collin Reyes to his eternal home. We worked out the details, and you've done a bang-up job." The noise of footfalls echoed as they proceeded down the stairs. Meghan glanced into her cell, a little surprised when the reverend didn't shove them into it.

At the bottom, they reached another iron door which stood ajar. The reverend pushed it open the rest of the way and guided Henry inside. Meghan followed because, for the moment, she had little else to do and was anxious to learn more about the interior of the cave. The hallway was dimly lit and the large room at the end stretched out as a dark space with no clear end.

"Oh yes, let's get lights on in here," he said. "Lights please."

The walls erupted in flames. A large altar table, similar to the one in the cell, fronted the room. Behind it, a cave disappeared into the wall. Opposite the cave, against the wall, secured by iron rings were three figures. A woman and two boys. The woman had been severely beaten and the right side of her face had swollen up. One of her shirt sleeves was torn and the arm looked like it was either dislocated or broken near the shoulder. The boys, appearing to be five-year old twins, didn't look like they had been beaten, but their clothing were dirty and torn from the ordeal. They kept their eyes locked on their father in a terrorized stare.

Henry let out a yelp at the sight of them. He ran to the woman and held her face in his hands, then turned to the boys and kissed their cheeks, while mumbling, "It's alright, honey, everything will be fine." The boys clung to their father, moaning.

The woman let out another whimper. That was all she could manage as her mouth had been sewn shut with large-diameter fishing line. Severely beaten, she cracked her eyes open to look at Henry.

"Man, I give you woman. I think those were the exact words I uttered at your wedding. Such a lovely bride. You were so handsome, Henry. It makes me wonder what happened to make your soul so dark and hateful."

Henry sobbed uncontrollably. He sat on the floor, holding his wife's feet which barely touched the ground. Although, to Meghan, it didn't matter since the woman didn't look like she'd stand on her own anyway.

Meghan found voice in the injustice being presented. "What the hell is this, Donny? What have you done to these people?"

"My dear lady, you, of all people, should probably be the last person to say anything. These people are practically family. Imagine what I'd do to someone I have no emotional attachment to."

"You're a monster!" Meghan shouted. "A horrible monster. Let her go and for God's sake, let these children go. You can't—"

The reverend backhanded her, sending Meghan crashing into the wall. She lay on the floor, momentarily stunned.

"Silence!" Donny commanded. "I told you that you are here to watch and nothing more."

"You said," Henry spoke meekly. "You said ... you'd let us go."

The reverend raised his eyebrows inquisitively. "No, I said nothing of the sort. I said that I'd let you go. No problem. All you have to do is choose."

Henry took his wife's hand. "Choose? Choose what? I don't ..." The sentence trailed off as he answered the question himself. "No, you can't mean ... that's not right. I can't choose a family member."

The reverend smiled. "Very well then, I guess the choice falls to me. Be a shame to break up a set of twins like that. Right, Henry?"

The woman squeaked out a barely audible word from in between the sutures, "No." It was faint, but loud enough that everyone turned toward her. Henry stood up and they looked into each other's eyes. Meghan sensed the unspoken communication of love passing between the two of them. What came next was inevitable.

Henry turned from her with renewed resolve. "I choose me then. Take me."

The reverend laughed. "It's precious really, a father choosing to sacrifice himself for his family. Touching and almost too cliché. But I'm afraid that isn't an option. No, the rules are clear in this matter. You have to choose one of them."

"But, this isn't fair. You said choose and I chose."

The reverend sat down on the top of the altar at the front of the room. "Of course it is. I made you a promise when you took over the store and you made one to me. You don't remember? Well, I do. You said you'd be faithful to our cause. One of us didn't live up to that promise." His eyes flicked from Henry, and his family. "However, I'm not unreasonable. After we're done here today, you can walk away from here a little wiser. You can leave town if you like and consider your debt to the people of Riapoke paid in full. It's up to you, choose one of the three. Quickly please, we can't stay here all night."

Henry exchanged one final look with his wife who could only hang from the wall of the cave lifelessly. "I'm sorry my love. We tried." Henry reached up to his wife's bleeding and heavily bruised face and kissed her tenderly. Holding her head for one final moment, they nodded to each other. "I choose Carol."

The reverend clapped his hands together. "Thank The Master. I wondered if we'd be here all night." From behind the altar, he took out an elongated knife and cut the ropes holding the children to the wall. They ran for their father and clung to him.

"Please, Donny, let the boys go," Meghan pleaded. "Let me take them to my cell or back up to your office. Don't make them watch this."

"Oh no, that'll never do. This is a good lesson for the boys to learn. You see, this will teach them the importance of following rules. I think it's important to learn the rules, don't you? I know you've taught that boy of yours to follow rules. Isn't that what they teach you in Boy Scouts? To be obedient? This is the same thing. If everyone just remained obedient, we wouldn't be here today. Who knows? If you followed the rules and stayed out of our little town, you and Kyle might be just about anywhere else right now."

Meghan had just enough time to process a change in the room's shadows before a large creature lunged at the helpless woman hanging from the wall. It put two monstrous paws flat against the wall on either side of her shoulders. The creature's immense size filled the space. Megan backed into the hallway, putting distance between herself and this shadowy creature now terrorizing the woman. It reminded her of the gargoyles she'd seen on the side of the large cathedrals, except this beast was much, much larger. Meghan hadn't seen anything like it before. She screamed at the sight.

The creature shot her a glare and howled in a booming voice, "Silence!"

Meghan was unsure if the things ability to speak or the look of the creature were more terrifying.

"I like this one," it said, turning back toward Henry's wife. "She's fresh meat. High priest, be a little more careful not to tenderize my meals so much next time."

Henry balled up into a corner of the room, helpless to do anything other than quiver and hold his sons' heads to his chest, shielding their eyes from the horror playing out. The boys whimpered as they clung to their father. Despite their young age, Meghan knew they understood their mother was about to die.

"Yes, my Lord. I will remember that for next time." The reverend knelt and bowed his head.

"What shall be your fate?" The creature asked Carol. A large lizard-like tongue protruded from its mouth and licked the side of her face. "Yes, you'll do nicely."

Forgetting her terror for the moment, Meghan pulled the letter opener from her waistband and charged at the creature. It was a bold move, but it could be the only chance she had to save the woman's life. Plunging the pointed office implement into the beast's chest cavity, it bent under the force of the strike. The beast used one of its enormous wings to sweep Meghan off her feet and sent her bouncing across the wall of the cave.

Turning toward Meghan, now scampering away from the creature, it laughed. "So tiresome, woman. Do you think you can kill me? In this form I'm indestructible. You'd better learn your place, or I am inclined to play with my dinner the next time I feed. Do I make myself clear?" It turned back to Carol. "Now, shopkeeper's wife ... where were we?"

Carol let out a shriek through the sutures holding her lips together. A few tore through the flesh as she let out an unholy cry. The shriek cut short as the creature tore into her exposed throat, sinking its teeth in. Blood spurted out, washing the walls and the floor. The creature chewed on the woman's windpipe, letting blood drip down its immense jaws. The creature continued to tear into the woman, ripping skin, muscle, and organs from the body, snarling in ravenous joy.

As it finished its meal, it scowled at Meghan. "Let's be clear on something. I control all of this. These are my people and they will obey my will. Your boy will come to understand this, in time. I promise he will."

Meghan forgot her own fear and terror at what she just witnessed. "You leave him the hell alone. Do you hear me? By every fiber of my being I swear I'll kill you."

The creature turned from Meghan and walked back toward the hole in the cave wall. "You'll kill me? Oh human, you amuse me. You are going to kill a living god?"

The reverend turned toward Henry and his children who still clung to their father. All three were reduced to stunned silence. "That's right boys, you stay with your father. He'll need you now that mommy is gone." He turned toward Meghan, "Isn't it sweet? The love of a child is the purest love there is."

Meghan slapped the reverend in the face. A ring on her finger caught the corner of his mouth, leaving blood streaming down. "You're a monster! A bully! You son-of-a-bitch!"

Regaining his composure from her assault, he shoved Meghan to the ground. "I suggest you remember that at any time I can gut that little boy of yours. You'd better learn some manners. Instead of being out with my daughter, he'll find himself chained to one of these walls. Let's see how you like watching your little boy being eaten alive."

The monster slunk back into a dark corner of the cave and into the even darker hole. Over its shoulder, before disappearing, it said, "Tisk ... tisk, High Priest. You need to learn to control your temper." Then it vanished into the blackness, as if the dark void swallowed the demon whole.

Donny waved at Henry. "You are free to leave. The boys stay in town with us, though. Remember, all children born under the approval of The Master remain the property of the town. You may leave anytime you wish. However, children always fare better when they have a parent to raise them."

He grabbed Meghan by the arm and shoved her up the stairs and back into her cell. "You'd best remember the lessons you learned today. It's too late for you, and that boy of yours could still find himself staring down at the blade of a knife as it enters his belly. Consider that the next time you decide you want to be so mouthy." He slammed the door shut and locked it before storming back up the stairs.

18

HALLOWEEN COMES EARLY IN RIAPOKE

Kyle observed the windows of the store fronts across the street, deeply lost in thought. "So, you're sure my mom is still alright?"

Matthew drew in a deep breath. "Honestly, I'm not sure of anything anymore. I think so. All I know is The Master has something planned for you. Not sure what, though. The Master was scheduled to be fed today and they already have someone in mind."

"What do you mean by 'fed'?" Mike chimed in, chewing on a chicken leg Matthew bought from the deli across the street to replace the food spilled during the confrontation with Bill.

"I never took part in that end of things," Matthew said. "I only apprehended the people under the cover of law. Senior elders were responsible for bringing a person to The Master every other month for feeding. He needs a live victim to keep up his strength, or at least that's what Donny tells us. I know a little more than I used to since becoming a deacon, but not as much as an elder or senior elder. I wish I knew more.

"There is a selection committee which meets once a week and decides how best to meet The Master's needs. Sometimes they take people from the surrounding hillsides and bring them into town for the kill. We get lots of hikers in town looking for supplies and stopping at the cafe. Other times we use a local citizen who has chosen to follow our rules."

Mike sat in silence for a moment, and then asked, "The house, down by the lake, what is it used for?"

"That's the processing house. When The Master becomes impatient, he makes us take people down there to remove their hearts. A man in town does the job. He loves the job a little too much, if you know what I mean. He seems to enjoy torturing people. I try to stay as far away from that place as possible." Matthew shivered at the thought.

Mike looked over at Kyle, whose face had gone pasty white, obviously shaken by this discussion. "I think that's enough for now, Matthew. We need a plan, and a good one. Unless I miss my guess, this isn't going to be a walk in the park."

"You don't know the half of it," Matthew said. He pulled a pad of paper out from the desk drawer and drew a rough sketch. "Here is the basic layout of the reverend's house. We'll need to get in and try to find Meghan. I have no idea where he'd hide her in that house. Someone must know something."

Kyle pointed to the crude map. "We didn't see anyone aside from Shelly and Elizabeth while we were in the house. It shouldn't be too hard to get back in."

Matthew shook his head. "You saw what they wanted you to see. Down in the basement is a security center which guards Donny at all times. There are cameras in every room. Every bedroom, bathroom, garage, and closet have sensors. Literally, the second someone does anything, they'll know. That is why I suspected nothing happened between Kyle and Elizabeth. Security watches everything."

As Matthew spoke, Mike wandered around the office, opening drawers and closets and examining their contents. Boxes containing everything from public safety supply company samples to information from the state fire marshal's office were shoved into every nook and cranny, waiting for someone to declare them old and unusable. In one box he found a set of uniforms from a supply company who'd promised to outfit Riapoke's non-existent sheriff's department. A letter on the top indicated they sent them two inspector's uniforms to try out.

Matthew continued, "And even if we could break our way in, we'd be discovered, and getting out might be impossible. They'd call the reverend, and he'd be likely to take drastic measures. We need a way to get in and—"

Mike interrupted, "And look like we belong there?"

Matthew looked puzzled. "I was going to say get out undetected. Not sure I understand your meaning."

Mike reached into the long-forgotten box and pulled out two shirts with matching pants. The shirts were light tan, and the pants a polyester green. He laid them down on the table and smoothed them out. "Matthew, do you know why it's possible for a man with a clipboard to go anywhere they want?"

"Okay, I'll bite. Enlighten me."

"Because a man with a clipboard looks important. Everyone just assumes he belongs there. No one bothers to question him. Sure, Mike and Kyle would definitely raise a stir if we tried to walk into that house, but inspectors Brown and Taylor might not raise any suspicions at all, especially if they were escorted by Officer Tanner."

Kyle's face brightened. "All we need are a couple of clipboards and official-looking badges, and we can go just about anywhere."

"Hold on a second," Matthew interrupted. "Are you suggesting we just waltz in there with clipboards in hand and hope like hell no one will notice us? I suppose it's simple enough to work, but kind of aballzy move."

"Actually," Mike said, "I think Kyle will have to stay in the vehicle when we get there. Remember, they've seen his face and will certainly recognize him. We can just say 'Agent Taylor' here is ill and is staying in the truck."

"Okay, I hate to admit it, but this idea has merit. This is going to take planning and those uniforms have been in their boxes since they were sent here. They don't have any patches or anything and we'll have to find a few to make them look official. It has to be something convincing and still obscure. Maybe Department of Interior patches?" he said, thinking out loud.

Matthew sat back down in one of the chairs. "You both know what this means, don't you?"

Kyle glanced back at Mike and then to Matthew. "We'll have our Halloween costumes early?"

Mike frowned at Kyle. "Don't think so, champ. I think what our friend here is saying is that after this point, the three of us are on our own. There's only two ways out and one is in a body bag."

The three sat in an uncomfortable silence, thinking over the implications of what they were about to do.

Kelley and Meghan would have told Mike to take Kyle as far away from this place as possible if they were there to consult. But right now, responsibility for the boy fell to him and both of them were surrounded by a town that institutionalized serial killing for an unholy demon.

Mike spoke up, "We should send Kyle back to the resort on a boat. He can bring help, and it would get him out of harms' way."

"No way," Kyle responded. "I know you think I'm just a kid, but my mom is out there somewhere in this hellhole and I need to find her. Besides, all we need is for someone to see me at the boat launch and this rescue operation turns into a fight for our lives."

Matthew fidgeted with a pen on the table. "The kid has a point. I know this town and these people. That pier is always busy this time of year and even if one person were to see the boat leave, or another boat passes him on the way in, this will come to a screeching halt. People around here are trained in the art of paranoia. Frankly, I'm shocked you even made it this far into town on your own."

"Okay, Kyle." Mike said, pointing at the teen. "When we get to the reverend's house, stay in the truck. You're going to stay as quiet as a church mouse. If anything goes wrong, I mean anything, you start that engine and take the highway out of town. You drive as fast as that truck will carry you until you hit the state line. Understood?"

Kyle rolled his eyes at Mike in response to the lecture, "Sure, Dad."

Mike frowned at the boy. "We're being serious, Kyle. Anything goes wrong, I want you out of here." He put a hand on Kyle's shoulder. "Deal?"

Kyle threw up his hands in indignation. "Fine, I got it."

Matthew stood up from the table. "Good. I'm going to call the house and arrange for a visiting team of inspectors from the Department of Interior to pay a call on the house. In the meantime, in that top drawer you'll find patches. There's a sewing kit in the closet. Get cracking. In about twelve hours, you two will be transformed into two of the best-looking federal agents the world has ever seen."

For a good portion of the night, they worked on hemming the uniforms to fit the two. Mike found a stash of insignia, rank, and shoulder patches sent to the department in hope for a patch exchange. Kyle turned out to be a wizard at sewing, blaming his mother for the talent. Making ends meet in the Johnston family often meant sewing patches on second-hand clothes. At two in the morning, they tried on their new uniforms. They were almost a perfect fit.

"Good job, Martha Stewart," Matthew said, punching Kyle in the arm. "You two need to take showers and get some rest. The cots in the cells aren't the most comfortable; however, you're only going to sleep for a few hours. I'll be back at sunrise with breakfast and shaving stuff. I'll need to run home and change myself. My uniform smells so bad I could almost wipe out the town by myself on stench alone."

Matthew left the two alone with their thoughts. They knew they didn't have a lot of time before the plan needed to take flight, and a few hours of sleep would do them both good. As they stretched out on the cots, Kyle asked, "Hey Mike?"

"Yeah, buddy?"

"Do you think my mom is alright?"

Mike hesitated, unsure how to answer. "I'm not sure, Kyle. I'll tell you what I think, though. I believe in my heart your mom is fine. I just think that right now she's sitting someplace, thinking about you. Right now, you are thinking about her. So you can say that right now you are together in thought at least."

"Hey, Mike?"

"Yeah, Kyle?"

"That is the sappiest load of horse shit I've ever heard in my entire life. Talk like that to my mom, and there will be no getting rid of her." Kyle laughed.

Mike laughed too, overcome by the silliness of the moment. "Let's get some sleep Kyle, we have your mom to rescue soon."

"Mike?"

"Yes?"

"Thank you."

Mike lay there, alone with his thoughts, trying to think how to respond. He may have just made Kyle a promise he couldn't keep. Deep inside his heart, he believed she was still all right. Even though Matthew's dour assessment probably lay closer to the truth.

He yawned and stretched his tired body. They needed this little break. Exhaustion led to mistakes, and they couldn't afford to make any. In the morning, they had to play the role of the perfect federal agents. The fake identification cards, very real badges, and leather belts and other police equipment lay in a pile on a desk. With the official looking garb, it should be easy to get into the house under the guise of an official inspection. Matthew told Shelly that they needed to gain access to the entire house to ensure they were compliant with ecological regulations. The simplicity of the plan was an asset. However, luck could play a deciding role in the ultimate outcome.

Turning his head on the small pillow, Mike heard soft snoring coming from the other bunk. He listened to the gentle rhythm of the boy's breathing for a while. The noise reminded him of Kelley. He wondered again, not for the first time, if his daughter was worried about him. Maybe she'd gone out looking for him. Mike prayed silently for the morning to come swiftly and for a successful mission.

———

MEGHAN TRIED to make herself comfortable on the rock-hewn floor of the cave. Having lost the concept of time or anything else for that matter, sleep could be coming in the middle of the day or night. The reverend had brought her a pillow, blanket, and additional food, but she refused to even make eye contact with him.

In the dark of her cell, she thought about Kyle, wondering if he was okay. She'd make sure he made it out of Riapoke, even if it meant sacrificing her own life. Tank's odd warning about the weird town came to mind, a warning that no longer seemed odd at all. If anything, it stuck in Meghan's chest like a knife.

She had an unmistakable feeling that Kyle was safe, wherever he was. Stretching out a hand, she envisioned touching him. For a moment, they would be together somehow. Meghan remembered reading something about how all the molecules of the world are connected. If that were true, then wherever they were, they still had a connection and he might sense her.

She found a relatively flat spot on the rocky floor and wrapped the blanket around herself. Even in this cold, wet, and forlorn cavern, sleep pushed out the thoughts of the evil lurking in the impossibly dark cave.

———

"ARE YOU KIDDING ME? How could you be so careless?" Donny screamed. "I gave you one thing to do and you couldn't handle a simple task that should have come almost as second nature." The scared teenage girl shrank from his anger, trying to disappear into the cushions of the sofa.

Tears streamed from Elizabeth's eyes. "I'm sorry, Daddy. I didn't mean to screw it up. I just thought—"

Donny leaned forward with a vicious glare. "You just thought? I'm not sure you did. You should have used that brain of yours! Too much time is spent hanging out with your friends and it's turned your brain to mush. You weren't even paying half attention to what I wanted you to do."

"You said not to let him leave the town. You wanted me to watch him. Now there is no way he'll leave town, and we can keep an eye on him. I don't see the problem here." She leaned forward on the couch, trying to defend her position.

Donny held his head in his hands. "Honey, you accused him of rape! Matthew arrested him. Now he's in jail, pending testing. And you know those tests will come back negative. We know this because his door was locked until after he got out of bed. I made sure they were locked. Tell me sweetie, what do you think The Master is going to say when we tell him Kyle hates you? You two are supposed to search for his mother together, fall in love, and stay in town. The plan is for the two of you to usher in a new era. Now Kyle isn't going to want to look at you, let alone spend any time with you." He circled the room. Instinctively fidgeting with a stress ball on the desk and squeezing it until his knuckles turned white.

She stood up from the couch. "I've got it, Daddy. I know how to fix this."

He sneered at her. "Oh please tell me your plan, oh great one."

"Okay, I screwed up. I admit it. We get Kyle back here and maybe drug his dinner. We lock him up here and then I'll work my girl charms on him. And then—"

Donny put a hand up, imploring her to stop. "Oh geez, just stop right there. I don't want you to do anything. Keep an eye open for Kyle and if you see him, you call me. For The Master's sake, don't talk to him. For tonight, Matthew says he's in a jail cell, pending test results."

"Dad, you're the high priest. Why don't you just tell that stooge to bring him back here?"

Donny shook his head. "Because, darling, he's the law in this town. Like it or not, I need cooperation from others, and people respect Matthew. You are going to have to learn that pushing people too hard could result in them pushing back. Better to control his authority than try to usurp it."

She nodded, lowering her head. "Sorry I messed this up, Daddy. I know you'll figure this out." She stood up and left the room, closing the office door behind her.

Donny sat back in his chair and contemplated the next move. There were a few hiccups, but things were still under control. The scare he put into Meghan ensured she'd cooperate for Kyle's sake. Kyle sat in the cell at the police station. The Master, still full of concern about the situation, was presently content. Waylon had been eliminated as a potential threat. Every loose thread appeared tied up and trimmed for the moment.

Yawning at the late hour, the trees across the driveway bent to the will of the strong wind. A storm brewed just over the horizon, common this time of year. If they were lucky enough, it'd be just a light rain.

The phone rang in his pocket, shocking him from his thoughts. "Hello? Oh, hello, Matthew. I thought about calling you. I wanted to know how our guest was getting along. Uh huh ... I see. Well good then."

Donny bantered on for a little while longer about several details he didn't care about while staring at a tree branch that fell into the driveway in the wind. He contemplated an expedient exit from the inane prattle of the conservation officer when a string of words caught his attention. "What's that? Inspectors from where? Oh yeah? Couldn't happen at a worse time. I suppose we get them in and get them out. I'll be ready in the morning, so we can get it over with. We've got a big day tomorrow and I don't want anything to screw it up. What's that? Yes, that's right, first thing in the morning."

Donny hit the call end button on the phone. The trees outside stopped moving as the wind gusts died down. "That might be the worst of it," Donny said to himself. He knew better, though. The storm would still come. This was just a brief respite from its fiery.

19

INVASIVE SPECIES

Matthew opened and closed the door to the station as gingerly as possible. The beds in the cells were hard to sleep on under the best of circumstances, having napped on them quite a few times. The night before he'd considered bringing Mike and Kyle back to his house to sleep in the guest rooms. Their presence might be difficult to explain to the neighbors.

He placed two large shopping bags he was carrying on the table in the center of the room. Out of one, he took out a bottle of juice and milk, unsure what Mike or Kyle wanted to drink. He also made a pot of coffee.

Kyle stretched out as Matthew worked at setting up a breakfast spread. Glancing over at the boy, it struck him how extraordinarily tall he was. His large feet hung over the edge of the metal cot bolted to the wall of the cell. Pouring himself a first cup of coffee, the idea of having a son played out in his imagination. Matthew saw a younger version of himself playing ball with a kid in the front yard of a nondescript house somewhere in the suburbs.

Taking a young boy out on a camping trip into the hills could be great fun. Matthew always loved the woods, especially camping. As a child, wandering the hills and forests around their home was a favorite pastime.

When he drove Kyle and his mother to Donny's house, he stole a furtive glance or two in the rear-view mirror. Meghan was attractive in a plain sort of way. Even dressed in a bikini top and cutoffs, she maintained a dignified air about her. Although quite a bit older than he, she'd be nice to get to know. That, however, was highly unlikely when this was resolved. After all, it was he who delivered Meghan and Kyle into the waiting clutches of Donny in the first place. Had he seen how all the pieces would fit together then, he could have saved a lot of heart ache.

He didn't want to frighten anyone with his opinion of their chances. The odds of them pulling this off, let alone making it out of town, were as close to impossible mathematically possible. Taking up this mission meant risking everything. Once they left for the reverend's house there was no turning back. His career in law enforcement and his standing in the church would be over. They had to try for the sake of giving the town its best chance at freedom.

Matthew remembered reading about the scorched-earth policy the Soviets employed during the Second World War. The same went for his personal, and newly declared, war against the Church of The Master. Even if he destroyed Donny, The Master would remain and start fresh. If the opportunity presented itself, The Master must die as well.

Last night he wrote two letters. One addressed to his mother and father and the second to his sister. In the letters he gave them specific instructions on what to do today. No matter the outcome of the impending battle, he wanted them to just leave town and never return. It was his insurance policy. By some miracle, if he survived, he'd find them. If not, he'd die knowing they were safe.

"Morning." Mike's voice interrupted Matthew's train of thought.

Matthew motioned to the paper bags. "I brought breakfast. Not sure what you wanted to drink, so I brought juice and milk. Got a couple of bagels and donuts. Nothing fancy. Enough to get us through today."

Mike watched Kyle sleeping soundly. "Should I wake the kid up?"

"No, let him sleep a bit more. We have time before we have to leave."—Matthew took a sip of coffee— "You know, Mike, I want to make sure you fully understand what we are about to do."

Mike lowered his voice to just above an audible whisper. "You're about to lose your badge, and I'll likely get disbarred for this. If we catch a few lucky breaks, we will save a woman I hardly know. If we don't, we'll never make it out of here alive. Sound about right?"

Matthew nodded. "Sounds about right."

"What do you think our chances are?"

"Realistically, only one in twenty might be optimistic. I don't want to sound harsh, but the odds aren't in our favor. Oh, that reminds me." Matthew reached into a desk drawer and fished around a bit, pulling out a revolver and a box of ammunition. "Ever used one of these?"

"A couple of times." Mike took the pistol from Matthew. "Pretty much just point and shoot, right?"

"Double action .38, you can pull through the hammer action and fire the weapon or pull back the hammer and squeeze the trigger. Here's the thing, don't pull it out unless we need it. I can guess what you must think of the people of Riapoke, but there are good people living here. People that I don't want to see get hurt. As you know, I'm breaking about a gazillion laws as it is. I draw the line at shooting innocent people."

"You don't exactly have the corner on risk here. I'm likely to get disbarred for this. Not to mention dead."

Matthew's mind flashed back to his final moments with Waylon. He'd have to square that with more competent authorities, likely standing trial for the murder of Waylon and whomever they dealt with along the way. The bloodshed wasn't over. The best thing now would be to try to keep Mike out of as much trouble as possible. No sense in ruining both their lives.

Behind the men a loud yawn broke the silence. Kyle sat up on the cot and peered over at them. "Oh, breakfast."

Mike smiled. "Do teenage boys ever think about anything other than food?"

Kyle frowned at them, "Yes, their mothers."

Mike felt like an ass. Kyle had more to lose in this fight than anyone else. At the end of all of this a young man might lose his mother and that thought likely terrified Kyle.

"Fair enough," Matthew said, dissipating the sudden tension in the air. "What do you say you gulp down juice, get dressed, and we can be on our way. We have a damsel in distress to save."

Kyle smiled at the idea. Matthew decided it was best to put as a positive spin on the situation as possible. Rehashing the discussion about the odds likely wouldn't help. It'd be better if Kyle didn't know how impossible the situation truly was.

A little while later, Kyle still chewed on a donut while buttoning up the shirt they altered to look like a Department of Interior uniform. Matthew inspected them and nodded his satisfaction. A leather belt with pouches and snaps completed the ensemble, making them look like official law enforcement personnel.

While Mike fastened the revolver into the holster on the belt, Matthew handed Kyle a dummy weapon that looked real enough to a casual observer.

"Hey, don't I get a real weapon?" he said, sounding a little put out.

Matthew frowned at the teen. "Really, Kyle, do I even have to justify that question with an answer?"

Mike chimed in, "Sorry kid, your mother would never forgive me if I let you walk around with a loaded gun."

"You guys are no fun at all."

"Ah, but I do have the perfect second prize," Matthew said.

"Oh yeah?"

Matthew threw Kyle his keys. "Yep, you get to drive the squad truck."

Mike glared at Matthew. "Really?"

"Sure," Matthew folded his arms. "Actually, it makes sense. If we need to get out of there fast, we want someone at the wheel who is already familiar with the truck. I don't want us fleeing for our lives with a kid at the wheel who has never driven the truck before. This way he gets a little more experience behind the wheel.

Kyle drove especially carefully, possibly because of nerves or in an attempt to impress the two men. The drive to the house was short. To Matthew the time moved along intolerably slow. His mind rehearsed every potential thing that could go wrong. Mike's worry about Meghan had obviously rubbed off on him.

When they arrived at the reverend's security gate, Matthew and Kyle switched places and Matthew pressed the button on the security intercom. A speaker crackled to life. Matthew knew, from his talks with the security staff, the video monitor on the front gate wasn't working, so he wasn't worried about the camera seeing Kyle.

"Hey, it's Matthew. We have an appointment."

"Good Morning Matthew. We've been expecting you," the voice over the speaker said.

"Excellent. We'll be as brief as possible."

The gates opened slowly, its rusty hinges creaking under the metallic strain of heavy steel. Matthew pulled the truck forward and parked in the space giving them the quickest exit out the driveway if they needed it. With a nod to Kyle, the boy slid over to the driver's position. The hairs on the back of Matthew's neck stood up as he nodded over to Mike sitting in the back seat. "Are you ready for this?"

"Not really. Sitting here isn't going to make me anymore ready though, so let's get on with it."

"Kyle," Matthew said, "whatever you do, don't get out of this truck. If anything happens, the police radio is set to channel 4. I want you to get on it and say, the weather service predicts a storm."

Kyle gave him a quizzical look. "A little cliché, don't you think?"

"No, you see the regular citywide radio channel gets some bleed over from channel 4, the weather channel. If you say, 'the weather service predicts a storm', we'll hear it and know to come back to the truck. Anyone else hearing it will just think it's a piece of the weather report and nothing more."

Kyle practiced reciting the line a few times. "The weather service predicts a storm ... the weather service predicts a storm. Got it."

"Kyle," Mike interjected, "if your mom is in there, we'll get her out."

Kyle didn't respond, remaining focused on the task at hand.

———

MIKE TOOK POINT, knocking on the door with an official-sounding rap. Although they'd practiced what he would say and thought the verbiage was set in his mind, the words suddenly escaped his mental grasp. Breaking into a sweat, panic set in as the sounds of footsteps approaching the door boomed in his eardrums. The lock made a metallic click as the deadbolt slid back. The first word eluded him. He remembered the middle part and not the first. Suddenly he could only remember the last thing he needed to say. Beads of sweat poured from him, cascading down his back, wetting his undershirt.

Regardless of his nerves, it was show time.

"Good Morning. You must be the inspector Matthew was telling us about." A grizzled man in his early sixties stood in front of them. The man looked a hundred and twenty pounds if he wore cement shoes.

Mike's brain finally, mercifully, engaged. "I am. My name is special agent Charles Mayhew, from the Department of Interior." He unclipped the identification badge from his shirt, handing it to the man.

"Names George Whimbly, head of security for the parsonage and church. Come in, by all means." Taking the badge and holding it up to a clipboard, George made a few notes with a pen and handed it back to Mike. "Seems like everything's in order. What did you say you needed to look at?"

Mike grasped at what to say. Opening his mouth, words came out as he silently prayed for his brain to engage and help make sense of it all. "At the department, we're looking into areas where there have been instances of the hemlock woolly adelgid. It's pretty invasive just over the state line in West Virginia, and we want to see how Virginia is handling them. I'm inspecting homes surrounded by trees to catch any signs they could be around. I'll want to look in every room if I can. It shouldn't take long."

The night before, Mike, Matthew and Kyle sat at the table and crafted the narrative surrounding their bogus reason for the visit. It wasn't unusual for forestry experts to come to the area to check for invasive species from time to time. The bug was a real insect. If anyone bothered to check their story, however, they'd likely find out government employees didn't normally scour the countryside looking for them and certainly don't inspect houses. They'd staked their lives on George, and the rest of the staff, not bothering to check.

George cocked his head to one side. "The woolly hemledge?"

Matthew chuckled. "No George, the hemlock woolly adelgid. It's a species of bug which has high incidences of infestation in West Virginia. Kills hemlock trees. Pretty bad for the ecology."

"Oh right," George said. "Hey, wait a minute, we're not in West Virginia."

"Well, that's true," Mike replied. "Bugs don't care about regulations telling them where they're supposed to go, and even less about state boundaries."

George nodded. "I suppose that's right, isn't it? Well, let's not waste the agent's time, Matthew. It isn't often we get federal guys out here." George motioned to the men, who followed them inside. They walked down a long hall that ended in a pair of beautifully crafted doors. "By the way, what's the deal with the other guy in the truck? Isn't he coming in?"

Mike and Matthew hadn't talked in great detail about how they'd explain leaving Kyle in the truck. "He's not well," Mike spoke up. "Caught the flu and is staying away from other people. He's an entomologist. Unless we find a bug body somewhere, he'd just be another person tracking dirt through the house."

171

20

THE HOUSE OF THE DEMON

Kyle sat quietly, and more than a little nervously, inside the truck. Struggling to keep a positive attitude, the situation looked dourer every minute that ticked by on the dashboard clock. If Mike and Matthew were successful, they'd bring out his mother. If not, then they'd have to switch to plan B. A plan they didn't, as yet, have. He took solace in the fact that they would know more soon.

He fidgeted with the truck's radio. Even though it looked like a normal radio, it only played one station featuring the sermons delivered by Donny Swenson. The reverend carried on about something, practically screaming about fire and brimstone.

Now I know the world wants you to believe in things you know aren't true. Be careful that you don't fall into the traps set before you, good people of The Master. He wants you to know that he loves you. So much, in fact, sometimes it hurts to punish those who are wicked. It is out of love that he punishes. It's to keep those in line who otherwise undo what he's built here.

Brothers and Sisters, The Master gives us all and asks so little. So I ask again, why would anyone want to leave? It defies logic. Everything we have here is perfect. We live in a proverbial Garden of Eden. I know there are those of you who are curious about the world outside of our little town. Although, I have to tell you, it's not what it should be. Lest ye' forget, I've seen it first-hand. People living in licentiousness! Brothers and sisters lying together as husband and wife, children acting as parents and parents acting as children. Men and women of the cloth who turn against their own flock for their own benefit. I've seen things—

Kyle snapped off the radio, having heard enough of Donny's nonsensical gibberish. While they had never been full-time church-goers, this didn't sound like the kind of preaching his family subscribed to.

Behind the wood line, the telltale noise of an approaching vehicle destroyed the silence left by the absence of Donny's babble. Trying to make himself as invisible as possible, Kyle folded his tall frame onto the floorboard, cramming himself into the tiny space. The act of hiding made him feel like he stood out even more.

He heard a car door slam shut, followed by Shelly's easily recognizable voice. They were too far away from him to make out any words.

Kyle froze in place as he heard footsteps approach the truck.

This is it, someone found me. We're all dead.

His eyes darted toward the dashboard and the radio handset sitting in its cradle. He wanted to pick it up and declare a storm moving in, but he convinced himself to calm down and relax. They were still okay. He was hidden behind the locked doors of the truck and there was no reason to panic ... yet.

Something rocked the truck, as if someone leaned up against the door, only inches from Kyle's head. "Hey John, how are you?" Donny's voice rang out.

"I know you're busy," he continued. "We need to have a ceremony." Donny paused for a moment, listening to the person on the other end. The volume on the cell phone was so loud Kyle could almost make out what the other man was saying, but not quite. What was clear is that the other man was protesting. "I know John. Look, we have to get this one done. We haven't had a quick turn-around ceremony like this in a while. The Master insists this one get done tonight."

Ceremony? Kyle thought. What kind of ceremony? He didn't

remember anyone talking about a ceremony while they were in the reverend's house.

"What's that? Oh no, I don't think that'll be necessary. We are going to keep this low key. A woman and her son wandered into town. The Master thinks it's the beginning of something big, and this has to be done quickly and quietly. The son isn't a tribute. We only need to keep him away and make sure he doesn't find out."

Kyle sat in stunned silence listening to Donny finish the phone call. They were planning something for his mother and him. Based on the conversation, he wondered what the reverend meant by saying he wanted to get her out of the way. If the comment meant what Kyle thought it did, they needed to move. Time was of the essence.

Kyle's eyes fell to the dashboard clock again. Another minute ticked by. How long had Mike and Matthew been inside the house? To him, it seemed like an eternity. One thing was for certain, his mother was still very much alive. Maybe not for long.

———

"SO, Agent Mayhew, how do you know if any of these small creatures are around?" George asked as they walked through the hallways of the house.

"Feces, and we find dead ones from time to time." Mike wasn't sure how convincing it sounded. George bought it though, with little reservation. Glancing over at Matthew, searching for any hint he was right or completely off base, gave him little comfort. Matthew maintained an impressive poker face as they walked.

"You know, I've always wanted to work for the Department of Interior," George continued, blissfully unaware that Mike knew absolutely nothing about government work. "My Uncle was a forestry guy for the better part of thirty years."

"Is that right?" Mike said. Walking past every room, Mike glanced inside for any possible sign of Meghan. So far, they'd come up empty. Kyle had given them a thorough rundown of which rooms they'd inhabited while staying in the house, so Mike knew where to look. Mike wasn't naive in thinking finding Meghan would be that easy, but he'd hoped to find a trace of Meghan. Perhaps a hairbrush or article of clothing to suggest her presence.

Matthew pushed open the door to the room that Kyle indicated Meghan slept in. The room smelled of pine soap and fresh linen, suggesting it had been freshly cleaned. His heart sank a little as one of their few leads dried up.

George continued their one-sided conversation. "Yep, I worked logging crime about forty miles from here for the forestry service. Caught a couple of poachers in the area. The last great adventure in government service if you ask me."

Mike pushed open the bedroom door where Kyle spent the night. In contrast to Meghan's room, this bed was still disheveled, and the toiletry items Kyle had been given to use were still laying on the dresser.

Mike eyed George. "You had visitors?"

"Oh yes, a woman and a boy the reverend had staying with us. I think the boy is returning ... not expecting the woman back."

Matthew asked, "Why's that?"

George looked at Matthew with one up-raised eyebrow. "Why's what?"

Matthew growled at George. "Why aren't you expecting her to return? A little odd, don't you think?"

"Well, he probably ..." George's voice trailed off, and he scowled at them. "Why do you care, Matthew?"

A bead of sweat broke out on Matthew's temple. He'd come dangerously close to overplaying his hand. "Now that you mention it, I really don't." Matthew stepped forward to the next room, feigning disinterest.

George shot Matthew an odd glance. Mike could tell the gears were mentally running through all the little details of their visit. Matthew mentioned that George had a law enforcement back-ground, and something apparently began looking fishy to him.

Matthew's hand radio crackled to life and through some static a faint whisper of a voice could be heard. "The national weather service just issued a storm watch for our area."

Not exactly what Kyle was supposed to say, but close enough. Mike turned around an extended a hand to George. "Well boys, I don't see any reason to continue wasting everyone's time. No sign of the critters here, and I don't think continuing our search will turn them up. Probably should just give it up and move onto another house. The department thanks you for your time George."

Mike's movement broke the uncomfortable stare-down between George and Matthew. George reluctantly took Mike's hand and shook it.

Matthew, on his way to the door, turned back toward George. "Thank you, George. See you at the ceremony huh?"

"How did you—," George stammered. "Sure, yeah. See you at the ceremony."

Mike followed Matthew out the front door. Both men gasped at the sight of Donny pacing the parking lot, involved in a heated conversation with someone. Kyle was nowhere in sight. Matthew wondered if he'd managed to get out of the truck and run into the woods in between his call for help and now.

"Hello Reverend. How are you this fine day?" Matthew called as he descended the stairs.

Mike noticed Matthew moved his hand to rest it on the grip of his weapon. With the other hand he gave Mike a signal to stay behind him.

"I'm fine. Who do we have here?" Donny glanced disinterestedly from his phone as he hit the end call button and slid it into the pocket of his dress shirt. "Oh, you must be the agent from the Department of Interior. Hopefully everything is in order?"

Thankful Donny failed to notice there was only one of them and not two. Mike played his part as boldly as possible. "Good day Sir, Agent Mayhew. We are looking into reports of an invasive species of insect. We are hoping to try to keep them out of Virginia if we can. They come over from the west. And yes, everything appears to be in order."

"You're looking in my home?" The reverend asked.

"Yes, Sir. You see, the critters burrow into wood like termites and live under the siding and other places. There is little we can do to stop them once they have a foothold, our only recourse is to fumigate." Mike hoped he sounded convincing. A law professor once advised him that a weak case can sometimes work if presented strongly enough. The jury, in this case the reverend, might just buy an extraordinary argument.

Donny was either underwhelmed by the information or wanted out of the conversation as quickly as possible. Mike glanced up at the window to see George looking down at them, vulture-like. Although still unsure what his suspicions were, George would likely share them as soon as the reverend walked in the door. George obviously suspected something was out of sorts.

"Reverend, we don't want to take up any more of your time." Matthew said, a nervous edge in his voice. "We need to get moving."

"Yes," Mike added. "Thank you so much, your staff was very helpful in speeding this along."

Donny waved his hand dismissively at the both of them. "I expect nothing less of my little team." Then he turned toward the house.

Matthew whispered, "We need to get out of here."

Mike wondered what became of Kyle. Standing on the top of the stairs he should have been clearly visible to them and there should have been no way he would have been invisible to Donny.

Walking to the passenger side, Mike breathed a sigh of relief as soon as he spied the boy, on the driver's side foot board; neatly folded to remain as small as possible.

Mike said over the top of the truck to Matthew, "Wait a second before you get in." Mike opened the door and motioned to Kyle to move over toward the passenger side. George, still at the window, would undoubtedly tell security to lock the gate if Kyle popped up. The old head of security was fairly scatterbrained, and it likely hadn't occurred to him to ask what happened to the entomologist.

For now, the plan remained largely intact.

Although George had suspicions, Matthew knew Donny thought George was lazy and borderline incompetent sometimes. More than once Matthew was asked to keep an eye on the aged chief of security. He'd voiced suspicions about other people in town, Donny dismissed them as being a figment of George's imagination, and they usually were. Matthew outranked him in the church hierarchy and was considered more trustworthy. Then again, suspicion and backstabbing became institutionalized since Donny instituted his brand of religion in this little town.

All breathed a collective sigh of relief the moment the truck sped away from the house. Far enough away from the front gate, Kyle crawled over the top of the seats and dropped into the back. Stopping at an intersection for a passing car, Mike asked, "So, what next?"

"Sorry for using the radio," Kyle said, somewhat sheepishly. "I just didn't know what else to do with him standing there. Plus, I overheard the reverend say something about my mom. He said a woman and her son who wandered into town and something about preparing for a ceremony."

Mike adjusted his leather duty belt. "You asked George about a ceremony, Matthew. What was the significance of that?"

Matthew made a discomforting face as he depressed the accelerator and the large truck roared to life. "It means we're running out of time. I think your mother is being held at the church. Unless I miss my guess, they plan to kill her at sundown."

Kyle's voice broke as he spoke. "Then we need to go now. Please."

"We're going to," Matthew said. "We have to be careful, or we're going to do more harm than good. There are things at the church which defy explanation."

Mike stared out the window at passing trees. "Well, I think you might want to give it a try. This whole situation could go south if we aren't careful."

Matthew turned the truck down a country road and pulled into the driveway of an abandoned house. "Okay, this is going to sound weird and fantastic, but I swear it is the truth. Riapoke isn't just a name, it is a sort of an eternal holding cell. Riapoke is an Indian word. It means, the devil or evil, depending on how you translate it. Legend has it that the Powhatan Indians, who once controlled this area, found the cave and discovered something living in it."

Kyle cocked his head to the side. "Thing living in it?"

"Yes, something supposedly immortal. The Indians knew to steer clear of the cave. Legend has it that Chief Powhatan himself went down to discover its secrets. After days of being down in the cave, he emerged and ordered the entire population to stay away. He even sent his daughter away from the area on a mission with some Europeans who landed here. He wanted to keep her safe. You know her as Pocahontas."

"The Pocahontas?" Kyle's eyes grew big as saucers.

"One and the same," Matthew continued. "I don't know if this thing is immortal or not, but this town is essentially built around it. Until about ten years ago, it wasn't that big of a deal. No one paid attention to it. Sure, some made sacrifices, mostly livestock. No big deal. Then the reverend came, and things changed."

"Changed? How so?" Mike asked.

"At first, little things. He exerted more control over the council's activities, and such. Soon Donny altered the church's constitution and changed the election cycle, allowing him control over the entire governing board. Eventually eroding all outside control of the church. Of course, everything done in the name of The Master, and therefore unquestioned. One time he disappeared into the cave for almost a full week. Donny Swenson went down, and the high priest of the church came out." Matthew paused for a moment, recalling an uncomfortable memory. "Not sure how to describe it. It was shortly after he came from that damn cave that ritualistic sacrifices of humans were being demanded. In the beginning, bones of the dead were returned to the families for Christian burial. That's when I exhumed one of the bodies and sent it in for testing."

Kyle interjected. "I'm guessing you were able to keep it a secret."

"Yes, I value my life. Also, it gave me something on Donny. So, I forged a bench warrant and used an outside construction company to dig up the plot. The remains were sent to a crime lab out of state. The body showed acute opisthotonos. That is the technical term for an extreme arching of the back. Common in strychnine poisoning. The toxicology report showed trace amounts in the marrow."

Mike asked, "A ritual sacrifice doesn't require poison, does it?"

"You asked the million-dollar question. One night I checked into anyone buying strychnine. I found out that a doctor by the name of Charles Wheatler had purchased the poison."

"Was there something specific about this guy you exhumed?" Mike looked puzzled. "I mean, why were you suspicious?"

"The guy was an older gentleman who'd stood in opposition to the changes Donny made and enforced with an iron fist. I'm sure the man died because he opposed Donny, and by extension The Master. He wasn't a sacrifice. This was murder plain and simple."

Mike looked out the truck window at an old outbuilding, seemingly lost in thought. "Did you talk to this Dr. Wheatler?"

Matthew frowned. "I didn't have to. Dr. Wheatler doesn't exist. That is one of the pseudonyms used by Donny Swenson. I've seen a prescription pad in his office at church with that name on it along with a dozen other aliases he's using."

Kyle interjected. "How has he been able to get away with this? Why is it that no one has tried to stop him?"

"Fear is a great motivator, Kyle," Mike said.

"If someone won't stop at murder to ensure their power remains intact, that tells you everything you need to know about your adversary." Matthew put the truck back in gear and backed out onto the main road before speeding away.

"We need to get my mom, and we need to get her now." A spike of terror laced Kyle's voice.

"I think you are absolutely right. It's time to finish this. Just understand that, the entire church building needs to burn along with it. You need to be ready to do the unthinkable to save her. Donny has a group of people called 'The Committee' who assist in the ceremonies, and they'll do anything to protect him. He has something solid on each of them and if they don't do his bidding, he'll exact revenge."

"How many are we talking?" Mike wondered out loud.

"The committee is made up of seven. But, with Waylon dead, only six remain." Matthew nodded to Mike. "You met George. He is the de facto leader. I suspect he'll be tied up at the house, he'll get here, but not until later. They'll all be armed and take pleasure in doing The Master's bidding. All committee members are required to commit a murder in the name of the high priest."

"What about The Master?" Kyle asked.

"Everyone thinks The Master is an omnipotent being. I've done research, and something does live down there, but I doubt it's actually immortal. Although Donny has convinced the town The Master's powers are limitless, that's true. Its ability to sense things are limited. Outside that cave, it's blind. Now, here's the important part, I think it can be hurt. Not by regular weapons though. There is a weapon of sorts we can use to make sure that thing never harms another living soul."

"What's that?" Mike asked, suspiciously.

"A necklace, with an amulet. I've only seen it once, when Donny wears it during ceremonies. It makes him invincible. Well, mostly. The amulet makes the wearer invincible to bullets, blades, and The Master himself. It puts a shield around the wearer and the area surrounding him. If The Master gets too close, it causes him pain. We can use it for our own protection. We just need to figure out how to get it away from Donny.

Kyle looked dubious. "If it protects Donny, then how do we take it from him?"

Matthew turned onto a narrower country road. "That protection doesn't extend to physical human contact. The three of us need to overpower him and take the amulet."

Kyle furrowed his brow in confusion. "I still don't understand."

Mike turned to Kyle. "We can kick his ass, but shooting him is out of the question as long as he has the amulet."

Kyle nodded in understanding, "Ah, got it."

"Don't get wrapped around the axle about the amulet for the moment. I'm not even sure where it is, but I suspect in Donny's office. I'll let you know what to do when the time comes. You both need to promise me that whatever I tell you to do, you'll do it. Most importantly, no one leaves that church until it's burning to the ground."

"Won't others try to stop us?" Kyle asked.

Matthew considered the question. "Probably just the committee members. The regular people of the town won't get involved unless specifically ordered to. They've been beaten into submission and behave more like sheep. If we're careful, no one will be able to call for help until it's too late. The committee members are beyond my control. If it comes down to it, I'll have to kill them. They won't stop any other way."

They drove on, lost in their own thoughts. That's when Kyle caught a glimpse of something out of the corner of his eye. A girl on a bicycle, looking dumbfounded at them as they slowly turned the corner onto the main road toward town. It was Elizabeth, and there was no mistaking the look of recognition on her face.

21

CRY HAVOC

" ... and here is another thing, Reverend. When Matthew pulled up to the intercom station to be let in, I looked at the monitor and I'd swear I saw three people in that truck. I even asked that government man about him. He gave me a story about him being sick. I didn't think about it until after they left, but only two people drove out of here." George finished the report and awaited further instructions.

"I thought the security monitor was broken."

George smiled, "We got it partially working. It's taking stills every five seconds. Need to get a guy out here to look at it."

Donny smiled and nodded at his head of security. "Thank you, George. You've shown me great loyalty today. The Master will be appreciative of your service. I need you to summon the committee to the church. Make sure everyone parks on the other side of the building. I don't want anyone to know you're there. Listen to me carefully, George. Matthew has turned on us. He's planning to disrupt the ceremony tonight. I want Matthew and the boy brought to me unharmed. Take whatever actions you think are necessary. I'm relying on you to stop him. Bring them before me, alive if you can, dead if you must. Do I make myself clear?"

George nodded.

Should Matthew and the two others return, they weren't to leave the property alive. Donny hoped the plan worked a little more smoothly than it had thus far. Unfortunately, he'd misjudged who played the part of the betrayer. He thought the problem was solved with Waylon dead. The situation wasn't all bad, now he had something additional to lord over Matthew. That little rat of a conservation officer would now die for his transgressions.

Matthew once had his complete confidence; that was until someone called to confirm the receipt of a body for an autopsy in a county morgue in West Virginia. Due to a difficult to read phone number, Donny received the phone call through the town's switchboard. It was too late to stop the report from being transmitted and he thought it better to let it go through. It signaled the beginning of the end for Matthew.

At first, Matthew's gall in exhuming a body and sending it out of state infuriated him. The Master theorized that Matthew should be brought closer rather than drive him away, adhering to the age-old wisdom of keeping your friends close and your enemies closer. They made Matthew a deacon in the church, and it gave Donny almost unfettered control of him.

As soon as The Committee had finished preparations at the church, George was to join the other members of the committee. The plan was simple, he wanted Matthew and the boy alive. The other man was to be used as feed for The Master. Once they were inside the cave it became a tomb, unless they died in a hail of gunfire.

Breathlessly, Elizabeth tumbled through the door, panting as she ran up to her father.

He scowled at his daughter. "Where's the fire, pumpkin?"

"Dad, I saw him!" she gasped.

"Who'd you see?"

"Kyle, with Matthew and another guy," she said, matter-of-factly. "They were all in Matthew's truck together. You said, you wanted me to keep an eye out for Kyle and I saw him. Did I do alright, Daddy?"

He gave her a paternal grin and pushed a lock of blond hair out of her face. "You did excellent, baby girl. Unfortunately, you are a little late. George already saw him in the truck."

She pushed out her bottom lip in a pout. "Aww, I wanted to find him."

"You did well. And, I am glad you kept your eyes open. Right now, George is getting things set for the ceremony tonight."

"Oooh ... can I come, Daddy? Please? I'd like to help out of I can."

"Really?" He smiled at her. For years he'd worked to desensitize her to the idea of killing. It was The Master's plan that someday she would take over as high priestess of the church. Starting with small animals, he'd managed to work his way up to where she observed whole ceremonies. The Master seemed to enjoy how she watched the proceedings. However, over the years and the introduction of hormones, she took on a darker bend. Tonight, for safety's sake, he preferred to keep her out of the cave. If something were to go wrong, he didn't want her in harm's way. Until Matthew and the others were bound to the iron rings in The Master's lair, he wanted Elizabeth nowhere near them.

Donny shook his head at her, "Sorry sweetie. You have to sit this one out. We don't have everything set and I don't want you in any danger." He thought back to her first ceremony. She watched intently, never blinking at the violence. She drank it all in.

And this is how you make a serial killer, Donny thought to himself.

———

MATTHEW UNLOCKED the church door with a dull thud. Along with George's suspicions, Elizabeth's sighting of Kyle would certainly raise the alarm. Time was a luxury they didn't have. Behind the altar a cave opening sat below the floor where The Master resided. However, the opening was inaccessible to most people. The reverend normally interacted with him by entering through a heavy steel door in the back of his office. Down a long passageway were a row of cells and storage caves allowing the reverend to keep people prisoner when the need arose. In sharp contrast to the police department jail cells, this was the real prison of the town. Or rather, it was Riapoke's version of death row.

The foyer of the church opened onto a huge sanctuary. The center of the floor was made of polished marble and had several slabs of brass encrusted symbols which marked the final resting places of prominent Powhatan leaders. Although the church maintained these were the real grave sites, Matthew doubted it since the sub-floor was suspended several feet over solid bedrock.

Two large central staircases, one on each side, led up either direction to a balcony overlooking the sanctuary. A register of pipes towered over the altar area. A small elevated platform, dwarfed by the sanctuary, held the organ consul. It was connected by stairs to a large choir loft.

Though he'd lost faith in The Master long ago, the grandeur of the church still filled Matthew with reverent awe.

"Where do we look?" Kyle broke the silence, anxious to begin the search.

"We need to get into the reverend's office," Matthew replied. "The door to the left of the altar leads to it. Inside there, we'll find another door taking us underground. A large cave is used to hold those waiting as tributes to The Master. Your mother is likely being held there."

Walking toward the office, they were suddenly stopped by loud voices outside the church. The voices sounded male. They were trying to be quiet and failing miserably, one person kept admonishing the others to 'keep it down'. Mike peeked out a small opening in the drapes, exclaiming, "Guys, we have company. And not a lot of time. Looks like five men coming this way."

Matthew grabbed Kyle by the arm. "Come, quickly."

The trio ran across the sanctuary. Matthew hastily pushed them toward the altar and through a small door behind the pews. The opening provided access to the space under the floor and the infrastructure supporting the sound system. Few people even knew it was there, and no one had been down there in years.

Matthew, wanting to stay in a position to cover them if their hiding place were discovered, took shelter inside a small closet filled with robes and extra chairs.

The door to the church opened and closed with a metallic scrape. Sounds of heavy boots echoed through the sanctuary. Matthew held his breath as they drew near.

A deep baritone voice rang out through the open space. "Well, now, isn't this nice? All of us together in the holy of holies. Our little sanctuary away from the rest of the world. C'mon out Matthew. I know you're in here somewhere. Who knows, if you give yourself up, we might go easy on you. The Master might only take your badge and not your life. What do you say?"

Matthew prayed Mike and Kyle would crawl as deep into the sub floor as they could. Accessing the space a few times over the years, he'd never explored it fully. Mike and Kyle weren't large men, and they could make it quite a distance under the building before they'd run out of space.

He backed away from the doors of the closet, hoping to find a better position to hide in case someone decided to check his hiding place.

He considered hiding within the folds of the thick robes hanging in the closet, when his foot stepped on a fluorescent bulb someone carelessly left on the floor. The bulb shattered with a loud pop. The noise rang out like a bell in Matthew's head. There was no way the others could've missed that.

Oh, crap.

The baritone voice growled again, "Well now, what do we have here? Someone's hiding in the closet, fellas. Let's have a look." Matthew knew he'd been caught. He only hoped Mike and Kyle found somewhere to hide. Drawing out his pistol, he waited for an opportune moment.

———

INSIDE THE CRAWLSPACE, Mike and Kyle heard a sudden gunshot and then a scuffle. He could only assume it was Matthew and the men. A sudden scream of pain and then ominous quiet weighed heavy on their shoulders.

Mike wished there was something he could do to help Matthew, but right now his responsibility was to protect the boy. They slithered down the natural curve of the rocky surface. The farther they got from the entrance to the crawlspace, the less dusty the air became. The rock changed from dry and warm to cool and wet.

The light should have faded as they crawled deeper into their hiding place and it did for a time. Then a light source in front of them took over. Dimly at first, and then a thin veil of light cascaded from an unknown source, reflecting off the polished surface of the rock. Kyle tapped Mike on the shoulder and motioned that they should go toward the light.

The light seeped up from a hole in the floor only a few feet in front of them. It was enough to illuminate the rocky floor and the underside of the building's superstructure. Peering down the hole, the light's source became apparent. Fire blazed forth from the rocks, generating an eerie, but welcome glow given the impenetrable darkness they sat in. The hole, large enough for them to fit through, led down to a stairway hewn out of the bedrock itself. They were at least seven feet up with a landing on solid rock. It might be possible to jump down without serious injury if they were careful.

Kyle hung his head down the hole and stared up the hallway. Kyle urged Mike to take a look as well. Mike saw what the boy spied. A door, the bottom of which was only partially lit by the firelight offered the possibility of escape. The sight provided an enticing reward for their efforts.

Mike silently indicated his intention to jump down, and then Kyle could follow. Mike dangled his legs over the hole and began lowering himself down as far as possible. If he'd close some of the distance before letting himself fall, it would minimize the likelihood of suffering a broken or sprained ankle. Most importantly, it might minimize the noise.

As he hung from the rock, anyone walking down the stairs would not miss a pair of legs dangling down. As if fate dealt them a crushing blow, the door in the hallway issued the grating metallic strike of a deadbolt retracting from an old door frame.

A man's voice rang out. "All the way down." The door opened slowly, and the shuffling of feet echoed across the cavern as people entered. "You gentlemen have rendered a fine service to The Master. He will be grateful."

"Keep moving, you traitor," a different voice added to the gruff chorus.

Mike's eyes grew as large as dinner plates. This was the point of no return. He'd have to climb back up without making any noise. Kyle reached for his hand and pulled. For a moment, nothing happened as Mike hung precariously in between the hole in the bedrock and the rock stairs below. With a tug, Kyle pulled Mike back up to the top.

Surprised by the boy's strength, Mike's legs disappeared over the top of the cavern lip before anyone had a chance to see either of them. Scooting over to the side, Mike cast a look of appreciation to Kyle.

Peering down at the floor, Mike noticed, with horror, the phony identification tag they made as part of his uniform had fallen off while Kyle pulled him back up. All it would take is for one of the men to notice the identification card and they would know something was wrong.

As the shuffling of the men's feet echoed down the stairs, Donny's voice boomed through the hallway. "Now boys, don't rough him up too bad. I want him in good shape tonight for the ceremony. You know, Matthew, if anyone had told me that you were the one who'd betray us, I'd have thought they were mad. I have to admit, when I discovered you'd sent that corpse out of state I was more than a little impressed. You managed it right from under my nose."

"Fuck you," Matthew hissed.

"Now ... now, Matthew. You're in the house of The Master, show respect. After all, as far as we know, no one has decided your fate. Why don't you just tell me where the boy is, and I'll go a little easier on you. He's not at the jail, so I can only conclude you stashed him somewhere."

As they dragged Matthew under the hole in the ceiling, he glanced up. For a moment, Matthew and Kyle's eyes met. The look must have lingered a little too long because one of the men raised their head to see what had drawn Matthew's attention. Thinking fast, Matthew yanked his arm away from the man and sucker punched him in the gut.

"Oh, you have some fight left in you, huh?" another goon, standing nearby said. The man punched Matthew in the ribs with a pair of brass knuckles. As he did, something fell from the captor's belt and skittered into the cell opposite the hole in the ceiling. In the firelight, Kyle and Mike could see it was Matthew's gun. They must have taken it during the scuffle upstairs. None of the men noticed it fell during the present scuffle.

Mike could only look down, helpless to act. Matthew was taking a considerable beating on their behalf. The look of pain on Matthew's face was intolerable. However, his act distracted the man and avoided a possible disaster. Matthew spit a mouthful of blood out onto the floor of the stairs and the wall. For now, they would just have to watch and listen from their overhead perch.

"Donny," Matthew's voice, gurgling with blood suddenly spoke. "Wait, Donny, ... listen."

"You have something to say, my dear Officer Tanner?" Donny turned on his heels and looked at the bleeding man.

"Yeah ... your men hit like fucking little girls." Matthew suddenly burst out laughing. "No ... no ... I take that back. Girl scouts could hit harder than that."

Donny's face turned red. "Take him to The Master's lair and make sure the ropes are good and tight." He leaned in close, "Let's see how much humor you have left in you after The Master has removed your spleen."

The group walked past the opening in the ceiling and down the passageway, disappearing from sight. Mike heard the opening of what sounded like another large metal door. A few moments later, Matthew's piercing, agonized scream echoed down the corridor.

22

PRISONER IN HELL

Meghan was exhausted. The combination of the humidity and the lack of anywhere to sit played on her psyche. She remembered seeing an old television show detailing a popular Soviet torture technique which involved never letting someone completely sit or stand. The victim was forced into holding an uncomfortable position in a room too small to stand up and a floor covered in spikes, so they couldn't sit down. Although the cell had no spikes, finding a place to sit or sleep comfortably proved elusive.

She ate what little food the reverend brought to her. Not tasty, but it was still something to eat and would keep her strength up. This could be the deciding factor if an opportunity for escape presented itself.

The cave, turned prison cell, lacked any creature comforts. In the corner, a few old crates were stacked up against the wall. She'd searched them thoroughly, finding only a few rusty nails and a long metal hinge loosely securing the top of one of the boxes. It could be fashioned into a weapon.

Rocks lay scattered on the floor near the wall, but none were large enough to be useful. Several rags lay strewn around the floor, and not much else. There were a few smaller openings in the wall, much too small for her frame to fit. Given enough time, a larger hole might be chipped out to slip through. However, she was sure she didn't have that kind of time.

In the distance, a door opened with a quick shriek. Based on the sounds, it was a group of men. A scuffle broke out, leaving one of the men to let out a terrible groan. Meghan spied up the hallway to see Donny walking in front of four men, dragging another man. The badly beaten men's clothing, torn and blood stained, was still recognizable as a uniform. It was the conservation officer who had arrested them the day before at the boat landing.

She yelled out to Donny, "What the hell are you doing to him?"

He stopped and turned toward her and stared through the bars. "The better question is, 'when are we going to be doing something similar to you?' Your time has just about run out. After I'm done with him, then it will be time for you to join us in The Master's lair."

He continued, "Oh, by the way, you'll be happy to know that brat of a son of yours and another guy know you're here. Don't worry, they'll be joining you shortly. My man on the outside didn't give me a name, but someone came over from the resort." Donny smirked at her.

A wave of fire and emotion welled up inside of Meghan. She drilled Donny with a piercing gaze that made him take a few steps back. "You leave Kyle alone!" She clutched the bars, her knuckles turning white. "Mess with him, and I swear by all that is holy you'll never find a hole deep enough to hide in, no rock large enough to hide behind, and no island remote enough to escape me. He's my entire world and hell hath no fury like a mother protecting her children."

Donny regained his composure. "My dear Meghan. It is sad to see you reduced to useless clichés. This isn't a Hollywood movie, you know. Look around you. There's nothing you can do. I had a plan for your boy. My own daughter kind of messed it up. What are you going to do? Kids, you know. If you'll forgive a cliché of my own. That's alright, now your son will be joining you at a feast of sorts. I won't tell you who the main course is, that'll spoil the surprise."

"You're sick, you know that?"

"I'm sick? Oh, dear woman. That makes me laugh. Outside our little town, people are slaughtered in the streets. Do you know that only a handful of the major metropolitan areas in the country account for almost all the murders which take place annually? Did you know that? Parents abandon children so they can go out and get wasted on recreational drugs. The honest people have to work two, sometimes three jobs just to make ends meet. And those buffoons in Washington keep making matters worse with their own greed, idolatry, and stupidity.

"During the last presidential election, one candidate should've been in prison and the other is an egotistical womanizer. And you think I'm sick? Just because I've found a way to keep my people safe from the outside world? You have no idea how hard it is, do you? The world would judge these people by laws invented by men. In the outside world our way of life would get us all thrown in prison because they simply don't understand what we're trying to build. The world wants what we already have. Our security. And they'll destroy anyone who challenges the existing authorities."

Meghan couldn't believe this lunatic had the nerve to rant at her, talking down to her in a sermon of sorts. How dare he lecture her? "You murder people for your so-called security!"

"A few people who violate our laws are punished, that is true. It's all for The Master, a real God. We owe it to him. You know what happens to those who break our rules, Meghan. Although you didn't do it intentionally, you broke our laws the moment you set foot on our dock. You and your son aren't supposed to be here. I can't make exceptions to the rules, now can I?"

"Then let us go. We promise to leave and never to return."

Donny let out a giant belly laugh. "Thank you, Mrs. Johnston, I haven't laughed that hard in a long time. You must take me for stupid or insane. I assure you, I'm neither of those things. How do you think that plays out? You'd go back to the resort, who of course didn't even notice the missing boat or your sudden disappearance for a few days? Then you'd just pack your things and head home? No, I don't see any of that scenario likely to play out. How about this scenario? You'd show up at the resort and immediately call the police. You tell them your story and then I have FBI agents all over my town, poking into the affairs of the good people of Riapoke. Which one of those scenarios do you think is more likely?"—he raised his hands like a balance comparing two weights—"I can't let that happen. No, I like things just the way they are. We already have a bit of a mess with this other guy showing up with Kyle. Who is he anyway?"

Meghan searched her memories of the past few days. She tried to remember anyone who might be enticed to come to her aid. They may have called the police when she and Kyle vanished with the boat. The police wouldn't just show up with one police officer and her son, though. The only other person who knew anything about her was Mike and they'd only just met. "I ... I really have no idea."

Donny leaned toward the bars. "Don't you dare lie to me. I can make all of this easy or hard. It's up to you. Now tell me, who the hell is that other guy with Kyle?"

"I tell you, I don't know."

Donny lurched forward and tried to grab Meghan by the shirt as she ducked out of the way. "Tell me!" He howled.

"I have no idea. It was only Kyle and me. But I will tell you this, I hope he guts you like a fish."

He stepped back, smoothing out his shirt. "I have to give you credit. Your fictionalized view of the world is making my day entertaining. However, you're in no position to make any kind of insinuation about who will be gutting who. Or is it whom? I can never remember." Donny backed away from the bars.

"Okay," he continued, "I'm not that concerned. Not sure I even care. It's only a matter of time before we have everything wrapped up." Toward the end of the stairway, the four men who brought Matthew down, stepped through the door to the cave and moved to lock it. "Don't lock the door, gentlemen. We'll be back soon enough." One of the men handed a large key ring to Donny.

"Well, Mrs. Johnston, I guess I'll be seeing you again later. I'm just waiting for a couple of other people to fall into my little web. Till then, I bid you adieu."

Meghan heard the men trudge up the stairs, followed by the telltale sound of the metal door opening and closing. As soon as the metal lock fell into place, she sprinted to the corner of the room to the forgotten boxes.

There were two things that the reverend said which stuck in her mind. Kyle somehow brought someone from the resort. It was likely this person was made aware of their situation. The second thing Donny said is that he'd be back soon. And, if that was the case, something to defend herself might come in handy.

A few swift kicks to the mostly dry-rotted boxes reduced them to splintered planks. A few more well-placed kicks, and the metal hinge popped loose. There were other pieces of metal left behind, but they'd either rusted to a fine powder years ago or bent too easily. Meghan picked up the hinge and pulled out the remaining nails and slivers of wood that clung to it. The hinge mostly formed a decorative piece; however, one end tapered to a convenient point. Not sharp, but she didn't need it to be.

Meghan used the rough stones as a file and worked the piece of metal. With each pass, it took on a sharp, blade-like edge. Maybe it would take on enough of an edge to cut flesh, sever an artery, or pierce a vital organ.

In the distance, she heard what sounded like something heavy falling to the floor. Ignoring the commotion, she retreated behind the rock table, where she continued to work the metal. Maybe being hidden from sight would force anyone coming downstairs to have to enter the cell, which would give her a chance to make her escape.

23

THE GREAT ESCAPE

Mike helped the gangly teen lower himself to the floor of the stairway. They looked in both directions. As inviting as the door leading to the exit was, below them someplace, Matthew lay on the ground severely beaten. It was also possible one of these cells held Meghan.

Wordlessly, Kyle used his fingers in a 'V' shape, pointing at his eyes and then down the stairs, indicating Mike's responsibility was to watch his back as they made their way up the stairs to check the door.

Stopping for a brief moment, Mike reached over to Kyle and replaced the fake weapon in the holster with Matthew's weapon laying on the ground. Far from the way someone should be trained in how to handle a firearm, it was a revolver and required little to no training to pull the trigger. This situation was no longer just a search and rescue mission, rather a true fight for their lives.

Hugging the wall as they went, Mike glanced into the smaller rooms. Each had a rusted door, and in some cases, the doors had long since fallen off their hinges and lay against the wall inside the spaces. Another door rusted open years ago and likely hadn't moved since. The hallway was lit with the same eerie glow of the fires burning with heatless flames along the walls. The stairs were worn from years of use. It made Mike wonder about the original builders of this space. It was clear the once natural cave had been reshaped by time and human intervention.

Inside the small cells, boxes and barrels of all shapes and sizes lay on the floors or in racks. Like someone had forgotten these items had been stored down here. In one cell a collection of old wine bottles and casks, indicated a less nefarious use in the cave's history.

At the top of the stairs they found the door. Kyle carefully pushed his ear to the metal, listening for any sound coming from the other side. Mike checked as well and when both were satisfied they were alone for the moment, they turned back toward the lower expanse of the cave.

"I wonder how many cells are down here?" Mike asked in hushed tones.

Kyle absently looked into one of them. "Maybe ten or twenty? I wonder if my mom is in one of them."

"I sure hope so," Mike said. "I'm sorry. I just meant it would be great if we find her and got the hell out of here. I'll be a lot more relieved."

Kyle shook his head. "That's okay, I know what you meant. Don't be too hard on yourself. Believe me, I want nothing more than to get us out of here and back to that resort of yours. Besides, you owe my mom a date. I hope my mom is alright."

A hushed voice rang out of the cell behind them. "Oh yes honey, I'm just fine."

Kyle let out a gasp and pushed his way past Mike. He slammed into the bars of the cell door where, in the dim light, Meghan's smile shone like the sun. He reached his hands through the bars and embraced his mother.

"Oh thank God," she exclaimed. "You're the greatest thing I could ever see right now. I was so worried about you." She turned to face Mike. "Mike? You're the other guy who came to rescue me?"

He smiled at her. "Well, you do owe me a date."

"Mike, I'd do more than just give you a date if you get me out of here." Her words were followed by an awkward silence. "Okay, that came out wrong. Get me out of here please."

As if an invisible hand with keys worked the lock, the mechanism for the cell door sprung open.

Mike eyed the mechanism with suspicion. "Well, that's weird."

"Maybe the doors are remotely controlled?" Kyle opined. "I don't see any wires or anything."

Mike shook his head at the lock. "I don't like this. If someone is controlling the lock, they are likely already aware we're here. We'd better hurry and get Matthew. If he's still alive."

Meghan pushed the door open and stepped out onto the stairway. She hugged Kyle again, followed by an awkward hug from Mike. The three of them proceeded down to the bottom of the stairwell.

The steel door was formidable. Mike tried to push it open, without success. Kyle stepped forward and pushed on the door handle which gave an audible click and the door swung open. Kyle gave Mike a wry smile.

Behind the door a thirty-foot long hallway just large enough for two of them to walk shoulder to shoulder lay like a snake in the darkness. Lit by the same eerie yellow flame glowing from recesses in the wall like the rest of the underground cavern, it gave off an odd funereal vibe.

Approaching the end of the hallway, they peered into a large, dark room. Meghan recognized it as the room she'd been in earlier. She stared at the spot where the unfortunate woman met her savage end. Remembering the pool of blood and pieces of tissue left over after the woman was devoured, she cringed. Meghan wished she'd warned the others of the hideous beast inhabiting the space.

Not wanting to risk talking, she stopped Mike and Kyle, and put a finger to her lips to indicate they needed to stay quiet. Maybe it would be enough of a warning. Meghan reached into her waistband and pulled out the improvised knife.

Across from them, the body of Matthew hung from ropes secured to the rings set into the walls. Meghan ran to him, sighing in relief to find he was still breathing. If they moved fast enough, they could save his life.

She worked on Matthew's ropes with the piece of metal. The time spent sharpening the old hinge was worth it, as it tore through the well-worn ropes. Soon one hand was free, and she set to work on the other one.

The group exhaled anxiously as the second piece of rope gave way, freeing Matthew. Meghan guided his body down against the rock into a sitting position with his back against the wall. Mike ran over and put one arm under Matthew's shoulder and motioned for Kyle to do the same. As Kyle moved to lift Matthew, the door at the end of the hallway opened with a loud clang.

Mike pulled out the pistol and pointed it at the figure. Meghan watched in horror as Kyle pulled out a pistol of his own, but the argument of the morality of her son wielding a firearm was a moot point. Kyle and Mike gallantly stepped in front of the group, preparing to defend them.

"Are you ready for this?" Mike said to Kyle.

"I'd kill to protect my mother," Kyle said, with a noticeable tremor in his voice. "And you know what? I'd kill to protect you as well."

Mike felt blessed with his own daughter and seldom thought about having a son. At that moment, he regarded Kyle as his own flesh and blood. "No matter what happens, I am glad to know you, Kyle."

Two white-robed men entered the hallway, disturbing the eerie light seeping from the walls. Kyle recognized them as two of the men who'd brought Matthew down to the cellar in the first place. Behind them stepped Donny, clad in a black robe. Around his neck hung an amulet from a gold chain, glinting in the light from the walls.

Kyle nodded toward Mike and then the amulet. Mike nodded back in understanding.

Donny glided to a halt several yards away from them. "Well, we are all here now. Thank you for making this so much easier."

"Don't come any closer," Kyle said, with a shockingly composed determination.

"If it isn't my wayward son Kyle. You know, it isn't too late. You come over to me, and I'll see that no harm comes to your mother. I'll even forgive killing poor Bill. Completely unnecessary. He was only doing his job, you know."

Kyle raised his gun toward the trio. "Let us go. You have no right to keep us here!"

"Rights?" Donny laughed. "You're concerned about rights? Let's see, you violated the laws of our town, and now you are pointing a gun at me and my family here in my own church. I'll grant that my rules may be a little strict to you, but you have no right to lecture me about rules, boy."

Donny reached one hand up and grasped his amulet off his chest and held it out before him. "Seize them!"

The two men lurched forward as if being operated by remote control. Walking with an absent-minded determination, they would be on them in seconds.

Mike warned, "Stay back!"

When the two didn't stop, Mike and Kyle fired at almost the exact same moment with frightening effect. Both men crumpled into piles on the floor, like marionettes falling to the floor after their strings were cut. Their chests opened and left a sickening spray of blood painting the walls from an unseen exit wound.

Mike fired two more shots at Donny, his jaw dropping with the realization the bullets virtually vanished into an unseen void. "I'm sure I hit him! I don't know why he isn't down."

Kyle fired once at Donny as well. The reverend remained obstinately upright and grinning smugly at them from behind the amulet. "Me too! What the hell is going on here."

"Do you want to tell them, High Priest, or shall I?" A deep, guttural voice echoed up from a hole in the wall.

Donny knelt on one knee, still holding the amulet in front of him. "I would be honored to hear you speak, my master."

Kyle, regaining his senses, grabbed Mike by the arm and whispered, "Let's make a run for it. We can make it." He glanced over to his mother who nodded in agreement. But they couldn't leave Matthew behind. They'd come back expressly to save him.

Mike fired one more shot at Donny and picked up Matthew, while Kyle lifted the other side. The four ran forward. Even with the added weight, they eclipsed the distance between where they stood and the two bodies of the men they'd shot.

A black wall materialized in front of them.

They froze. As the wall transformed into a large demon. Its long claws and wings scraped against the side of the cavern. The horns on its head almost touched the top of the cave. Cloven feet looked vaguely human but covered in fur and grotesque warts.

Retreating to their previous position, they set Matthew back down with a groan. His injuries weren't helped by the sudden burst of motion.

A snarl formed on the disfigured demon's face as it spoke to them. "Leaving so soon? That's a little impolite, don't you think?" The beast laughed. "I insist you stay and hear the story. It's a good one." The demon waved its hand, and the three fell to the floor, pushed down by an unseen power.

24

WHEN IMMORTALITY ENDS

"Do you have any idea what it's like being immortal? No, of course you don't." The demon paced the length of the room, drool wetting the sides of his lips, his arched back covered in thick spines resembling stiff hair. "I can tell you it sounds like more fun than it actually is. I was once mortal, a human of flesh and blood. When I was born, the spirits thought it would be fun to name me Matchitehew." The beast chuckled at the name. "You may not get the joke. It means 'he who has an evil heart'. Funny, isn't it?"

"Seems fitting," Kyle offered, with obvious disdain.

The demon shot back, "Silence, young one. Or maybe it'll be easier for you to keep quiet with your tongue removed."

Kyle nervously stepped back as Meghan cast a maternal glance, begging her son to keep his mouth shut.

"So, where was I? Oh yes, Matchitehew. Because of something as arbitrary as a name, I had to be faster, stronger, and smarter than the others. A great hunter and trapper, I also grew into the great warrior that I am. More ruthless than the other braves, I demanded they respect me. Alas, when it came time to select seats on the tribal council, I was denied my birthright. Some said it was because I was too violent. But I knew the truth. They were jealous they didn't have the courage to do what needed to be done."

"Denied what was rightfully yours, my Master," Donny spoke up, still staring at the ground, kneeling in supplication.

"Indeed. So, I did what any red-blooded boy would do. One night I snuck into another tribe's camp and killed them all. One by one, I held them down and slit their throats, from the oldest man to the youngest child. The blood soaked the pelts which made up the beds they slept in stood as my mark, the mark of Matchitehew. I even took a few of their women before slitting their throats to make sure I showed my enemies what would await them if they dared challenge me. I wanted to show the Powhatan what a real warrior should act like. That feeble idiot Powhatan was never a warrior. I'll grant you, he was a gifted diplomat, but never a warrior."

"But you were caught?" Mike said.

The demon still paced the room, leathery wings folded behind his back and massive, muscular, arms outstretched, scraping its long nails against the rocks. "Yes, you are correct. I was caught. That idiot chief and his slut of a daughter tricked me into a tent where many warriors waited to beat me down and bind me. They treated me like a common criminal. They should've thanked me and made me chief. Instead, they accused me of murder and upsetting the balance of nature. I ask you, is it not nature's balance that a brave and strong warrior should rise up and take his rightful place as chief of them all?"

Mike, remembering the gun in his hand, pointed it at the demon. "I don't care what your beef is, you're going to let us go, right now."

The demon regarded the man for a moment. "Do you really think those weapons will harm me? Did they hurt my High Priest?"

Kyle watched Donny, still kneeling on the floor of the cavern. Since the bizarre conversation began, the high priest hadn't moved a muscle. The amulet, held out in front of his chest, took on an unearthly glow. Kyle recalled Matthew's story of the necklace.

"Of course, they won't," the demon continued. "The high priest has an amulet to protect him. It bestows, to its bearer, a veil of protection equal to only my own. It's imbued with the same magic that put this spell on me. The irony of his situation is that he holds the power to keep me imprisoned in his hands and is completely unable to recognize that power. The white man values the wrong things. Always looking for a leader and being too fearful to lead themselves.

"There is a legend, spoken at my trial, and again at my imprison-ment. Two strangers would arrive, and one of my own would turn. This signals the end of my confinement, and also my death. They weren't counting on my witless idiot of a priest. The first time that fool wandered down here, I had him. His mind and will were mine to control. Even now, he's nothing more than my puppet. When I ascend, I'll take his life and burn this city to the ground. This arrangement no longer suits my needs."

Kyle grimaced as he realized the demon loved to talk about himself. Although terrifying, the demon was nothing more than a self-important blowhard who believed he was robbed of a birthright he'd neither deserved nor earned.

While the demon waxed poetic, Kyle took small, unobtrusive steps toward Donny. The amulet held the key to everything and offered a sort of protection. The demon indicated its power matched his own. It'd buy everyone enough time to get out of there, and away from the demon. He had to time it perfectly. It was an all or nothing attempt.

The demon droned on. "... now I stay here, year after year, waiting for sustenance enough to return me to my true form. The first thing I shall do when I am back in my human form is dig up the bones of Powhatan and grind them up. That false chief robbed me of my peace, so why should he get his? My only disappointment was my little matchmaking attempt between you and Elizabeth. I figured having two people under my control might be useful. Oh well, can't have everything I suppose."

The demon continued pontificating and pacing the cave. For a split-second it turned its back to Kyle.

This was his chance. Kyle took three long strides, covering the distance between himself and Donny. Not slowing, he snatched the amulet out of Donny's hands and slipped the chain over his head before anyone had a chance to react to his movement. Donny still hadn't even moved until Kyle jumped over him. Kyle whipped around, pointing Matthew's gun at Donny and squeezed the trigger, a fiery tongue jumped from the weapon and the concussive noise reverberated off the walls of the cavern. The smoke and smell of burnt gunpowder choked the air. Donny fell forward, landing with a sickening splat on the hard stones, blood and pieces of cranium painted the floor in front of the fresh corpse.

Undeterred, Kyle jumped over the body of the slain reverend and past the dumbstruck demon, taking a position in front of Elizabeth and Matthew. "Go find your souls somewhere else. We're not your dinner tonight."

The native American, turned demon, smiled at the boy. "Too bad I didn't kill you first. You're a smart one. You took out my high priest by identifying the one weakness in my plan. I give you credit for that, boy. But what you don't realize is the amulet will only work here. Once outside the immediate vicinity of the cave it's worthless." Rising to his full height, the demon walked over to the still exsanguinating body of Donny. For a moment he stared at the lifeless corpse of his fallen high priest. "A good servant. Too bad it ended this way."

Kyle looked at his mother, Mike, and a broken, slouching Matthew.

Positioning himself between them and the demon, the amulet provided an uncrossable barrier. For the moment, it was impossible for the creature to hurt any of them. Kyle hoped.

"I don't think you understand me," Kyle said, momentarily feeling brave. "Now that I have the amulet, we're leaving here. You get to stay down here, rotting for another few hundred years. Who knows, maybe longer?"

Undeterred, the demon reached down and flipped Donny over. The high priest's face was coated in blood as the warm liquid came to a rest in a depression in the stone floor. "Once again, boy, you've miscalculated. In many ways, you and I suffer from the same malady. I was too smug, too sure of myself. I neglected to take out those who challenged me first. There is a piece of information you're missing. Don't feel bad, it's something that you couldn't know."

Kyle shot another nervous glance at Mike and his mother, who just shook their heads in response. None of them knew what the demon was referring to.

"Pity. You almost had me. In order to serve my time, I must live here for the total amount of the lifetimes I took. Or, trade something of value, particularly the hearts of the living. It was a little loophole built in when Powhatan and his daughter concocted this prison for me. One heart for one person I killed. No one ever thought I'd be able to pull it off. But they had to build in the loophole to maintain balance in their spell. You'd say that they had to give me a sporting chance. And I've done that for quite a while now. For the longest time, getting people down here was difficult. A few settlers looking for a good place to live, children wandering the woods looking for adventure, hunters looking for prey, the cave explorer looking for a new challenge. Then someone came along and founded the town of Riapoke. I assure you, an accident. Stupid white man, they didn't know what the Algonquin word meant. No interest or patience in learning about the world around them. They just thought the name was the Indian word for this area. Little did they know Riapoke is this place's very nature.

"Then I realized the good fortune of this situation. After all, why should I work so hard to find people when I could make someone do the work for me? Mankind's stupidity, it would seem, has grown over the years. Now, with your cell phones and computers, there is no way to keep yourself from falling into my web, especially since I had the good reverend here providing me as many hearts as I wanted. How many lives have I sacrificed to atone for my sins?"

Kyle did some gruesome mental math. Hundreds of years of suckering people down this cave, to their doom, gave the beast the opportunity to acquire many, many hearts. If Donny, and the townspeople helped him then his macabre quota must nearly be filled.

The demon chuckled. "Don't overtax your mind, young one. Here's the secret I'm dying to tell you: Your mother is special. In her breast beats the last heart I needed before I can transform and leave this cave. According to prophecy, this woman is my final victim. She either spells my doom, or my salvation."

Mike stood up from kneeling next to Matthew. "Well, you've failed. We have the amulet."

"Again, the white man fails to see the truth before him. Her heart is ideal, but not necessarily only her heart. Any heart will do." Plunging a clawed hand into Donny's chest cavity with a crunch of bone and rending of sinew, it made a sickening sucking noise. After rooting around for a few moments, he withdrew his claw, in it he held Donny's heart. "Perfect, and even still warm. High priest, your service is much appreciated."

Mike released Matthew and grabbed Meghan, holding her close to him. Kyle took several steps backward, shielding them. For a moment, everyone stood in silence.

The demon crammed the remains of Donny's heart into his mouth, chewed, and swallowed it with a sickening gulp. Blood coated his lips which curled into a sinister sneer.

Two small points of light shot out from the corners of the room and swirled around the creature, slowly at first and then gaining speed as they continued their aerial dance. The light enveloped him, becoming so intense the four had to shield their eyes. More light flowed from the walls and the demon's enormous body morphed in appearance. Horns disappeared, retracting into his head. The leathery black wings faded from view and the black flesh of his face replaced with tan skin. His enormous size diminished as well.

One last blazing flash preceded the swirling lights suddenly disappearing. In place of the demon, stood a man, about the size of Kyle. Dressed in leather pants, held up by a belt, and mukluks. Pulling a long-handled ax out from the belt of his breechcloth and leggings, he said, "Now you see me as I truly am. No longer a hideous beast. I am, as my own people know me. I am Matchitehew, the rightful heir to the Powhatan tribe. I will rise up and take my place at its head."

Mike became aware of Matthew pulling on his pant leg. "Leave me," Matthew's raspy voice called out from the floor.

Mike looked down at him in disbelief. "He'll kill you."

Matthew struggled to sit up. Blood seeped through the remains of the uniform shirt. One of Matthew's eyes had swollen shut. "I'm dead no matter what you do. Finish this for me."

"He's right, you know," Matchitehew hissed. "The second you leave him, he'll be dead. You can't protect him, and I owe him a fitting death. The amulet only goes so far. Flee, little ants ... flee. I like a good chase."

Mike held his hand up. "Why don't you just let us go? You have your freedom. You don't need to hurt anyone else."

Matchitehew walked around the perimeter of the cave, pointing the double-headed ax at them. "It's not that simple. You see, I have a lot to do, starting with tying up proverbial loose ends. I can't just have you walking around telling people who I am. You know my little secret. It's a hell of a story too. I mean, a member of the Powhatan tribe, sentenced to live as a demon under the earth for centuries. No, I can't afford that."

Without warning, Matchitehew lunged at the four cowering against the wall. Kyle, still holding the amulet braced for the impact of the ax as it made an arc toward him. Within two feet of the ax connecting, a ball of light flew from the amulet and hit Matchitehew in the chest, sending him flying across the room. The Indian got up from the floor and brushed himself off, shaking his head and frowning at Kyle as he did.

"Nice try," Kyle said, trying to hide his own surprise at surviving the initial confrontation.

Matchitehew laughed. "The amulet still has power, but it fades quickly, now that I've broken the curse. Soon, it will be nothing more than a mere trinket. Do you know what I would trade for that amulet? A few leaves of tobacco. That's all it costs back in my day.

Today, probably worth a fortune as Powhatan art. Perhaps I'll sell it as an antique after I get out of here."

"You have to leave me now." Matthew insisted. "I did what I came to do, and this is your chance to escape."

Mike grabbed Kyle by the arm while pulling Meghan to her feet. "Let's go."

"But he'll die," Kyle protested.

Matthew coughed up a splotch of blood. "Go, and don't look back."

Meghan gave Matthew a long hug and whispered something in his ear. Then Mike, Kyle, and Meghan moved toward the hallway. Kyle kept the amulet between them and the angry Indian.

As they moved away from Matthew, Matchitehew moved in closer to their fallen comrade. "That's right, run," he mocked. "Run as fast as you can. It won't be far enough. You'll have to face me, and I will take great pleasure in killing you."

Entering the hallway, the trio looked back at Matthew as Matchitehew raised his ax high in the air. Matthew mustered every ounce of his remaining strength and shoved the metal hinge Meghan slipped to him straight into Matchitehew's rib cage. He screamed in pain as he brought the ax down on Matthew. With a sickening thud, the ax made frighteningly short work of Matthew's skull.

Matchitehew held his side as he hit him repeatedly, chopping the corpse out of pure anger. Pulling out the shiv from his side, he snarled, "Pathetic attempt. Did you think this piece of rusted metal could kill me?"

It did do damage. Although Matchitehew still presented a terrifying image, Matthew's dying act proved their nemesis was no longer invincible. He was mortal. Vulnerable. Killable.

25

ASCENSION

The trio ran down the hallway, as Matchitehew laughed and shouted something about running away like scared children. They made their way to the steel door, hoping to lock from the outside, keeping Matchitehew contained. Someone locked the deadbolt with the door still open and took the keys so there was no way to close it.

"Upstairs, quick," Mike pointed at the stairs. He worried the door at the top might be locked, making their escape attempt short-lived. If the door stood locked, he'd be forced to fight a savage warrior with no compulsion about killing them all, a contest he'd surely lose.

The three bounded up the stairs as quickly as possible. Behind them, the footfalls of Matchitehew echoed through the corridor. He was quick on his feet for someone who'd spent half millennia in a cave. Mike wondered if Matthew's last act of defiance had done any permanent damage to their pursuer. Maybe they'd be lucky, and he'd die of blood loss or an unusually aggressive case of sepsis.

As the top of the stairs, his heart sank as the door stood defiantly closed. Kyle reached it first and tried to push it open, but the door would not budge.

Behind them, Matchitehew stalked them, step by step. He slowed down when he realized his prey suddenly found itself cornered. "What's the matter? Did you forget to take Donny's keys?" Matchitehew smiled at them, menacingly.

Still holding the handle, Kyle was caught off guard by the door suddenly springing open with a surprising amount of force, pulling him with it. On the other side of the door, a startled George tried to get out of Kyle's way. Mike and Meghan jumped through the door, following Kyle. Mike slammed the door closed with a metallic boom and leaned into it to keep it shut.

"What the hell!" George barked in panic at their sudden appearance. As an afterthought, he pulled out an old revolver.

Mike spit out, "Lock the door, quick."

George, still stunned, said, "Where's Matthew!"

"Dam it, lock the door!" Kyle scrambled to his feet and grabbed the keys out of Georges' hand. He deftly inserted the key into the lock, closing the deadbolt.

"Hey, you're that government agent from the house," George said, pointing the revolver at Mike. "Where's Matthew and Donny?"

Mike grabbed George by the hand and pulled him up out of the chair. "We don't have time for a pleasant reunion, George. We need to get out of here."

George stammered, "Just hold on a second! You're not going anyplace! Where's the reverend?" George waved the gun around the room as if it were a natural, and clumsy, extension of his hand.

Just then, a dull thud knocked on the door. The handle twisted, but with the deadbolt engaged the door refused to budge. Matchitehew shrieked in anger. "You think you're so smart, don't you! No matter, it'll only hold for a little while."

An ear-piercing, thunderous, metallic boom shook the room as Matchitehew smashed the door with the ax, attempting to break through. The four of them watched in horror as the metal started to bend under the repeated blows. At this rate, the door would likely hold for several minutes, but that was it.

Kyle, looking down at his chest, grabbed the still glowing amulet and removed it. Exchanging glances with Mike and his mother. His eyes flew wide in recognition as he ran to the door and hung the amulet from an old nail affixed to the top of the door frame. From the other side came a piercing scream, followed by unintelligible words sounding like they might be native American swear words.

"You little—" Matchitehew shouted, then calmed himself. "Smart kid. Okay, you have me trapped. For now. You seem to have forgotten the amulet will lose its power and I have the mortal remains of my high priest here ... and his keys. If I were you, I'd be running for my life right now." They heard the muffled steps of Matchitehew's moccasined feet running down the stairs.

George stared in disbelief. "What the hell is on the other side of the door?"

"You wouldn't believe us if we told you." Meghan grabbed Kyle by the arm and dragged him toward the door of the office. "Come on Mike, we need to get out of here."

Mike grabbed the keys out of Kyle's hands and unlocked the outer door of the office. The amulet's glow already faded so they needed to move. The four of them stumbled out into the sanctuary. Looking around the marble flooring in the center, a corpse lay supine on the floor in front of the closet. The man could be confused for someone taking a midday nap if it weren't for the gaping gunshot wound to his chest and the pool of blood surrounding him like a crimson lake. Mike understood where the gunshot they heard earlier went. Matthew got one of them before they could apprehend him.

"Wait a minute," George shouted, remembering the gun in his hand. He trained it on Kyle. "Someone explain to me what the hell's going on around here! I'm head of security and, for the moment, the man in charge!"

Meghan threw her hands up in exasperation. "Okay, listen here, whoever you are."

"George," Mike said.

"Fine then! George, Donny is dead, that thing you heard in there is, or was, The Master and right now, he is set on killing all of us if we don't put distance between us and him. The Master isn't a demon, he's a disgruntled native American warrior who's just broken a centuries old curse put under by some sort of chief."

"Chief Powhatan," Kyle offered.

"And, as you can probably hear, he's not in the best of moods. So, either stay here or come with us. But, if you come with us, we need to go now!" The words flew out of Meghan's mouth before she had time to think about what she was saying.

"Who are you people?" George stared at them in disbelief. "Do you take me for an idiot? I mean this could be the worst lie I've ever heard in my life. You people have to be—"

Mike grabbed George's arm, and stared straight into his eyes. "Look, George, you don't have to believe her. In a few minutes, that amulet Kyle put on the door won't protect us any longer and you can ask him yourself. We won't be here though. I don't care if you think we're crazy or not. Soon we are going to run out of options, and you don't want to see what that looks like."

George stood dumbfounded. "Okay, so, what do you want to do?"

Meghan put her hand on George's forearm. "George, we need to get out of here as quickly as possible. Preferably before anyone notices us. Then we need to get out of town. I suggest you do the same."

A splash of red liquid appeared across Meghan's face. George's eyes widened to the size of saucers. He looked down where the blade of a stone ax stuck out an inch from the center of his chest. He fell to his knees and then down on his face with a groan.

"Get out of town. Probably not a bad idea." The voice of Matchitehew echoed from the corner of the room.

"The hole in the rock, Mike," Kyle said.

"Right you are, Kyle." Matchitehew smiled at them. "You are such a smart little brave. I'm impressed. Pity I have to end your life. I pulled myself up through the hole in the ceiling of the walkway in the cave. I've had hundreds of years to study my granite prison. I know every nook and cranny of this place. But now, I tire of this little game. It's time for you to die and for me to go free."

He pulled the ax from George and raised it above his head, yelling something incoherent in his native language. Reflexively, Mike pulled Meghan and Kyle behind him.

A shot rang out, followed by the stinging smell of burnt gunpowder. Matchitehew dropped his ax and fell to the floor, clutching his arm and shrieking in pain.

They turned to see George, a wisp of smoke curling around his upturned head. He'd mustered up every last ounce of life to take one shot at Matchitehew. The Indian's magic was still too strong for the shot to be fatal, but it did hurt him.

Not wasting any time, the three of them ran down the aisle and out the double doors of the building as Matchitehew raised his ax and finished George with frightening efficiency. The sound of crunching bone and squishing flesh filled the enormous sanctuary space.

The three tumbled out into the parking lot. They ran toward Matthew's truck, parked near the entrance. "Get in!" Mike shouted, pulling the driver's side door open and turning the key, still dangling from the ignition. The large truck roared to life just as the church doors flew open to expose Matchitehew, covered in George's blood as well as his own from the seeping gunshot wound.

"Mike, get us out of here!" Kyle shouted.

Mike slammed the truck into gear and hit the gas, reversing the truck backward and away from Matchitehew. Mike hit the brakes while jerking the steering wheel, sending the front end of the truck around, so they were facing away from the church. Mike hit the gas again and the big truck accelerated forward, putting blissful distance between them and the enraged Indian.

"Mike," Meghan begged, grabbing him by the arm. "We can't just leave!"

Mike gawked at her. Shocked to think that she'd even ask to delay the escape. "Are you out of your mind?"

"She's right, Mike," Kyle said, leaning forward from the back seat. "We need to kill him. We can't leave him free to roam the world. No one will ever be safe."

26

MATCHITEHEW

Mike glanced up at the rear-view mirror at the moving figure he knew was Matchitehew, chasing after them. There was no way he could ever keep up with the truck. The easiest thing to do would be to keep driving, leaving him behind. But at what cost?

He knew Meghan and Kyle were right. Leaving the ancient, bloodthirsty man alive would be a lethal mistake, condemning untold innocents to pay the price for his giving in to fear. This being, black-hearted and violent, must be dealt with immediately. Even if they could just cut and run, what kind of life would they expect to lead? With Matchitehew walking the earth, they would spend the rest of their lives glancing down dark alleys and over their shoulders in perpetual fear.

He shook his head. "You know, my life was pretty boring before you two showed up." —He smiled at Meghan— "Kyle, how many rounds do you have left in your pistol?"

"Three," Kyle said, checking the cylinder.

"I think I have two. That is five between us. Mike handed Kyle his remaining two rounds. I hope we won't need it." Mike slammed the truck into reverse and hit the gas pedal, swinging the truck around to aim at Matchitehew. The hunted now become the hunters.

The truck engine roared, issuing a challenge to its prey. It leapt forward on all four tires like a cat who'd just discovered a mouse. They held their breath as they anticipated the impact of metal upon flesh and bone when, at the last moment, Matchitehew jumped up in the air and pushed off the cab of the truck, landing behind them as they flew by.

Mike and Meghan exchanged confused glances as Mike brought the truck around to face where the Indian should have landed.

"Well, that was unexpected," Kyle said.

Matchitehew ran toward the truck as Mike, once again, hit the gas pedal, sending the truck lurching forward. The Indian jumped out of the way and took a swipe at the driver's side door which sent a spider-web of cracks through the safety glass. Mike pushed the glass out into the parking lot as Matchitehew stepped out into the rear-view mirror's gaze of the truck.

"Keep your distance," Meghan warned. "If he tries that again, he might actually hurt you."

Mike brought the truck to a halt on the opposite side of the parking lot from Matchitehew. All three stared while the enraged Indian appeared to be staring right back at them. A showdown, odds favoring neither side.

Mike hit the gas again and the giant engine roared to life. Much to their surprise, Matchitehew stood rock-still, simply, smiling back at them as if he'd anticipated their next move.

"Hold on," Mike yelled over the roar of the engine. "I'm going to try something."

"Hell of a time for an experiment, don't you think?" Meghan yelled.

Mike fixed his eyes on Matchitehew and ignored her comment. "Just hang on, alright?"

The truck picked up speed as it crossed the enormous parking lot. Matchitehew stood unmoving. When they were twenty feet from the unflappable Indian, Mike slammed on the brakes and put the truck in a slide with the back of the truck swinging out toward their intended victim like a bat hitting a baseball.

In the flurry of tire smoke and noise, they lost sight of him. They expected to hear a loud thud against the quarter panel of the truck, or at least some noise to indicate they hit their mark. The noise never came, and the truck skidded sideways to a halt in the empty parking lot. Examining the expanse of the lot, Mike didn't see an indication anyone or anything had been hit.

"What the hell happened?" Mike said. "He couldn't have just disappeared."

Meghan was just about to respond when one of the rear windows exploded into the passenger cabin of the truck. Meghan screamed while looking back to see Matchitehew standing, ax in hand, preparing to take another swing.

"Oh shit!" Mike yelled out. He gunned the engine, which caught Matchitehew off guard and sent him crashing to the truck bed.

"Kyle, watch him, tell me when he stands back up!" Mike said.

Matchitehew seemed disoriented for a moment, then flashed Kyle an eerie grin before getting back to his feet.

"Now, Mike!" Kyle shouted.

Mike slammed on the brakes as hard as he could, sending Matchitehew careening into and over the top of the truck cab. Instead of seeing the body of the Indian flying over the hood, again he vanished.

"This guy is beginning to annoy the crap out of me!" Mike yelled, traversing another third of the parking lot. Mike swerved the truck around to face the front of the church once again. Matchitehew was nowhere to be seen.

Kyle was first to break the terrifying silence. "What happened? We should've creamed him. I mean, splatsville. Where did he go?"

"Mike, I don't like this," Meghan said, nervously tugging at her hair.

A deafening screech interrupted the discussion as a sudden crease in the roof developed. Unbelievably, Matchitehew knelt on the roof of the truck cab. Another hit and the blade end of his ax appeared through a small slit in the metal. The overhead light knocked free and dangled in between Mike and Kyle.

"Mike, watch out!" Meghan screamed.

Kyle fired twice straight up, filling the cab with smoke, causing the Indian to momentarily stop.

"Oh shit!" Mike hit the gas hard and Matchitehew fell into the back of the truck. Kyle fired the remaining three rounds through the busted-out window until the weapon clicked on empty cylinders.

Meghan screamed as she watched the enraged Indian leap forward, picking up where he'd left off. The sound of metal crushing and scraping against the stone blade was deafening. Although the aluminum was hard, the expertly honed blade of the ax sliced through it with little resistance.

Without warning, the blade struck Kyle on the side of his head, sending blood everywhere. Meghan and Mike both screamed for Kyle as the boy slumped lifelessly against the side of the door, unconscious.

The truck picked up speed, on a trajectory toward the church. Matchitehew, now with room to work, cackled like a madman as ax strikes to the cab came closer and closer to hitting Mike.

"Meghan, hold on!" Mike yelled, moments before the truck crashed into the front of the church building. Chaos erupted as the sounds of wood splintering, metal being torn from metal, and glass shattering overtook the sounds of the engine. The airbags punched Mike in the face so hard he lost control of the truck. Kyle, although belted in, slouched into one corner of the truck cab, blood oozing from his scalp. The rear-door airbag kept him from sliding any further toward the floor.

The truck cleared the doors of the church and made it down the three steps into the open sanctuary. Pews were sent sprawling everywhere as hymnals flew in every direction. A screeching noise echoed off the once-hallowed walls of Donny's church as the rubber on the tires fought against the friction between them and the marble floor.

After the large vehicle came to a stop. Mike scanned the interior of the church for any sign of their attacker. Blood, presumably from Kyle's head wound, was everywhere in the cab.

Meghan stirred in the passenger seat.

"Are you alright?" Mike said, opening her door.

"I think so." Then she saw the blood escaping from Kyle's head. "Kyle, oh my dear boy, Kyle. Mike, help him! Please!" Meghan let out a helpless whimper as a stream of blood seeped from the gash in her son's head.

Mike grabbed the now empty gun from the floor of the truck and stepped out into the sanctuary. Helping Meghan bring Kyle out of the truck and setting him down on the pew, he was relieved to hear the boy breathing.

The sanctuary looked like a war zone. In addition to pieces of pews and hymnals everywhere, radiator fluid seeped onto the floor, producing a sickening smell. The top of the truck could be mistaken for a tuna fish can being opened by someone who forgot a can opener. Pieces of metal were bent into odd shapes. A bead of blood streaked across the remains of the truck roof. Mike expected to see some sort of sign as to what happened to their adversary.

Kyle's bleeding needed medical attention, as soon as possible; however, the boy's bleeding looked worse than it was. The ax only abraded his skin.

Meghan pulled off his tattered shirt and held it against his wound to stop the bleeding. "My boy," she said, over and over again.

"He'll be alright, I think. Head wounds bleed like hell. We need to get him to a hospital." He was about to pick up Kyle when he felt a presence behind him. Grabbing the handle of the empty pistol, he wielded around and pointed it at the altar, pretending it still had rounds to fire.

Behind them, stood a tall, old man. Dressed in conservative clothes. Most likely in his sixties, he had long gray hair. His skin, grizzled and wrinkled with age, was a deep tan, as if he'd spent too much of his time out in the sun. He smiled at them and put his hands up in the air. "There's no need to harm me. Especially with a bullet-less gun. I am here to help."

At that moment, the oddity of the situation struck Mike. They'd just battled some sort of native American demon and now a weird guy shows up and tells them he is here to help. He blinked several times, convinced the newcomer was a figment of his imagination. "Where the hell were you about ten minutes ago when we needed your help?"

"I was watching," the man simply answered. "Don't worry about your son, he'll be fine."

The man stepped forward. Mike wanted to hold the gun on him; however, the man didn't feel like he posed a threat. The stranger exuded a calming presence. This man felt more like an old friend or relative, which was strange as Mike knew he had never seen the man before.

Meghan also watched the man, as mesmerized by his approach as Mike. Kneeling near the boy, the stranger pulled out an old leather pouch from his pocket. He extracted a small plastic bag containing dried leaves which he crushed into the palm of his hand. He whispered a small chant and rubbed it on Kyle's wounds. "Witch hazel, it'll slow the bleeding. It looks far worse than it is."

"Who are you? Why are you here?" Mike shook himself from his dumbstruck condition.

The man stood up and straightened his clothing. "I'm called Johnathan Longhorn, the last of my people. I'm the descendant of the shaman who put the curse on Matchitehew. Like many of those you would call shaman, this is where we lived. This land is sacred. We were charged with watching over Matchitehew, ensuring his continued imprisonment was our charge."

Meghan, still cradling Kyle's head scowled at Johnathan. "You didn't do a very good job."

"I fear the lady is correct," Johnathan said with a heavy sigh. "About fifteen years ago, we lost the amulet which allowed us to enter the cave. The amulet is also the other half of the magic keeping him imprisoned. When the amulet resurfaced, I tried to return, but the so-called reverend refused to allow me back in town. Earlier today, I sensed his spirit released from the grips of the demon. Your actions were a catalyst, setting things in motion. I knew my time had arrived."

Mike looked at Kyle. The boy rested comfortably for the moment. Although he didn't know anything about witch hazel, the bleeding slowed considerably. "Well, you're too late. That Indian ran off."

"So sure about that, are you? That's the problem with this generation. You rely only on what you see and don't trust your instincts. Yes, he is physically gone, and you made sure of that; however, his spirit is far from released."

Meghan stared blankly. "What are you talking about? Please, explain this to me. What is my boy suffering for? Why did we do all of this?" A twinge of hysteria colored her voice.

The old man smiled at her. "Be at peace, Meghan." Seeing her surprised expression, he added, "Yes, I know your name. I know all your names. They were written in stone hundreds of years ago, the same stone which held Matchitehew at bay. The entire story of this was written the day Matchitehew entered his prison. And today it comes to an end. For his part, Kyle represents the earth spirit, the one who reclaimed the stone. The one called Mike, represents the sea spirit who came by water. It is he who released Matchitehew from his earthly bond."

Mike interrupted, "What the hell does that mean?"

"You killed him." The old man held up a finger like a teacher clarifying a point to his pupil.

"What about me? Why did I go through all of this?" Meghan asked.

"Ah, Meghan, you are the sky spirit; the vessel who carried the earth spirit who retakes the stone and restores balance to this land. According to the prophecy, you were also the sacrifice that the boy wouldn't accept. In short, your son would die to protect you and that is the purest love. Now you must go. This story is coming to its conclusion."

Mike spoke up again. "One more question. How was it possible Matchitehew convinced all those people to help him ... to kill for him?"

"Matchitehew understood what many of us still struggle with. Everyone has a weakness for one of the deadly sins. Most people give into pride. Many others give into lust. Still others, avarice. Humans, be they Indian, white, black, or any other shade are all the same. If we don't know enough to watch for stumbling blocks in life, we'll trip over them. That high priest wanted a comfortable life and took the easy way, with promises of power if he only gave a little more every time. Until, one day, Matchitehew took it all. Don't be blind to the world around you, or you'll risk falling into the same trap."

The old man dug into his jacket pocket, pulled out a set of keys and threw them to Mike. "The boy will survive. However, you must get him to a doctor. He'll need stitches and stronger medicine than I can provide. You'll find a Jeep in the parking lot waiting for you. When you are done, leave the keys at the desk at the resort. I'll want my car back, at some point."

"But what about you?" Meghan asked. At the very least, they owed the old man a ride. It didn't seem right to just leave him here.

Shaking his head, he said, "Sky spirit, our pathways will only cross once in this life and never again. I have one last act I must complete to ensure Matchitehew is bound to his fate. There is something that must be done to erase the evil which has taken place here. A sacrifice must be made to bring the Gods Okee and Ahone into alignment. I bid you farewell, take care of each other."

Meghan abruptly stood. Glancing at Kyle, she implored, "Mike, he's right, we need to leave."

Mike picked up Kyle and carried his unconscious body through the remains of the church building. Stepping out of the gaping hole left by the truck, Mike turned around to see the man making a hasty pile out of the hymnals and saying something while holding his hands up in the air. The books instantly burst into flames.

Outside, they found the Jeep. Mike put Kyle in the back seat and buckled him. The boy stirred faintly but didn't open his eyes.

Leaving the parking lot and turning onto the main road, a thunderous explosion rocked the area and caused the Jeep to vibrate. Mike glanced up into the rear-view mirror to see the church building engulfed in flames. The small fire Johnathan had set shouldn't have spread that quickly, nor cause any kind of large explosion. However, after the day he had, Mike wasn't about to question anything anymore.

Five minutes later, a sign bearing the words "Now Leaving Riapoke" appeared on the side of the road. Mike allowed himself a relieved smile as he rocketed over the bridge which marked the city limit.

27

THE DEEP SLEEP

Kyle's head throbbed like someone had taken a tire iron to it. How long had he'd been out? It could have been days or weeks. It was anyone's guess. Eyes shut against the blinding fluorescent lights of the room, the smell that filtered through the haze suggested a hospital. Out in the hallway, nurses talked with doctors from time to time in phrases and words indicating Kyle suffered a "temporary coma". Then a different, more familiar sensation overtook all others. Someone was holding his hand.

He cautiously opened one eye and focused on the darkest thing in the room, as the light momentarily sent a searing pain through his head. Gradually he opened both eyes. He looked down at his hand, to see his mother holding it. She was fast asleep, awkwardly resting her head on the side of the bed.

"Mom?" he said, feeling bad for waking his sleeping mother.

She picked her head up from the side of the bed and smiled. "Oh, Kyle, sweetie. My dear sweet boy. You're awake."

Kyle's mind continued to reboot and flashed of the last event before waking up in the hospital bed. Some sort of battle with the Indian and then everything went black. "What happened? Did we win? Where's Mike?"

She laughed. "Yes, we won. Mike will be here in about an hour, he'll be happy to see you're awake. I'm just glad you're okay. I was so worried. How are you feeling?"

Kyle rubbed the side of his head. "I think the proper phrase is, like crap on a cracker."

A young woman walked into the door carrying two paper cups with lids on them. It took a moment to recognize Mike's daughter Kelley.

She did a double take and smiled at him. "You're awake! You had us worried for a while there, bro."

Kyle looked at her quizzically. "Bro?"

"Well, not yet. Don't worry, you and I'll talk after the adults are gone." She smiled at Kyle. "But I'm happy to see you upright and talking."

Meghan squeezed Kyle's hand. "You've been out for two weeks with one hell of a head wound. Kelley helped me stand watch. I wanted familiar faces in the room when you woke up."

Kelley sat down in the chair on the other side of the bed and poured him a cup of water from a small carafe. "You gave us quite a scare there, hero boy."

He took a sip of the water as she held a straw for him. "What?" he managed to croak out, surprised at how dry his throat felt.

Meghan spoke up, "Had you not taken the amulet when you did, none of us would be alive to tell the tale. You saved us. But, rest for now. I'll tell the doctor you're awake."

Meghan left the room, and Kelley leaned in close. "Okay, I'm only going to say this once, and if you repeat it, I'll swear you are lying." She smiled and put her hand on Kyle's shoulder. "Thank you for saving my dad, Kyle." She gave him a kiss on the forehead. "You're going to make a great step-brother."

The doctor came in and asked a few questions, after which, Kyle drifted off to sleep. On one side he felt his mother's hand, and in the other hand he felt Kelley's. He'd have to remember to press Kelley for details when he woke up.

————

"MATCHITEHEW, you have committed a great evil. How do you answer this tribunal?" a muscular man in a headdress asked. Surrounding him, other native American men sat. On their heads they wore feathered headdresses of different length and ornamentation. They watched the man in the center with deference. His presence commanded respect.

Matchitehew, facing the one sitting in the center of the circle, tried to stand up. However, the leather bindings holding his hands in place also bound him to the floor. Instead, he puffed out his chest. "This court has no authority over me. I'm the rightful heir to all that is our destiny. You have no right to pass any kind of judgment over me, Powhatan."

Powhatan, un-phased by the outburst, calmly reached forward and slapped him across the face. "You will address me as chief!"

"I will do nothing of the sort. I took back what you stole from me."

Powhatan shook his head. "You killed innocent people for your own personal gain. Did you think you'd get away with that?" His face remained stoic, as if resigned to Matchitehew's obstinacy. "All of us must ultimately answer for the good and bad in our lives."

"I killed the white man, who has no problem stealing from us. You are too blind or just too stupid to see that."

The chief shook his head. "This is what you never understood. People of all tribes must learn to live in harmony. Anyone trying to gain power over the other will upset the natural balance of things." He frowned at Matchitehew. "I had such high hopes for you. I loved you like a son. All you had to do was atone for your sins to be allowed back into the great circle. Instead of accepting your punishment, you committed an even worse crime. Now the Earth, Water, and Sky Gods have passed their judgment on you. Your fate has been sealed."

The fire in the center of the room leapt skyward and everyone, save Matchitehew, vanished. Finding that his bindings vanished as well, he jumped up and ran out of the tent. He came to a skidding halt outside. A mere foot from the tent was a cliff which dropped into infinity. The speck he now inhabited, floated in seemingly endless space. Around him, a grassy plateau covering thirty feet in diameter made up the extent of his world. A dark sky dotted with a million stars surrounded in every direction. In the distance, too far away to reach, other pieces of land floated just as aimlessly as his own.

"You can't do this to me!" He screamed at the top of his lungs. "I'm the rightful chief of the Powhatan nation! I'm the leader."

A fire burst forth from the center of the grass. The flames laughed, mocking him. "And your wish is granted, you are now the leader of your own tribe. Name it what you want. From now on, you answer only to me."

Matchitehew felt a sudden pang of fear, as the dancing, flickering flames alternated between red, yellow, and blue. "Who are you? What do you want from me?"

Flames rose up in response to the question. The voice laughed again. "It isn't what I want from you. Rather, it is what you want from me. As Powhatan explained, the Earth, Water, and Sky Gods have decided you are to be mine. Your punishment is sealed."

Matchitehew sneered at the fire. "You think this is the end? I escaped once and I'll escape again. No prison can hold me."

"So, even now, at the end of it all, you are too self-centered to understand. Too blind to see what your own ambitions have bought you."

"Who are you? What is your name that you should speak to me in such a manner?" Matchitehew screamed out in anger.

Fire from the center shot into the air. The light flashed so bright it caused him to cover his eyes. When the flash receded, in the center of what was the fire pit, a man stood made entirely of flame. He wore a brightly colored warbonnet which extended down his back and disappeared into the ground behind him. "I go by many names. I'm called The Tormentor, Fallen Angel, Mephistopheles, Beelzebub, The Beast, and countless other names. For you, I have a special name. You may call me, Riapoke."

The End

ACKNOWLEDGMENTS

Once again, I have slogged through the art and craft of writing to bring you a tale. Naturally, I have to thank tons of people for their love and support during this process. Of course, Riapoke couldn't even exist without my wife who supports my obsession of writing; although, I am sure there have been nights where she wanted to take my keyboard and beat me over the head with it and run off to be with her other husband who we are sure is a pool boy named Juan in California. Her love and understanding is a huge part of this book. I also have to thank my children for putting up with all of this! The character of Kyle is drawn heavily off my son Thomas. As all my kids get older, the prouder I am of their accomplishments, and I am pretty dam proud of them anyway.

There's no way I could've made it to this stage if it weren't for my beta readers, who stand at the anvil of literary creation and beat the storyline until it approaches something readable. They do it for the love of reading, and that's what makes them all the more amazing. I need to send a huge shout out to my fellow writers at the Independent Authors Support and Discussion group who patiently answer questions and encourage me daily. I also want to thank my editor, who believes in my abilities. His help, encouragement, and support are absolutely critical. To him I say, be patient, I'll get this whole writing thing correct someday.

MOST IMPORTANTLY! I need to thank you, the reading public. Ultimately, you ordered or bought this book over all others in the world. You are the reason I write. You could've chosen to read anything, but you chose to read Riapoke, and I want to tell each and every one of you that it means the world to me.

This book is dedicated to all the independent authors out there struggling every day to bring their imagination to life. Stick with it, future generations will thank you.

OTHER BOOKS BY BRYAN NOWAK

No Name

The Dramatic Dead (Dirk Bentley Mystery Series, book one)

Riapoke

Crimson Tassels

The Bagorian Chronicles

Visit Bryan online:
www.bryannowak.com

facebook.com/Bryanthewriter
twitter.com/Bryan_TheWriter

Made in the USA
Coppell, TX
11 May 2022

77675555R00134